I0556627

The T-Stat Missions
The Fight For Home

By Llewellyn Burgess

DEDICATION

Dedicated to all those who have helped me along the long windy road of life.

CONTENTS

Llewellyn Burgess

ACKNOWLEDGMENTS

Thanks to Zi-Lynn Ho for doing the cover art.

1 THE SECRET QUARRY

"Marina..." Sarah said wistfully as she watched Marina cry softly with her head in her hands. "I'm really sorry," she wanted to say, but the words would not come out of her mouth. After a few tries she got up from the helm chair and stood next to Marina. She briefly paused before leaning over and embraced Marina. "We'll help you get them back," she said softly to Marina. "We'll help you get them back." Marina did not respond but leaned into Sarah and continued crying. The others on the bridge nodded towards Sarah and returned to monitoring the RAINE's travelling.

Down in the hanger, the mechanics were congregating near the ATF. "Fae, with the destruction of the Osmerian home planet, doesn't that mean the war is over?" a Generian mechanic asked Fae.

"I suppose so," Fae nodded.

"But wouldn't that mean we'd have to return home?" another one added.

"It would, but I doubt this mechina would be welcomed back very well," Fae responded. Then she added with a sigh, "Well we'd be able to go back to Generia, the issue would still be our Terran counterparts wouldn't and its highly unlikely they'd be back allowed on any Terran settlement either."

"Probably not," Sonluth said as he entered the hanger area and overheard the conversation. "No matter what happens now, anything short of destroying the Silician aggressors would result in us dying."

"But that's not the worse part," Jace interjected. "The worst part is that the UTSF doesn't know about the destruction of the Osmerian home planet. After all, the UTSF lacks any co-ordinates into Osmerian Space. Every mechina they've sent into the area has been destroyed. And since the Silicians have been playing the helpless and defenseless race they aren't its only matter of time before they turn on the UTSF. And the UTSF won't even see it coming."

"So what do we do?" the Generian mechanic asked. "As a Generian I won't feel comfortable running forever."

"None of us would," Sonluth remarked. "We are currently heading to an abandoned quarry where the commander was told we could find the Osmerian Secret Weapon from Project Nebula."

"How do we know it's not a trap?" one of the mechanics asked.

"It's a risk we'll have to take," Sonluth said. "If we ever want to face this problem all we can do is move forward."

"Easy for *you* to say," another mechanic yelled as he pointed towards Sonluth. "*You* don't have anything valuable in the Terran system. I heard you were just going to go back into mercenary work after you finished with us. And you'll probably benefit a lot from the resulting chaos if the Silicians take over."

"Is that all?" Sonluth asked coolly after the mechanic finished. "It is true, I normally don't like to get involved with these types of things, but I also like to always successfully complete jobs. My job right now is to keep this ship safe, and safe it shall be, so long as I draw breath."

"He's right," Fae spoke up. "I know morale is plummeting due to recent events, but there is no sense arguing or breeding mistrust between us. Right now, we all need to trust the decisions of our commander, and have faith in each other." Everyone solemnly agreed with Fae, and went quiet. There was nothing more to say until they arrived at the quarry. They were being cornered, and cornered into a difficult space. All they could do is trust their fellow crew members and carry on in the face of odds that continued to be stacked against them as the days went by.

The group disbursed and Jace and Sonluth headed back towards the pilot quarters.

"This has been on rough ride," Jace commented.

"It has," Sonluth responded, "and it's still not over yet. Although, I have to admit, this crew is holding out a lot better than most others I've seen. The irony here being that the UTSF assembled this group as an experimental crew, who would follow the book, but it turns out that this group has grown into a superior fighting force that seems to be able to keep one step ahead of everyone."

Jace nodded, "So true. Even with the losses, they still keep going, although I don't know how long they'd hold out now. Like Fae said, morale on this mechina is extremely low. Losing two pilots, watching a planet be destroyed, escaping capture not once, but twice, having your own commander and in one case father turn on you, I think this mechina has had suffered more misfortune than anyone should be allowed to have in a lifetime."

"Yet, we are all still here. No one has deserted, no one has mutinied. They possess the discipline the UTSF originally wanted to train people with, yet they still hold on to civilian morals," Sonluth said. "Once again, the irony being most experienced soldiers would have either cracked or simply started genocide. But this crew has held it together. From Fae and the mechanics, all the way up to Sarah and the bridge. The question is, what happens when one of the central people snap or hesitate."

"Let's not think about that," Jace said with a grimace. "We have enough on our hands; there is no need to add more."

"I suppose so, but in the meantime, we better be prepared. No matter the end result, this ship is going to go out with a bang."

"Agreed," Jace responded. "Hopefully it'll be a good bang and we'll all see this through to the end."

"We will. I have faith in this young and inexperienced crew," Sonluth said as he mimicked the mannerisms of Commander John Collins.

Jace let out a small laugh as he entered his room. "Isn't that the truth?" Once Jace had gone inside, Sonluth followed suit, eventually going down to his lab to work to tinker with the Omega Drive.

The mechina remained unusually quiet until the target planet came into view. There was very little atmosphere, but as the RAINE began descending towards the co-ordinates of the quarry the ship was pinged by multiple sources.

"Believe it or not, we're being pinged," Vlad said dryly.

"Nothing seems to surprise me anymore," Sarah sighed. She ordered Marina to break off her descent and Megumi tried to open up a communication link with whatever was targeting them. After a few minutes there was a response on the radio.

"You are a UTSF vessel. State your name and reason for approaching our quarry," a voice said.

"Not this again…" Sarah muttered. Then she spoke on the radio. "This is the UTSF Battlemechina RAINE. I am Commander Sarah Collins, and we have been sent here from Osmeria to investigate a weapon that was developed to beat back the Silicians."

"And just why would the Osmerians tell a UTSF vessel about something like that?" the voice asked.

"Its times like this I hate protocol," Sarah thought to herself with a sigh. She shook the thought off spoke in an audible tone, "Why can't they just take our word and let us land."

"Because that would potentially make them as dumb as the Trojans," Lucius commented.

"I didn't need a response," Sarah frowned. She then took a deep breath and held the button to speak through the radio. "Look, I don't have a good reason other than the one I gave you. However, if you want to be so cautious, would it make you feel better if we sent a small envoy down to reassure you that we are friendly and mean you no harm?"

There was a short silence over the radio before a response came through. "Alright, you can send down three people to act as an envoy. However, should they try any funny business they will be killed on the spot, and you will not be permitted to land."

"Sounds like a deal," Sarah responded. She then turned shut off the radio channel and let out a large sigh. "Now I have to pick three people…"

"As dangerous as this may sound, how about you send one Generian, one Terran and Marina," Lucius suggested. "That way you could appeal to whoever maybe down there."

"And who says I want to go?" Marina fired back.

"Calm down Marina," Sarah ordered. "I know you've been through a lot lately, but we all have. Lucius might have a point sending down a mixed team as we don't know who we are dealing with."

"I know…" Marina sighed.

"You don't have to go if you don't want," Sarah said. "You have taken the most lately, and if you think you aren't up to doing an envoy mission I will not force you."

"No… I'll go," Marina interrupted Sarah. "You guys might not be Osmerian, but you still treat me as a good friend. This mission is for the betterment of the ship, and maybe even the betterment of my fellow Osmerians."

"Okay," Sarah said. "Now, who else to send with you."

"Fae is the most approachable Generian, probably because of her line of work and experience," Kazumi suggested. "For Terrans you could either send Sonluth for intimidation purposes, or you could send one of us, but I'm pretty sure most of us lack diplomacy skills."

"If that's the case, then I'll go," Sarah said. "It will also show the guys in the quarry that we don't mean any harm if we are sending the commanding officer down."

"Good plan," Vlad nodded. "However, you might need to keep track of time. Fae is keeping the mechanics under control, and that aside, we don't know if the Silicians are tracking us."

"We'll make it as fast as possible," Sarah responded. "Besides it doesn't sound like we'd be welcome down there for too long anyways. Then she turned to Marina, "okay, let's go get Fae and head down. Vlad and Kazumi, you two are in charge until I get back."

"Yes ma'am!" the two echoed. Sarah and Marina then went down to the hanger to search for Fae.

"It would appear she's not here," Sarah said after they had searched around the hanger for ten minutes.

"Hey, do any of you know where Fae is?" Marina hailed out to the nearest group of mechanics.

"She went to do some electrical work near the power room," Ned answered. "She said there was a need to make the wiring more efficient and improve response times." The duo looked at each other before responding back to Ned.

"Ok, thanks," Sarah responded before her and Marina moved off towards the power room.

Sure enough, they found Fae down in the electronics room, where she was digging through a pile of wires and clips.

"Fae?" Sarah called out as the approached her work area.

"Oh, hey Commander, what brings you down here?" Fae asked without taking her eyes off what she was doing.

"There is a military or at least a guerilla force at the quarry, and we three are going down to negotiate a landing," Sarah explained.

"Well, I'm kind of busy at the moment," Fae responded as she clipped a wire in place. "I noticed that the Osmerians had switched around some of our electrical work, so I'm trying to fix it without interrupting anything. I'm also not involving any of the crew so that this doesn't cause a panic."

"Well, if you don't want to go, can you suggest anyone else to go?" Sarah asked.

"I do," Fae responded as she leaned back to wipe some sweat off her brow. "There should be a Generian mechanic called Ned. He went with us to retrieve the syncer chip back on Generia. He's a little gullible most days, but I'm sure he won't cause too much of a stir during your envoy mission. I left him checking over the mechina in the hanger."

"Okay, we'll do that." Then she added as she began to walk off, "Good luck with the repairs."

"Thanks, and good luck to you too."

Marina and Sarah walked back up out of the electronics room and back to the hanger. Sarah found Ned scratching his head as he looked from his clipboard to the ATF.

"Excuse me Ned," Sarah spoke as they got close to him.

"I didn't do it! It wasn't me, *honest!*" he jumped as he heard someone call his name from behind him. "Oh, Commander it's you," he said as he tried to catch his breath.

"I thought you were Fae."

"Do I want to know what you're doing that would elicit that type of response?" Sarah frowned.

"I can't find all the parts on this list," Ned sulked. "And if I go to Fae and tell her I can't find it, I know she'll magically produce it and then she'd chew me out again."

"Let me see?" Sarah motioned towards his clipboard. He handed it over and Sarah and Marina looked at the piece of paper. A few moments later Sarah smiled and handed the clipboard back. "You're safe; it's the wrong ATF model. Zee's ATF is a zero series; the one on your sheet is the one hundred series."

"What? Really?" Ned said as he accepted the clipboard back from Sarah. He looked at the sheet and then located the registration number on its landing gear. "Wow, you're right," he said with a heavy sigh of relief. "But why would they give me the wrong sheet," he wailed.

"Most definitely a little gullible," Marina said with a small laugh to which Sarah elbowed her in the side.

"In any case Ned, we need to go down to the quarry to negotiate a landing, and Fae suggested you come along so we can have a full spectrum representation of our ship. Besides, it'll serve as a nice distraction from your obviously stressful job." Marina started to laugh at the last comment which prompted another elbow to the side from Sarah.

"Well if Fae suggested, I guess it wouldn't hurt to go along," Ned responded. "Are you *sure* she said I can go along?"

"Of course she did, the only person probably less naïve on this ship other than you is her," Marina muttered. Sarah heard the comment and elbowed her again, but this time Marina blocked Sarah's elbow with her upper arm.

"Are you alright?" Ned asked Sarah as she winced in pain.

"She'll be fine," Marina said with a smile. "But are you ready to go out? The sooner we can negotiate, the sooner we can land and be out of harm's way.

"You make a good point," Ned said. He handed his clipboard off to another mechanic next to the ATF and the trio left the RAINE in a small transport mechina. As per protocol, they broadcasted a neutral signal to show that they didn't intend on taking any aggressive actions. However, the quarry inhabitants kept their weapons trained on the mechina right up until they reached the entrance gate. Once there, a small militia opened the gate for them and locked it behind them. Once that was locked, the militia carried out an extensive external search of the mechina, including running scans over it. Once they had finished that, they opened the air lock and allowed the transport mechina in.

"Keep your hands up where we can see them!" the militia escorting them ordered once the air lock was closed. The trio from the RAINE disembarked and came out with hands up and was pat down for weapons. Marina and Sarah both had their standard issue side arm and Ned had a pocket knife, but nothing that would overly concern a security check. Once the people who pat them down withdrew another man approached the trio.

"I'm sorry for the rough treatment, but as I'm sure you know one can never be too safe," the man spoke. "My name is Commander Tadashi and I will speak with you concerning your visit here."

"Very well," Sarah replied. "I'm Commander Sarah Collins

of the Battlemechina RAINE. We were directed here by an Osmerian commander before the Silicians destroyed the planet. He instructed us there were weapons here that could stand up to the Silicians."

"You do realize how dumb your story sounds?" Commander Tadashi frowned and crossed his arms. "An Osmerian gives the location of an anti-Silician weapon to a Terran commander."

"Yes I'm aware of how dumb it sounds, but it's the truth," Sarah responded. "There is no other way to describe our current situation. We've been attacked by Terran and Silician Forces, as well as assisted Generian and Osmerian Forces. We are in a complete reversal of our normal role in this war, which is how we arrived at your doorstep."

"Well, while we were waiting for your arrival, we did some research on the UTSF. Although you all do wear UTSF uniforms, there is no record of your ship in the UTSF database," Tadashi said bluntly. "So I am inclined to believe you are lying. Your fish story also doesn't help with your predicament. But even if you are lying, I'll give you a chance to return to your toy boat and go back out to space and never come here again."

"I'm sorry Commander, we can't do that," Sarah responded. "Whether you kill us or the Silicians kill us, it doesn't matter anymore. Right now, you're the only person blocking us from getting something we could use to survive. So trust me when I tell you, threats like that to us mean nothing. We are already backed into a corner, and a person is most volatile when backed into a corner."

"You dare to threaten us?" Tadashi thundered. He then signaled for those standing behind him to ready their weapons. "You guys certainly have guts, but you should know very well that you can't possibly win against us. We'd simply kill you here and then destroy that floating piece of metal you call some fancy battlemechina name."

"But wait," Ned interrupted as he jumped in front of Sarah. "Aren't you a Terran? Why are *you* so far out here guarding an Osmerian Secret weapon?"

"Who says I'm a Terran?" Tadashi demanded as he narrowed his gaze on Ned.

"You're not a Generian, because you lack the build of one, and you're not Osmerian otherwise you would know who she is," Ned said pointing at Marina. "That leaves you to either be Terran or Silician, both of which would be suspicious if you were guarding an Osmerian outpost."

"Very deductive," Tadashi replied taking a step back from Ned. "I am indeed a Terran. Your commander is most definitely Terran, as I know her father turned coat on us. Your last member… I honestly thought was Terran, until you spoke just now. But tell me, why is she important as an Osmerian?"

"I can let you know once we get permission to land," Marina snapped. "Speaking of which, if you did all this research, where does it say Sarah should be? After all, she *did* mention her name during the radio conversation, and since you know her so well, I'm sure you probably checked her profile."

"That I did," Tadashi shifted his position as he continued; "It says she's KIA."

"Well I'm *obviously* right here in front of you," Sarah whined.

"A person claiming to be Sarah Collins is right here in

front of me," Tadashi said. "There is no definite…"

"That is enough!" a woman's voice came from behind Tadashi.

"Commander Mistral!" Tadashi said with a jump before moving to the side. A woman walked forward, and Sarah immediately recognized her.

"Arianna," she said with a heavy sigh of relief.

"Good to see you still remember," Arianna responded. "I'm also happy to see you guys made it out here in one piece, although happy being an operative word, given the circumstances that have brought you here."

"You know her?" Ned asked.

"She visited the ship back in Generia," Marina whispered to Ned before adding in an inaudible tone, "Although meeting her way out here explains how she's kept hidden for so long."

"You've met with them before?" Tadashi asked Arianna.

Arianna nodded. "Yes I have, although, had you guys brought down Sonluth then Tadashi here might not have given you such a hard time."

"Sonluth works for the UTSF again?" Tadashi asked as creases formed on his forehead.

"Only temporarily, or so he says," Arianna responded to Tadashi before turning to face Sarah, "But enough of that, I take it you guys came down to check on the weapon."

Sarah responded with a smile and a nod, "Yes, that's why we are here. But first, can we get permission to land our mechina? It is out in orbit and would easily be picked up by patrolling mechina."

"Sure you can land. I suggest you land at the docks on the far side of the quarry so that you wouldn't be easily detected if a mechina did a random visual search."

Sarah happily agreed and didn't waste any time returning to the RAINE and getting it safely down to the docks. Once docked, Arianna and Tadashi met Sarah outside the RAINE on the docks. Sonluth, Fae and Marina also joined her.

"So I hear you showed your true colours Princess," Arianna said as Marina came into earshot when disembarking the RAINE.

"Princess?" Tadashi asked. "Why is the Osmerian Princess on a Terran ship?"

"You honestly think the guys in the Nav Department would refuse accepting a female member?" Arianna remarked.

"Well… no…" Tadashi responded quietly as he looked at the floor and then over to Marina. "But she must have been like one of one hundred."

"That she was, but like I said before, if you're not male and blatantly not Terran you could have gotten in as a 'Terran Female', because those guys were always looking to have femininity in their ranks," Arianna said with exaggerated hand motions. Tadashi muttered something under his breath, but Arianna chose to ignore it and continue. "But either way, she did a good job in hiding her tracks. The Osmerian Rebel forces did try to locate you, and would have given up if only the Royal Guards didn't insist you were alive until they found your dead body."

"You wouldn't have guessed that by the way we were treated," Sarah remarked.

"You're just not used to Osmerian heavy-handedness," Arianna responded with a slight chuckle. "Besides, I'm sure Marina herself is pretty good example of what Osmerian behavior is like, unless she's added coy to her pseudo-Terran resume."

"At least I didn't bring one home," Marina interjected.

"Are you still upset about that?" Arianna said with a frown. "It's not my fault I wasn't next in line and thus afforded the freedoms of dating away from the spotlight, so long as the suitor wasn't Silician. But enough of that, let's go down below to the weapon stash." The group nodded and followed Tadashi and Arianna to an elevator marked 'Shaft 947: Authorized Personnel Only'. The shaft was well lit, and even the trip down was well lit. Unlike normal mine shafts, this one appeared to have steel and concrete reinforcement and looked more like an elevator in a high rise building instead of a lift in an old mining shaft. Near the bottom of the shaft, Arianna instructed everyone to get off and they walked a little bit to a large bunker door.

"I'm not even going to ask how that got down here," Sarah remarked.

"It's not that hard," Tadashi responded. "All we had to do was blow out a cavern and line it with the usual bunker material. Also since it is underground already it helps keep it even more fortified." Sarah just nodded in agreement since she didn't want to give the impression that she wasn't listening and cause him to repeat himself in a longer and more drawn out way. While he was explaining the specs of the bunker, Arianna flipped a cover and punched in a code. The door then slowly began to creak open. Inside opened up to a much larger space than anyone expected. Near the entrance was a huge computer bank and one person was there seemingly monitoring the screens.

"Mandy, you've got visitors," Arianna announced. The person at the screens turned around slowly and spoke.

"Hello," they chorused.

"Mandy here is a mandaroid," Arianna explained. "She stays down here and monitors the weapons, despite her disposition with using them."

"Mandaroid?" Sarah asked. "Sounds like an android, but she most definitely doesn't look like an android."

"I'm technically not an android," Mandy responded with a polite smile. "Although I do contain mechanical components, I am still crafted mostly using the same biological materials that are found in a normal Terran. I also possess most of the problems and joys of being a Terran, but to some degree I can finely attune some of my senses better as I am still partially mechanical."

"I see…" Sarah responded.

"But do not worry; I won't do anything too rash," Mandy replied with her same polite smile.

"That's for sure," Arianna remarked with an eye roll. Then she added in a more audible tone, "But they are here to check up on the V-Cannons."

"The V-Cannons?" Mandy said as her eyes opened wide. "Why would you want *those*?"

"We need them to…" Sarah wanted to say 'kill' but Arianna cut her off.

"They need them for self defense purposes," Arianna interrupted.

"Self Defense?" Mandy asked as she tilted her head a little.

"They are being attacked by bad people, and they need them to survive being attacked," Arianna explained.

"Oh," Mandy responded as she pondered what Arianna had just said. Then she broke out into a smile. "Okay, I guess you can use them!"

"What was that all about?" Sarah whispered to Arianna.

"Mandy does not like killing things. Well not without a valid reason. We've kept her quite sheltered here, and as a result she likes to think things can be solved without violence. Her attitude towards fighting is like Newton's Law, every action deserves and equal and opposite reaction. In other words, she will never strike first, but if she is struck, she will retaliate with what she calls 'an equal response'."

"But if that's the case, why is she down here?" Sarah asked.

"She's in charge on monitoring them. She also determines who gets to use them as she's one of maybe five mechanics still alive who can install, repair and operate them," Arianna explained.

"Ummm… Commander Blizzarin," Mandy interrupted Sarah and Arianna's whispering. "Do they have anyone on their ship that can use these?"

"Use them yes, but to make sure they are properly installed and maintained, you're going along with them," Arianna responded.

"But... but... what about here?" Mandy asked, a look of perplexity crossing her face.

"We'll be fine," Arianna reassured her. "Besides, it's about time you got out and saw more of the universe."

"But..."

"Don't be such a child," Arianna remarked as she put her finger on Mandy's lips. "You're going with them, it's an order."

"Okay, understood," Mandy responded with a heavy sigh as her shoulders drooped a little.

"Was that really necessary?" Sarah asked Tadashi.

"If Arianna says it, you don't question it," Tadashi responded without taking his eyes off Arianna. "Well, unless you're Mandy. Mandy can get away with a few extra things, but then again, Mandy would also suffer bigger punishments than what Arianna would normally issue."

"So it's almost like a mother child relationship," Sarah thought to herself. "Maybe because she misses being a mother, and letting her son get away from her too soon."

"Commander, if we are moving to their ship, where is the computer equipment going?" Mandy asked in her normal voice tone.

"She bounced back from that quickly," Fae remarked.

"Its one of those things she can do because she's partially mechanical," Tadashi responded.

"You won't need most of it," Arianna responded to

Mandy's question. "Fae and Sonluth both have access to computers that can probably help you monitor things. And if they can't help, I'm sure their ship's Weapons Department can help you out."

"Okay," Mandy said as she nodded her head. She then turned to Sonluth and Fae. "There are two main Vector Canons and about five smaller ones. The five smaller ones can act as normal defensive fire on your main battle mechina. One of the two main canons is small enough to put on a personal mechina, while the other can only be equipped to a large battlemechina of either BA or FS class, or something of similar size."

"How long would installation take?" Fae asked.

"On the personalized mechina a day or so, give or take difficulties with calibration. The ones going onto your main battlemechina would take at least two days, and maybe another day for calibration." Mandy responded.

"Uh-huh," Fae replied slowly before adding, "So when would we be able to get started, and what size crew would you need to assist you?"

"I can start right away," Mandy beamed. "As for crew size it seems like you and Sonluth would be all I need."

"That's it?"Fae blurted out. "Surely you jest."

"Jest?" Mandy tilted her head to the side.

"You're not serious." Sonluth sighed and shook his head, more as a comment in disbelief of Mandy not having heard the phrase before oppose to trying to provide an explanation.

"No I am quite serious," Mandy said as she continued to smile. "It doesn't require a large crew if a few people know what they are doing. Additionally, a larger crew may hamper our ability to work quick and efficiently."

"That sounds like a robotic comment," Marina quipped.

"Robot is not the proper term used to describe me. I'm a mandaroid," Mandy corrected Marina as she waved her index finger.

"Okay, okay, I get it," Marina said as she shook her head and walked away a little.

Arianna then spoke to Sarah. "So where do you intend on going once you leave here?"

"Maybe try pre-empting the Silicians."

"I thought you would say that," Arianna said with a small laugh. "But have you not learned anything from the Osmerians?"

"I'm not sure what you are getting at."

"Divided you can't beat the Silicians. In other words, she's suggesting we go back to our own system to iron out problems, and then attack the Silicians as a united front," Sonluth explained.

"But wouldn't that wipe out our own infrastructure?" Sarah asked.

"That depends on how you go about uniting the Terrans," Arianna spoke, "but it would give you the resolve, supplies and numbers you need to take on the Silicians. It would also prevent you from being caught between a rock and a hard place. Think of it this way, even if you were to beat the Silicians on your own, where would you go? You'd still have to go back to UTSF controlled space and face them eventually. That is why, if you unite them first, even if you wipe out the current chain of command, you will still be able to get support from what is left." Then she grinned to herself as she though, "Wiping out the current chain of command sounds like a good idea, even without the experience a fresh start with no weeds is better than having to weed them out later."

"That does make sense, but tell me something, how come you haven't gone after the UTSF? By the sounds of things you had plenty of reason to do so, *and* you had the fire power."

"We lack the manpower to do it," Arianna said as her smirk melted off her face. "Leaving here would have revealed our location to the UTSF, something they would have *really* loved. We may have some fire power, but it is all attached to this quarry. We don't have a mobile mechina force to challenge and then hide from the UTSF. Trust me, if I could, I would have taken on the UTSF a long time ago," her voice trailed off into a sigh. "Had things be different I may have contemplated a do or die mission at taking over the UTSF, but it just never presented itself." She shook her head and perked up before continuing, "You guys still have the Central Armada?"

Sarah nodded, "Yes. Just before the war it was stationed just ahead of the asteroid belt. Now that you mention it, I haven't heard much about them recently either. Even during our initial fighting in Pluto and Mars."

Arianna did a double take, "*Really*?"

Sarah nodded, "Uh-huh, they assisted us at neither Pluto nor Mars."

Arianna shook her head and laughed to herself, "Maybe

they took on heavy casualties and were relying on testing you guys out under fire. Who knows; even when Leo was on the fleet he kept their movements secret from me." Arianna then spoke in a lighter tone. "Well, I've got to go up and prepare a few things. You guys can help Mandy to install your brand new Vector Canons. And feel free to ask her anything, she's pretty much the encyclopedia on them."

"Got it," Sarah responded. Arianna then walked off with Tadashi and the others began the long task of helping Mandy transfer the equipment over to the RAINE.

"Are you sure you want to send her off just like that?" Tadashi asked Arianna while they were in the lift away from everyone else.

Arianna nodded. "Yeah, she'll be fine. I have faith in the crew of the RAINE, and my son."

"Speaking on that… are you sure you don't want to go see him?"

"No. Doing so would only get him angry, and that is the last thing that crew needs right now," Arianna said as she leaned back on the wall and looked upward. "That aside, he has grown up independently of me. Even if I did speak to him, there is nothing I could say to him. Not even all the times I've kept him safe, because, he just doesn't remember, or doesn't know."

"But shouldn't you at least tell them about the Central Fleet?"

Arianna's gaze shifted back down to Tadashi, "No. The best thing about the RAINE's crew is they are acting off instinct. By us telling them the Central Fleet was the aggressors may cause them to become further enraged or distrustful. Allowing them to find things out is part of the joy of discovery. Some things you learn from books, yet things stick with you more when you learn by doing for yourself. After all is said and done, we can tell them, or you can have a few good stories to tell your children," Arianna said with a bit of laughter.

"I will never understand you as a mother," Tadashi commented. "Sometimes I think you are the coldest parent in the universe; you let both Saku and now Mandy go from under your wings, yet from a distance, you've still managed to love and nurture them as if you never left them. You're like a mother weasel; you will happily bring a scorpion to your children so they can play and learn how to handle it, but if things get out of hand you'll intervene."

"That's just how I am," Arianna said. "After all, I did have to trick my only child into thinking I died so I could protect him infinitely better than had I stayed there with him."

"Yeah, but what about Mandy? You do realize she looks up to you like a parent."

"And that is exactly why I need to send her away," Arianna responded. "Otherwise she'll become too attached and I'll never be able to get rid of her. Not only that, if I were to die, I'm not even sure how she'd respond. I need her to go out and experience death before it comes to that. That way her integrated system will be able to comprehend death and her losing someone close to her won't completely destroy her."

"I see…" Tadashi said dryly. He then added with a sigh, "How is it you always manage to think of these things? As a soldier I could never think of half these plans and ideas that you come up with."

"Because the military is about on time and straight lines; they forget to tell you that the road of life is paved with winds and turns. Once you figure that out, you can think on anything."

"I'll try to remember that," Tadashi said as the lift reached his stop. "Thank you commander, this has been a most interesting discussion." He saluted and left before Arianna could complain about him needing to salute her.

The RAINE didn't need many supplies as they still had a lot of the supplies gathered from Osmeria. Since the main concentration was on bringing the Vector Canons online, work was carried out rather quickly. After watching the first mini-canon get installed, the other mechanics were able to mimic the process and assist with simultaneously installing the remainder of the mini-cannons. The whole system was up and running halfway through the second day. They then proceeded on installing the main canon onto the RAINE, which was a little tricky as they had to rewire and reroute the energy for the Gravitron Canon. After another day, they had the main canon installed on the RAINE. As for the second main canon, Mandy suggested using the FRAMEs, ATF or the GENOVA unit. She suggested against using the Ingrids as the pilots would feel the G-Forces exerted on them when they shot off the canon. Both Forte and Jace relied on agility, thus neither wanted it deployed on their craft. Rosita also did not want it deployed on hers as the weight of the canon would require her to recalibrate her booster system. That left the ATF, which would again limit the craft's maneuverability, however it would not impact its current booster set up or weapon capacity. By the time they reached this decision it was late in the day, so they didn't start much preparatory work on the installation.

Late that night, there was a strange transmission on the bridge of the RAINE. No one was expecting anything, so no one was there when it occurred. All it involved was a small radio transmission, and that was all that it took to make one

Pluto Commander *very* happy.

CHAPTER 2: VASAL'S REVENGE

"Sir! We have located the RAINE!" a communications officer spoke quickly with a salute to Commander Vasal. "They appear to be somewhere located in an abandoned moon quarry in the 235th quadrant of Sector W. It does not appear the RAINE is on battle alert. Do you want us to give the order to attack?"

"Attack? No, not yet. I want to be there personally when that mechina goes down," Vasal responded. A grin came across his face as he continued, "Let's gather half the fleet and jump out to them. If they really aren't on battle alert, they'll never suspect we found them, and I'll be rid of them for embarrassing me."

"Aye Commander!" the soldier said with a salute. He then issued the order to mobilize half the Pluto Fleet, which included seven BA class and twenty one FS class battle mechina. The movements of Pluto did not go unnoticed as John Collins and Qui Fen both noted the sudden mobilization of the Pluto Fleet. However, they did nothing to hinder or intercept the Pluto Fleet. As a matter of fact, they made sure the Pluto Fleet had a clear path towards their destination vector and cleared the path of all Silician and Terran traffic.

Early the next morning Arianna was woken up by Tadashi banging on her door.

"Why so early in the morning?" Arianna yawned as she opened her door.

"Sorry to disrupt your sleep, but there is a massive UTSF presence building up nearby." Tadashi reported. "We've tried to contact them numerous times, but they are using a UTSF encrypted channel."

"So in other words, they are waiting for a response from another UTSF mechina," Arianna yawned. "Tell our forces to standby. Do not make any aggressive movements and inform Commander Sarah that her mechina is under attack. The UTSF has come out in force to take back the RAINE."

"Yes ma'am," Tadashi responded as he turned and left. "Dear, I'll never understand how you could wake up so early in the morning," Arianna mumbled to herself as she dragged her feet back to her bed. She looked at her pillows and sheets before letting out a deep sigh, "I guess I wouldn't be much of a leader if I went back to bed. Goddamn nobility habits that make me want to sleep in but refuse to let me abandon people under my care." She then turned away from her bed and grabbed some clothes out of her closet and threw them on before heading out.

By now, Tadashi had reached the communications room and relayed Arianna's messages to both Sarah and the other units on the ground.

"They're *what*!!" Sarah exclaimed as she received the message.

"I don't know," Tadashi responded. "All I'm doing is delivering the message from the commander to you."

"Fine, we'll scramble. Thanks for the heads up," Sarah responded. She quickly raised the battle code to red and all the pilots were put on standby and the rest of the crew on high battle alert.

"How'd they find us?" Kazumi asked as she booted up her console. "We're hidden from view, and sonar can't pick us up in here."

"Encrypted Message," Marina sighed.

"Well put it up," Sarah ordered.

"No, I mean that's how they found us," Marina reported. "They must have been still searching for us after disappearing from Pluto. The search crafts randomly send out encrypted transmissions which are automatically picked up by UTSF crafts. It's a safety measure to prevent enemy Trojans or if the target ship has been disabled." Marina then showed them something on the screen. "Here it is, 0300 hours, we were radioed by vessel PC 2340, asking if we needed assistance."

"And that's *all* it took?" Sarah asked.

"Apparently so."

"Sonar and sensors coming online; communications feed from the quarry base established." Kazumi announced. "There are no less then four BA class and fifteen FS class battlemechina amassing about one hundred miles from here."

"Did they bring the whole fleet to take us in?" Vladimir whistled.

"It would appear so," Sarah bit her lip as she saw the screen light up where the fleet was massing. She then radioed down to the hanger. "How is the electronic work going Fae?"

"Not too bad commander, we're just getting the Gravitron Canon online, but the Vector Canon will take a while yet. Your shields will also be at 80% proficiency if you activate them now. We are trying to work as quickly as we can."

"Okay, do it as safe and quickly as you can. No pressure, but we've got a large party from Pluto outside waiting for us."

"No problem," Fae said. "The pilots are all free to launch as we've cleared out the pathway to the catapults."

"Good to know," Sarah responded. "Place them on standby to await further orders."

"Yes ma'am," Fae responded before Sarah cut off the comm. link.

"How are your battle preparations?" Arianna asked Sarah over the radio.

"Not bad, our crew is virtually combat ready."

"We can buy you some time or provide a distraction for you. If need be I'll personally go out to take care of some of the fleet for you."

"Thanks Arianna, but try to keep safe as long as you can."

"You too," Arianna responded and then was gone. What Sarah didn't know was that Arianna had managed to unencrypted the channel and was now able to listen in to the conversations on the radio. Arianna knowing that the original Commander Vasal had been killed years ago was very cautious about this current Commander Vasal of the Pluto Fleet. She bided her time for a while until she was able to figure out who it was.

"Long time no hear Commander Visage. Along way from home aren't you," Arianna asked.

"Sir! Our channel has been compromised!" she heard one of the soldiers yell out.

"It doesn't matter. She's the wife of one of the greatest heroes of the UTSF." She heard Visage respond before addressing her personally on the radio. "I'm looking for something that belongs to me old friend. I heard from a little bird that you have it. Would you mind being a dear and hand it back over to me?"

"Friend? Ha! We were *never* friends. And I have no idea what you could possibly be talking about. Ships come and go all the time and it looks like you have *ample* ships with you right now."

"Ummm... Commander, is it safe to provoke the UTSF like that?" Tadashi asked.

"We're just buying the RAINE time," Arianna responded. "Our fates were sealed when they arrived in the sector. All we can do is stave them off long enough for the others to escape."

"So why open the channel?" Tadashi asked.

"Remember how you said I like to protect my children? Well this is one of those cases. The Fleet will not open fire so long as they don't know our full battle capabilities. However, as my last order to you, get everyone to the escape pods. I suspect, once they build enough confidence they will call our bluff and open fire on us."

"As you wish Commander, but I'm coming back afterwards," Tadashi yelled back as he ran off. "Don't die until I get back."

"I won't," Arianna yelled back. Then she grinned to herself, "Silly boy."

"Arianna, you aren't making this easy on yourself. I'd hate to tell Leo I sent his loving not to mention pretty wife to the afterlife."

"And I'll tell you like he'd tell you. Flattery will get you nowhere," came Arianna's sharp response.

"Well, I'm sure you have others down there with you. I'm sure you wouldn't want to bring harm to them." Visage said with a hint of concern.

"Aww, thanks for their concern," Arianna responded, "But they are like my children, very durable and *very* independent. If you came down here they'd shred you to bits. Oops did I say that out loud, I'm sorry, I forgot, you guys don't *come* out to battles. Let me rephrase, if they came out to visit you *then* you'd be ripped to shreds. Well if I gave them the order anyways."

Visage grumbled and actively grit his teeth together at Arianna's comment.

"Why not simply open fire on them?" Visage's weapon's officer asked. "They can't possibly have more fire power than us right now.

"No, simply opening fire maybe just what she wants," Visage thundered. "While we offload our arsenal in front, it would give the perfect cover for an escape from the rear, which would make this exercise pointless if the RAINE escaped. He leaned over on his fist, "I'm well aware of your tactical prowess, and I'm guessing you have something the RAINE wants. I severely doubt you've been hiding them all this time," Visage muttered to himself. "Yet it must be something extremely important for you to open a channel and taunt me." He banged his fist down causing his bridge crew to jump, "Dammit Arianna, why are you here. This would have been so much simpler if you were out of the equation."

"The order to evacuate has been made," Tadashi reported as he returned back to the communications center.

"Good," Arianna responded as she gazed out to where the Pluto fleet was amassing. "They still aren't moving, not sure if it's because of me or because they still aren't sure where the RAINE is." She then turned to Tadashi, "And just why aren't you going to the escape capsules? You still are part of 'everyone here'"

"Ever since I enrolled in the UTSF Academy, I heard all about you and your late husband Leo. Ever since then I wanted to be just like you two. When I finally met with you, I've always stayed in your shadow, hoping to learn what it is that makes you a great leader. I've seen this company through a lot of things, yet you always seem to keep things running smoothly. However, Mandy and Saku have showed me what really makes you such a good leader. And to honour that, I will stay with you until the end. Until one of us draws our last breath, I will be at your side, ready to serve you in whatever way I can."

"You'll be a good leader some day," Arianna said with a grin as she shifted her focus back to the gathering fleet. "Once you get over your fawning."

"I beg your pardon?" Tadashi asked not hearing clearly what Arianna said.

"Nothing, nothing at all," Arianna responded still smiling to herself. "Just watch and learn, so you'll know what to do after I'm gone."

"Commander Mistral, we too share Tadashi's sentiments," A radio communications came over an internal line. "You have done so much for us; we do not wish to abandon you when it is your time of need. We will stay here and do battle until the last man is left standing."

Arianna was a little surprised at the over welling of faith.

Like her, none of the others on the colony had been trained military personnel. For them to stay and fight instead of runaway she felt her lips quivering and her eyes began to water. She made sure Tadashi couldn't see her face as she cleared her throat and steadied her voice, "Fine; if that's the way you want it, then our forces will hold our ground. No one leaves until the RAINE is safely away from here. Its safety is priority and you have permission to shoot anything that pursues it." Her smile returned to her face as she added, "When I give the word its open season on the Pluto Fleet." There was a cheer over the radio, and onboard the RAINE they noticed the change in atmosphere.

"It would appear the members of the quarry have taken up arms," Kazumi reported as numerous sonar sources went off. "We can at least be sure to have some cover fire as we head out."

"Alright," Sarah nodded. She almost felt as if she was going to jump and hug the nearest person to her. However she simply afforded herself a grin as she oversaw the final preparations to move out.

"The RAINE has finally begun to move," Tadashi reported as the RAINE began to clear its docking bay.

"I'm going out," Arianna responded.

"But why?" Tadashi demanded.

"Because those guys are going to need more then ground based support," Arianna responded. "Tell the RAINE to hold position until they hear shots fired. Once that happens, they can leave."

"Yes ma'am," Tadashi sighed.

"Don't you sigh at me," Arianna roared.

"Sorry, it won't happen again," Tadashi quickly responded as he braced himself.

There was a moment of silence between the two before Arianna's features softened. "I know you think this foolhardy, but as a leader your priority is making sure all objectives are met. Consider that your lesson for the day. Now get your head in the battle and hold down the fort until I get back. You're in charge now. Don't let me down."

"Yes ma'am," Tadashi said with a salute. Arianna simply shook her head and left the room to board her mechina in the docks. Tadashi quickly relayed Arianna's orders to Sarah.

"Alright, but we'll help you push back the Pluto Fleet," Sarah responded.

"No you won't. The Commander has ordered us that your safe withdrawal is priority. So within those orders, I can guarantee that you won't be able to stay and fight."

"But we can engage them better then you."

"No!" Tadashi responded sternly. "We have our orders. If you want to help out, respect our commander's decision and leave." He then cut off the radio communication.

"So what are we doing commander?" Kazumi asked as Marina held the RAINE's current position.

"We'll follow their wishes..." Sarah said with a sigh. "I'd love to help them out and I'm sure we can, but they want us to escape above all else."

"Well, even for us, taking on a force this size maybe a little over our head," Vladimir countered. "There are a *lot* of larger class ships out there. Taking them on here might be a pyrrhic victory and we'd be forced to stay here and potentially fight more waves of UTSF fighters, not to mention Silicians."

"Wait!" Lucius exclaimed as he nearly jumped out of his chair. "If the majority of the Pluto Fleet is out here, then there is probably not much left back at the base."

"Wow… you may have a point there," Sarah mused. "By moving such a large force out here, we can start our Solar System Campaign off without much trouble if the fleet is out here."

"But do you think the Pluto Garrison really left themselves *that* open?" Vladimir asked. "You think the Central Defense Fleet or even the Saturn Fleet would move to cover Pluto?"

"Knowing him, he's probably come after you without notifying the rest of the UTSF," Arianna's voice came over the radio. A humanoid mechina with what seemed like wing thrusters then approached from the stern. Neither sonar nor radar picked it up as it flew right next to them.

"How are you doing that?" Kazumi asked.

"The same way you got into Osmerian Space undetected, my mechina has the same capabilities as the prototype," Arianna responded. Then she added. "But we can discuss that later. I'm going to fly up to the Pluto Fleet. When I let you know I'm close to the fleet, I will give Tadashi a message and get you to move. Once you leave here, head straight for Pluto. Even if by some miracle the central fleet is there, they can't send a huge entourage without clearance from HQ. Pluto will serve as a beach head of sorts. After neutralizing Pluto, you will be forced to take out the garrison in Saturn. Otherwise they will come out to reinforce the Central Fleet, which I suggest luring near or inside the meteor belt. Once the central fleet takes on severe losses they will retreat back to either the Earth or the moon. If you've played your cards right, and with a bit of luck, you will be able to easily take over Martian Space. The base where the RAINE originally departed will be your final resupply base before you take on the UTSF for one final stand at the moon."

"You make it sound reasonably easy," Marina commented.

"On paper, it is," Arianna responded. "That's what the military does; make things easy to read as they follow set patterns. I will hold out here as long as I can. It should buy you enough time to approach and severely damage any resistance left at Pluto. Once you take over Pluto, unless the Silician Forces come, you should be able to retreat back there if you should run into any trouble."

"But we don't have the man power to run Pluto Base and the RAINE."

"There's no need," Arianna responded. "The Pluto Base can be fully automated. It only has people there for times it will need to over-ride commands, like say if it wants to shoot at you. The base defenses can't do that unless the controller tells it that you are now an enemy and not a friendly. So they need to keep a skeleton crew there. The only others you will probably run into are crew members of the mechina that they left behind."

"So you're saying that all we know about the Pluto Base is just hype?" Sarah asked.

"Oh, no, not hardly," Arianna responded. "If you take too long, they will switch over the system, and if that happens you guys will have hell on your hands."

"How long you think a switch would take?" Marina asked.

"Thirty minutes maybe," Arianna said with a shrug. "Depends on who is left at the base. But enough talk, that is the best strategy I can give you. Take care of yourselves and my children. They are getting restless, so I better go out and give you guys a diversion."

"Thanks commander. We will, make it back safely," Sarah said quietly. She then opened a radio channel to Tadashi. "Good luck. We'll see you in a week or so at UTSF headquarters."

"You too," Tadashi responded. "Sorry about the initial rough treatment. I'm looking forward to the party."

"It would appear they are hiding the RAINE," Vasal said thoughtfully as Arianna's mechina revealed itself. "Fleet open fire on the approaching mechina. If they wish to taunt us with only one then we'll show them our might. Those who do not have a clear shot at the mechina advance towards the planet."

"Ground forces prepare to open fire," Tadashi ordered. He then radioed to the RAINE. "The fighting has started. You are free to advance out of the docks. We will provide covering fire."

"Alright! Activate full camouflage, and begin moving out," Sarah ordered. "Marina, can you start punching in co-ordinates before we clear the opening?"

"I can, but we still can't initiate until we get outside," Marina responded. "But that's not what I'm worried about."

"What can be worse?" Sarah asked.

"This colony is far enough out that we will need to make

two jumps, even using the fastest way in the nav book. In between that hour layover, the Pluto Fleet will mostly likely use that same co-ordinate to try pursue us. However, we could try an alternate path, but I'm not sure if it's completely safe."

"Marina," Sarah interrupted her. "We've trusted you all this time. You put in random co-ordinates before to escape from the Pluto Fleet. As far as I'm concerned, that is all you'd be doing this time as well. When you think about it, if you didn't say anything just now and put in proper co-ordinates, we'd never know, and assume you always knew what you were doing." There was a small silence before Marina spoke.

"You're right. I shouldn't doubt myself. Thanks commander," she said with a small smile. She punched in a few numbers and prepared to move the RAINE towards the proper jump point.

"The RAINE is emerging!" Visage's communications officer said to him. "It's coming out at the far side of the quarry. Do you want us to shift tactics?"

"Shoot that mechina down!" Visage ordered. "No matter what happens, we can always take it back in pieces and say the enemy did it! No one mocks the Pluto Fleet and gets away with it!" The ships advancing onto the quarry tried to alter their course, but were met with heavy fire.

"Commander, the advance ships can't alter their course without taking heavy fire as they change formation," the officer reported.

"I see... Arianna knew they'd come out over there. So she set it up so that we'd advance too far to turn around. Good plan Arianna, but not quite good enough," Visage thought. Then he issued his orders. "Rear mechinas head towards the RAINE as fast as you can. Ignore everything else! I want that mechina! Helmsman! Advance and send out our mechina! We'll handle Arianna ourselves!"

"Weak," Arianna thought with a grin as she noticed the switch in tactics. She was about to attack the ships that were going after the RAINE when Visage's escort and mechina opened fire on her causing her to break of her attack. It was an obvious blind volley as not many of the shots were on target, and she knew her camouflage didn't drop unless she was hit or if she used a weapon. "Trying to force me to drop my cammo eh," Arianna said to herself. "I might not have trained like all you guys did, but I'm still not dumb enough to fall for that. But still, even if it is blind firing, I can't approach the second group unless I take him out." She then radioed in to Tadashi. "Tadashi, check if any of the long range gunners have clear shots at Visage's escort group. They have shields up and I need a stronger gun to test and see how strong they really are."

"Understood," Tadashi responded.

"And tell the RAINE make it quick, they've got company inbound."

"Will do," Tadashi responded once again. Tadashi relayed both messages while Arianna held her position to see if any of her forces had a clear shot on Visage. "Commander, the ground troops are unable to get a clear shot as they are blocked by the advance units."

"Understood. I'll get a hole punched in formation, just be ready to fire when they see it." Arianna then flew in between Visage's escort group and the advancing group. Since all their shields were concentrated on the front to deal with the ground cover, Arianna was able to easily open fire on them and do some heavy damage to them before they could recover their shields.

"Fire! Kill her now!" Visage ordered.

"But sir! If we open fire on her now any shots that miss her would hit our allies," the weapon officer responded.

"I don't care! Make sure you hit her before she put that camouflage back up," Visage ordered.

"Yes, sir!" the officer responded. He then began preparation to fire on Arianna. She broke off her attack and began taking evasive action to avoid being hit as well as bringing back up her camouflage. Visage's detachment fired on Arianna, whose camouflage came up just as the volley should have hit her. She had positioned herself quite close to the advancing fleet members that they didn't have time to react as to if the attack would miss its intended target. Whether it hit her or not, it had the effect Arianna wanted. The blast for the attack punched a hole in the advancing fleet's formation. The long range gunners had a clear shot at Visage and wasted no time locking on and firing off shot towards Visage's detachment.

"The RAINE is preparing to jump!" the communications officer exclaimed to Visage.

"What! On what co-ordinate? There's nothing over in that direction," Visage fired back.

"I can't tell sir," the helmsman confirmed. "They are literally jumping into nowhere. Even in the navigation book there is no jump for their current location. We took the only jump in the navigation book to get here."

"We got incoming fire!" the weapon officer interrupted. "The quarry has opened fire on us, probably in retaliation for taking down their commander. We have shields up but most energy was diverted to weapons fire."

"Tell that advance group to close up so they can't fire on us again!" Visage ordered as the volley closed in on his ship's position. The advancing ships closed up their ranks as ordered, and were starting to get in range of using their own weapons on the ground forces. The volleys hit Visage's detachment without them trying to evade. The other smaller mechinas had broken formation as they either were trying to confirm the destruction of Arianna's mechina or simply to get out of the line of fire from the incoming volley. As the weapon officer had predicted the shields didn't provide much cover and the volley did a fair amount of damage to the mechina.

"No major damage to report," The communication officer reported after taking the hit. "Although I wouldn't advise taking another hit like that."

"Neither would I," Arianna interrupted the radio conversation.

"What! How did you avoid that volley!" Visage demanded.

"My little secret, but here's something I'm sure Vasal would be happy to give you," Arianna said as she reappeared a few meters behind Visage's command mechina. She launched a short flurry of attacks and then disappeared again before the other support mechinas could get a lock on her.

"Do you want me pull back the advancing divisions?" the communications officer asked as they recovered from Arianna's attack.

"No!" Visage yelled defiantly. "Launch all available firepower at that quarry. I want Arianna to witness my military might!"

"Nuh-uh," Arianna rebuffed Visage as she took out a swath of Visage's support mechinas. The advancing fleet was now in range of their normal weapons and was about to open fire when a huge barrage of missiles launched from the quarry. They were instantly wiped out as their shields had already taken serious damage from their steady advance. They also could not evade the barrage as their formation could not be broken fast enough.

"Godspeed Commander Arianna," Sarah said as the RAINE had now completed preparations and initiated their jump. The pursuing mechinas tried to take shots but they were too late as the RAINE disappeared into the abyss of space.

"Argh!" Visage yelled in disgust. "Find out where they went!" he ordered his communications officers. "All other mechina fire at *everything*!"

The fleet then opened fire onto the quarry. Unknown to them, most of the controls were buried deep beneath the surface, so casualties were kept to a minimum. While the dust was still clearing from the fleet's attack, Tadashi issued an order to return fire and the quarry opened fire with armaments it had kept underground during the initial waves of attacks. Arianna was also going about picking off Visage's support mechinas so that soon it was only his mechina and a two other FS class mechinas left in his detachment.

"Main cannon is fully charged and ready to fire," the weapons officer reported.

"Good," Visage said. "Fire!" The cannon fired and this blast was strong enough to take out a good portion of the quarry's defenses.

"Commander... Mistral... we can't... take a shot... like that... again," came Tadashi's broken up communication.

"You've done enough, evacuate, *now*!" Arianna responded back.

"Understood," Tadashi responded and the radio went quiet.

"First you take Leo and now you take my unit... no, my friends. You have a lot to answer for, and I'm going to start you down the road to do so!" Arianna growled

"Now who's losing their cool?" Visage asked with a smirk.

"Arrogant to the end," Arianna remarked. "I already know your mechina can't take much more damage. Even if the rest of your fleet kills me, you still won't make it out of this alive." She appeared a little above Visage's mechina and launched one final flurry of attacks that would use up the last of her ammunition. The mechinas originally dispatched to pursue the RAINE managed to get locks on her mechina this time around as she intended on using all her remaining ammunition on Visage's mechina and made no attempt to avoid their fire. The initial shots started to hit her as she fired off her last missile. A large chain reaction then confirmed the sound she wanted to hear as Visage's mechina exploded and was destroyed.

"Good bye Saku my dear son. I'm proud to have a son like you. I'll be at your father's side watching over you," Arianna whispered as the barrage disabled her mechina and then in one brilliant blue flash it blew up.

"No... Commander Mistral..." Tadashi said fighting back the tears as both he and the surviving members under

Arianna's command saw the brilliant light that was Arianna's mechina.

CHAPTER 3: THE RAINE STRIKES BACK

Unaware of the Arianna's fate the crewmembers of the RAINE came out of their first jump unscathed. They tried a long distance communication back to the quarry, but there was no response. Marina assumed this was most likely due to their extreme distance away from most radio carrying devices and the signal might not be able to reach them. The pilots were then put on standby and the RAINE lead a nervous one hour vigil as they waited for the Jump drives to cool down and restore themselves.

"Marina, be honest with me. Do you think they made it out alright?" Sarah asked to break the nervous silence on the bridge.

"I'm sure they did," Marina responded quietly without making eye contact. "They were still holding out quite well when we left, I'm sure they're still doing fine."

"You're right," Sarah sighed. Then she added, "How are our preparations going?"

"They're okay," Kazumi responded. "Electronics have been fully restored. Mandy has completed the electrical work for the main Vector Canon. Hydraulics have confirmed their repairs are also up to scratch and have worked to protect the circuits and hydraulics from being easily damaged. Fae also says she's rewired the backup wiring for times we do take damage."

"All sensors are acting nominally," Vladimir reported. "Weapons systems and emergency measures are also in good condition. We can also increase weapon charge even when shields are at full as the power output was increased by twenty percent." Vladimir heard Sarah sigh at the end of his report so he added. "Commander, don't worry, everything will be alright. We have strong allies and a strong crew. We'll not easily give up the ship!"

"Thanks Vlad," Sarah said as she recognized the quote Vlad was trying to use. "But never did I ever think that I'd go up against the UTSF. The group I still technically still work for. Not only that, I'm potentially going to be going up people I once went school with, not to mention--" there was a short pause before she continued, "dad."

"I see your plight..." Vladimir responded rather despondently.

"Commander, your father would never fight you," Marina told her. "Think of him as an enemy who looks like the man you once knew as your father. Don't hesitate to do anything at this stage. I know how you feel since I had to attack some of my fellow Osmerians who I'm sworn to protect. It's hard to switch like that, but sometimes these things happen. Just know, we're all behind you, and we'll support you. And that can give you the resolve you need to overcome this."

"Umhmm, thanks guys," Sarah said with a weak smile. A little buzzer went off a few minutes later.

"That's our cue," Marina said. "The jump drives are ready again, once we jump there's no turning back, are you guys ready?"

"Let's do this!" Sarah said with renewed confidence. She then got on the intercom to address the whole crew. "Crew of the RAINE, as your captain and commander, I'd like to thank you all for your help and support during this mission. In a few minutes we'll be undertaking one of our most difficult assignments yet, reorganizing the UTSF. Once we jump, we'll be back in our home Solar System. I know some of you will run into family and friends, but... so will I. And with your help and resolve I hope to get this over with as fast as possible. Think of it as upholding our oath to protect our family, friends and our race as Terrans, and Generians. Your friends and family will understand, and if they respect us they may even join us. So go out and show them what a *real* United Terran Space Force does!" This speech sent the ship into a cheering frenzy, and the overall low morale aboard the RAINE began to turn around and start rising. Sarah's speech seemed to have the desired effect, and Sarah was very pleased as she issued the order to Marina to bring up the camouflage and begin the jump sequence.

"Our commander has matured into a fine leader," Sonluth grinned to himself.

"The whole crew has," Jace added. "I think we've all changed a little during this voyage. Never would I ever have expected to be a rebel against the UTSF, and here we are, in high spirits, one jump away from doing just that. One ship against the strength and might that is the UTSF."

As they came out of the jump in Pluto Space, they made a quick scan of the area and it was as Arianna had said; there were almost no physical defenses at the Pluto Garrison.

"Aww, I guess this means we don't get to test out our new Vector Cannon," Vladmir pouted.

"No," Sarah said as she narrowed her eyes at Vladmir. "We're trying to keep casualties to a minimum." She then spoke through the radio. "Members of the Pluto Garrison, this is the RAINE. While we do not intend to needlessly shed blood, we ask that you surrender peacefully to us without any further resistance."

"You are indeed very brave, or very foolish. You are currently placed between us and potential reinforcements." There was a pause before the person continued, "However, you are in luck. We are receiving flight logs to indicate that the majority of our fleet was decimated in search of your mechina, thus no reinforcements can be expected. As per your request we will surrender without any aggression."

"Yes," Sarah cheered softly with a fist pump.

"Excuse me?"

"Ahem," Sarah cleared her throat. "Yes we are pleased with your decision we will be landing shortly to officially accept your surrender."

"I can confirm the logs commander," Kazumi said as Sarah ended the radio communication. "These logs are indeed authentic and they all end with chain explosions, which probably resulted in the destruction of the mechina. It would appear Arianna and her crew destroyed Commander Visage's Fleet."

"Alright!" Sarah cheered as a broad smile crossed her face. "So far so good," she said to herself as Marina commenced the docking sequence. "Arianna held up her side and we intend to do the same."

"Welcome to the Pluto Garrison, I am Officer Mike Proteus and as the highest ranking officer of the garrison I officially surrender unconditionally to Sarah Collins of the RAINE," he said as he extended a hand out to Sarah.

"Your surrender is accepted and appreciated. As said before we will not harm you nor those serving under you."

"That is greatly appreciated," Proteus responded. "Commander Vasal left here in a storm, bound and determined to get you regardless of the costs."

"You mean Visage."

"Visage?" Proteus asked. "He was banished years ago as a traitor."

"Well, that's who you've been following all this time," Sarah responded.

"I thought something was wrong with him. Initially I just thought it was the stress of the new post, but this revelation would go a long way in explaining things," he muttered to himself before addressing Sarah again. "Commander… Sarah was it? I apologize on behalf of the Pluto Garrison for causing so much trouble for you."

"Think nothing of it, you were just following orders."

"Thank you. The survivors from the battle are jumping back now. They have also confirmed that Commander Vasal slash Visage was killed in combat. They also said they will not resist and are at your command when they return to base."

"Okay," Sarah nodded. Proteus saluted and then left the area and Sarah turned to her crew behind her. "We're getting a lot of help. It's almost too good to be true how these guys just switched sides like that."

"It probably is," Vladimir responded. "The crew certainly aren't taking any chances."

"The crew never takes *any* chances," Marina remarked. "They haven't let their guard down much since we left here the last time."

"So true," Sarah chuckled.

"Sadly we're still going to have to trust them when we

depart," Lucius responded. "After all we can't spare much manpower to handle the upkeep of this station, and it will work as a good base and early warning."

"Speaking of which, once the survivors get in, we could switch their and our signal frequency. Then reprogram the automated system to recognize it as a friendly signal," Megumi suggested.

"That might be a good suggestion," Vladimir added. "I don't think the UTSF knows we're back yet. We might have some time to reconfigure things."

"What's the time frame are we looking at?" Sarah asked. "Because we want to move while we still got surprise on our side. I do not wish to move after the Central Fleet has moved, and I don't know the specifications of the Saturn Fleet."

"We can probably look that information up," Marina said. "This mechina *is* a library for the UTSF."

"Oh yeah," Sarah responded as she turned to Vladmir. "Okay Vlad, gather Mandy, Fae and a small group of mechanics from this base and prepare to reconfigure the security interface." She then turned towards Marina and continued, "Marina and Kazumi, I'm putting you in charge of drafting information on the Saturn and Central Fleets." Lastly she turned to Megumi, "Megumi, keep an eye out for anything suspicious. If anything shows up while we are reconfiguring we might only have the ships to defend ourselves with."

"Yes commander!" they echoed. They all then disbursed to their designated duties, while Sarah plopped down in her chair. "Dad, why can't we go back to working together? What happened that we wound up on such different paths,"

Sarah said as she leaned back in her chair, staring at the ceiling and let out a long sigh. She leaned forward and put her head in her hands, "Why do things have to be so complicated."

Vlad and Lucius quickly located Fae and Mandy working on some fine tuning for the electrical work on the V-Cannon. "Why such a weird formula? Five A seven A? Why not just thirteen A?" Fae was asking Mandy as they approached.

"Perhaps thirteen was viewed as an unlucky number," Mandy responded.

"Sorry to cut into your work ladies, but the commander has asked us to switch over the electronic recognition system of the RAINE and the Pluto Base."

"Oh that is an intelligent idea!" Mandy chimed with a clap.

"And we can do that on our limited time schedule?" Fae asked.

"Indeed we can," Vladmir affirmed. "It isn't a complete overhaul, just setting up an alternate frequency pattern so that we can target the UTSF, but they would be unable to target us."

"I estimate the job should take maybe sixty to seventy minutes to set up," Mandy said.

"Well if it's *only* an hour or so worth of work, what are we waiting for?" Fae remarked sarcastically.

"Let us finish this job first. We should be ready to go in approximately five to ten minutes," Mandy said.

"Less if you help out," Fae added. Vladmir chuckled a little as he knelt down to help out the two complete their electrical work.

Two hours later Vladmir radioed up to Maiku, "Ping test the new system and let me know the response."

Maiku booted up the weapon system and ran a few dummy target tests before responding back to Vladmir. "Appears to recognize the base and RAINE as allied. Other mechina in the base still on the UTSF signal are recognized as enemy targets. We are able to lock onto them with all of our systems."

"Good. Disengage the weapon system and we'll shut down the one in Pluto as well. Advise commander to put the station on a heightened alert as we'll not be able to actively shoot down anything while it's in this limbo stage. Mandy assures us it will only be down ten to fifteen minutes tops."

"I heard that loud and clear," Sarah responded. "We'll expand our sensor range to at least detect potential incoming threats sooner than usual. Proteus, can you put your smaller mechinas on active duty and perimeter maintenance while the system is being switched?"

"We can certainly do that," he responded.

"Good, we'll maintain a twenty minute vigil and hopefully nothing will fly through in the twenty minute window."

Everything went quiet as the system was shut down. However about nine minutes into the operation sensors made contact with something.

"Commander, we got mechina inbound," Megumi announced. "Trying to verify their identity as they are also not responding to radio transmissions. Their origin is outside of the solar system, so we can assume they are not from either the Central or the Saturn Fleet."

"Could it be ships returning from a sortie?" Sarah asked.

"I've tried every known UTSF signal and they still aren't responding, so I'm assuming they aren't UTSF vessels."

"Or are they?" Maiku responded as he switched the weapons to auxiliary power. "Remember we are switching identification signals. They could very well be UTSF that are not responding due to our identification signal."

"This is the Silician 14th Attack Battalion," a voice finally came over the radio. "We request assistance with resupplying and refueling as we pass through this system."

"It's the Silicians," Marina sighed. "They don't seem to be hostile though, so I'm assuming it's a normal squadron."

"You may be right," Sarah responded. "Activate the camouflage and put the pilots on standby. Give them permission to resupply, but tell them the commander is out. Act normally, as if this is a normal resupplying stop. If they ask any questions, bluff as best you can, and remember, everything is undergoing maintenance."

"Yes ma'am!" Marina responded. She forwarded the message to everyone both on the RAINE and on the base. The RAINE brought up its active camouflage and the Silician 14th Attack Battalion was given permission to dock for resupplying and refueling. As was customary, the Silicians were given free reign of the base and for the most part the operation went smoothly. Julian and his crew kept a nervous vigil as they watched the Silician movements on the dock surrounding the RAINE. All of the pilots also stayed onboard the RAINE. Kazumi kept track of radio traffic, noting the Silicians didn't appear to be on combat alert and as they were not using an encrypted frequency. For several hours one could hear a pin drop on the RAINE as the anxious minutes ticked away. Finally after what seemed like an eternity, the Silicians began returning to their mechina.

"We thank the Pluto Garrison for the supplies and fuel," the Silicians said as they departed.

"We are always willing to help our allies," the Proteus responded. "May your fleet prosper in the face of adversity."

"Good luck with your outpost, Silcian Fourteenth Attack Battalion over and out," the Silicians responded as they advanced away from Pluto.

"That went pretty good," Sarah said with a sigh of relief as the Silicians disappeared out of sensor range.

"Yeah." Kazumi added and was about to turn off the radio when someone started speaking again.

"So what's the news Deathwing?"

"No sign of the RAINE or Commander Visage. They say that he went out on a sortie," another responded. "There was no suspicious activity on the base other then routine maintenance."

"Maintenance? Did they give a reason?"

"They said it was a regularly scheduled maintenance. It was put in the calendar by the UTSF."

"Commander John Collins, can you expound on this?"

"Well Fen, each station does have certain time frames for maintenance. However, I am not aware of Pluto's schedule, although I can find it out. We have not received any word from Visage either, although we don't expect any since he did leave on his own free will."

"Deathwing, return back to our system, we will leave the finding of the RAINE until Visage gets back."

"Aye commander!" came the response as the Silicians prepared to jump.

"That could have ended badly," Sarah cringed. "We had the deathwing down here and didn't know it."

"At least we didn't have to test the name," Maiku remarked. "For now they are gone back to their own system. That should give us a head start towards the Saturn Fleet. Even if they do come back, hopefully we'll be punching through Saturn by then."

"Speaking of the Saturn Fleet, you found any information yet?" Sarah asked.

"Yep," Marina nodded. "They are apparently a mid-sized force based near the North Pole of Saturn. Their specialty is high gravity and high pressure combat. Their fleet is mixed Terran and Silician combatants, but more Terrans then Silicians. They have two major battlemechinas and one command battle mechina. They are lead by a Commander Jules who is considered a very aggressive commander."

"So payback huh?" Sarah mused.

"For?" Marina asked.

"He's the guy from Sector J who tried to capture us. We owe him a beating for trying to kill us back then. Mind you he did give us some valuable information, but still he also took away one of our crew members *and* tried to kill us."

"I thought that was Commander Collins idea," Kazumi remarked.

"He was there too, but he really didn't do much other then annoy us from the inside. But we'll be able to face him too. Dad... no Commander Collins... is in either the Central Fleet or Earth Sphere Defense Fleet," Sarah said as she shook off the sentiment. "Okay, gather up the crew, we're going to depart before the Silicians come back. Thank the Pluto Garrison, and tell them we're trusting them to have our backs."

"Got it," Kazumi said as she began sending out messages both on the intercom and over the short range radio to Pluto. Twenty minutes later the RAINE was ready to depart. As they prepared to leave the whole Pluto Garrison came out to give them a proper send off.

"Crew of the RAINE, you have our thanks. For ridding us of our false commander, and showing us there are others among us that want change. We thank you for not firing on us, first after we fired on you and secondly when you took us over. You have spared the lives of many, of our friends, family and comrades. Godspeed, and good luck. We will hold down the fort here until you return to us."

"You're very welcome," Sarah responded after the short speech was over. "May you not have to employ your defenses while we are gone. We will see you at the victory party."

"Salute!" Proteus ordered and the whole garrison saluted as the RAINE departed. The RAINE crew was quite impressed with their send off, but there wasn't much time to talk about it as they were preparing to jump towards Saturn.

"Okay, pilots we are expecting somewhat heavy

resistance once we come out of this jump. Fae, as much as I don't want to, you will probably have to deploy with Saku. Do *not* try anything rash. Vladimir, Lucius and Maiku, I want the weapons fully charged and ready to fire as soon as we get out of this. Megumi, only put up front shields to full so that the weapons can have more energy to charge with. We are going up against Commander Jules, who is noted for his aggressive tactics. We are *not* playing defense on this one. We are being the aggressors. I want as much of that fleet wiped out before they can retaliate! Mechanics, remain on standby with ammunition, fuel and supplies for all the mechina, including the weapons onboard the RAINE. We will make this as quick and painless as possible, everyone understood?" The loud cheer that responded was confirmation enough that everyone understood.

"That was very well done," Vladimir commented. "I had my doubts at the start of this, but you have developed into a fine commander that I am honoured to serve under."

"Thanks Vlad," Sarah responded and then added. "This fleet isn't as big as the Central Fleet, but it'll be a good warm up for them. Speaking of which, how'd the signal turn over go?"

"Good," Kazumi responded. "Marina kept the old UTSF one so that we can mess up their targeting systems, and Fae and Mandy also increased the output on the engines so we are apparently more mobile."

"That explains a few things," Marina remarked. "We are quite a bit more agile than most other mechinas in our class. They also managed to reduce the timer on the jump engines, or is that a side effect of their added mobility?"

"No, that was an addition as well, although it is not fully complete." Kazumi responded. "There is also an additional defense mechanism installed. The weapon consoles are now outfitted with small remote shooters. You can use them to manually intercept projectiles or small unmanned mechinas who may have defenses against our sensors."

"Good to know," Vlad remarked. Just as he said that Saturn came into view.

"Alright you all know your orders! Attack!" Sarah yelled.

The Saturn Fleet was in a usual defense formation that the UTSF employed to act as a defensive barrier, but generally only in one direction. Marina, having already done research on the Saturn Fleet knew about this formation and had punched in co-ordinates to flank this wall formation. Due to the formation the fleet was in, they had a hard time maneuvering and returning fire as their formation made it difficult to switch from defense to offense quickly. The RAINE's ability to mimic their friendly signal while still setting it as an enemy signal further hampered the fleet's ability to retaliate. Between the RAINE's cannon fire and the quick teamwork of the pilots, the tally of destroyed mechinas quickly piled up.

"Seventy Percent of Saturn Fleet destroyed. Of those that remain sixty percent are damaged and another ten percent have been disabled," Kazumi announced.

"Commander Jules of the Saturn Fleet. This is Commander Sarah from the UTSF RAINE. Your fleet has been severely crippled and we ask for your peaceful surrender or face further casualties," Sarah announced on the radio. There was a short pause before a response came back.

"Commander Sarah, you have indeed come a long way. When I last saw you in Sector J I never expected I'd see you develop into a commander of this caliber. However, I can not just surrender to you. I know your intentions, and as such I can't allow you to pass beyond this planet. I will hold this line until Silician or UTSF reinforcements come. You may have had the element of surprise initially, but now one ship still can't beat sheer numbers. Not to mention your mechina can't handle the pressure in Saturn. Once we retreat into Saturn's gravitational field, you won't be able to attack us, and we'll be safe to attack you again if you leave us," Jules responded as the remnants of his fleet began retreating.

"Do not pursue!" Sarah ordered as the pilots gave chase.

"Why not?"

"Jules has raised his fleet's shields; additionally we aren't aware of how well your mechina will react to the pull of Saturn's gravity. Return to the hanger immediately." She then turned to Marina, "Marina, you're a member of one of the best navigational teams ever to exist. Can we not maneuver close enough to keep them in range of our weapons?" Sarah asked.

"I can try," Marina responded as she advanced forward. There was a sudden pull forward as the RAINE touched the boundary of Saturn's gravitational field. Marina reflexively pulled up and out of it.

"See, you can't destroy us," Jules said triumphantly. "And a little bird just told me the Central Fleet is on their way."

"Dammit, we can't afford to have them get here," Sarah muttered. "Marina! Status report."

"Commander, you are asking for a tall order," Marina responded. "You want me to dive into a strong gravity field *and* hold the ship steady long enough for someone to fire something."

"Can you not do it?" Sarah asked.

"I can try," Mairna sighed, "but I make no promises." Marina once again advanced the RAINE into the gravitational field of Saturn. After a few minutes, they ran into a phenomenon that felt like turbulence.

"What was that?" Sarah asked as the RAINE started shaking violently.

"That's gravity trying to kill us." Marina responded. "I'm trying my best to keep us out of it."

"One thousand meters until we are in range of the V-Cannon," Vladmir announced as Marina tried to steady her advance.

"Shields at forty percent," Kazumi added. "Electronics and Hydraulics holding stable."

"I commend you for your determination," Jules said. "But you will be within our weapon range in eleven hundred meters. And judging by the erratic movements, I'm sure we'd be able to get our shot off first."

"Don't be so sure," Sarah responded. She was going to mention their attack range was longer but Vladimir stopped her.

"Don't mention that to him. That is one hundred meters we *need*. Besides, if he started to advance now, we might be in trouble," Vladimir explained. More turbulent like shaking ensued as Marina struggled to gain control of the RAINE against the increasing gravity.

"The shields can no longer be deployed," Kazumi announced. "The force of gravity is too strong."

"So Vlad, when we get within range, we will only get one shot off," Marina spoke as she continued fighting for control. "No pressure of course."

"None given," Vlad responded. "In four hundred meters we're going to blow the remnants of that fleet into the next universe."

"Commander, we got damage in the fourth quadrant," Fae radioed in. "We're trying to repair it, but this gravity is making it difficult."

"Keep damage to a minimum," Sarah responded. "Don't worry about fixing it completely if it's due to the gravity. We're in for a rough ride, do the best you can."

"Understood," Fae responded.

"Hang in there," Sarah whispered as she closed her eyes. The RAINE continued to shake violently.

"We are in firing range," Vladimir announced. "Hold her steady."

"Working on it!" Marina yelled as she fought for control of the RAINE. A few tense moments went by as Marina adjusted and readjusted the thrusters on the RAINE to try and make it steady enough for Vladimir to fire.

"Giving up?" Jules asked as the RAINE stalled its advance. No one onboard the RAINE responded as it continued to steady itself.

"There," Marina yelled as she managed to find a precarious balance to hold the RAINE steady.

"Fire!" Sarah ordered. Vladimir didn't waste no time and fired without even locking onto any particular mechina in the fleet. The recoil from the V-Cannon blast knocked the RAINE back a bit as Marina didn't have the mechina completely stabilized.

"Sorry about that," Marina said as Sarah fell to the floor. "We were stabilized for positioning, but not for fire recoil."

"Ugh, that's alright," Sarah said as she struggled to her feet.

"Advance!" Jules shrieked. "Kill them! Wipe that mechina out of existence!" The small remainder of Jules fleet advanced towards the RAINE.

"Approximately three hundred seconds until Jules gets within range of his weapons," Kazumi announced.

"That short eh?" Sarah said with a headshake. "Recharge on the V-Cannon and status of the Gravitron Canon?"

"We can't fire the Gravitron Canon; there is too much gravity present," Vladimir responded. "As for the V-Canon, due to our set of circumstances, we're going to need thirty seconds after we get in range of their weapons."

"Marina, can you do anything about that?" Sarah asked.

"Believe me commander I'm trying," Marina responded. "But we are slowly being drawn in. The designers of this mechina didn't have gravity on their minds when they built it. Or at least not this type of gravity."

"Transfer energy from the shields!" Sarah ordered. "They aren't up, we should be able to increase recharge speed with that!"

"Good   idea!"   Kazumi   echoed.   She   immediately

transferred energy that was set aside from the shields to recharging the weapons. She transferred so much energy that the ration of energy between weapons and shields were nine to one. The control console required a manual override as such a task was not normally meant to occur.

"Much better," Vladimir noted once the transfer was complete. "We can have this up in thirty seconds."

"Better make it quick," Megumi noted. "We've been stalled and were down to twenty seconds before we get in range of the Saturn Fleet."

"Unless Marina you want to just let us get caught in the gravity field," Maiku suggested. A sharp glance from Marina indicated to him that he needed to explain himself. "Boost towards them and we might be able to get a surprise attack off. And by surprise attack, we'll have to cover two hundred meters before they can respond and we can take them down with some of our mid-range weapons."

"In theory, that's acceptable," Marina said as she continued to fight against Saturn's gravity. "Hurling ourselves toward them at this gravitational pull would give us fifteen seconds. Within those fifteen seconds we have to pray they aren't fast enough to react *and* you guys would have to already be pushing the button at fifteen seconds."

"Leave that to us," Vladimir said. "Just can you do it?"

"Of course I can," Marina responded. "But how do you expect to get out of this if we go in any further?"

"Contact in 15 seconds," Kazumi interrupted.

"Jump out!" Sarah exclaimed. "Didn't the timer resets get shortened?"

"They did…" Marina responded. "Okay Vlad, Lucius, Maiku, you got one shot at this. You will have five seconds to lock on and hit them. Otherwise we'll have to leave them here."

"Five seconds is all we'll need," Vladimir responded.

"Alright then. Hang on to your seats and don't let go. It's going to be a quick fifteen seconds," Marina said as she released the reverse thrust and instead propelled herself towards Jules' fleet.

The Saturn Fleet showed no change in tactics as the RAINE barreled towards them and continued to shift into their attacking formation. The next ten seconds were a blur as everyone on the bridge frantically worked to getting the operation done completely. Everyone held onto something that was strapped to the ground and no one dared move or even breathe. All anyone ever remembered was a lot of turbulence, a sudden flash, and they were back out in beyond Saturn's rings.

"Did we get them?" Sarah asked.

"I don't know," Marina said as she exhaled and allowed herself to lean back in her chair. "I didn't take note of us hitting anything. I was just concerned with getting us out of there," she continued as she dried off her sweating palms.

"I think we got them," Vladimir said hesitantly. "There is no way to tell for sure since we jumped before our shots made contact."

"Vlad… this is the safety of a whole ship and crew. Are you sure you can't tell?" Sarah asked.

"No," Vladimir responded. "Even our weapon logs can't

determine, but it's at a sixty percent success rate."

"Which makes it forty percent failure," Sarah sighed. "Well we better hope the sixty percent is what counted here." She then got up to leave the bridge.

"Where are you going?" Kazumi asked.

"To assess the damage. We may have to return to Pluto after this, but I want to see first hand what problems we have, as well as any injuries from that rough flight. Until I get back, stay within the debris of Saturn's Ring, just in case Jules survived or the Central Fleet comes," Sarah responded as she walked out.

"Phew. Well… I'm glad *that's* over," Marina said as she slumped down in her chair. "That is one of the most dangerous moves I've had to do in a while."

"Yeah…" Vladimir said despondently. "Let's just hope we hit our target."

"Let's change the topic," Megumi suggested. "I don't want to think about not hitting those last few mechinas, because sixty percent is not really a comfortable number to be working with."

"Agreed," Lucius said. The bridge then fell silent as they began their checks and balances wanting to believe that they had indeed successfully accomplished their goal and there weren't any remnants of the Saturn Fleet.

CHAPTER 4: PARENT VS CHILD

By now, Sarah had made it down to the hanger. She found Fae trying to organize the mechanics into different division to deal with the gravity damage.

"How bad is it?" Sarah asked Fae.

"Not too bad," Fae sighed. "Considering how reckless we just were. Most of it is superficial, but there was some damage done to the shield generators. Some of the mechanics have also reported injuries through that rough ride. You might want to check that situation for yourself in the medical wing."

"Point taken," Sarah responded. "Sorry about the rough ride, hopefully we won't have to do *that* again."

"Hopefully," Fae responded. "Because that caught all of us off-guard."

Sarah nodded and left the hanger area. She quickly made her way to the medical wing to get a report from them. As Fae had predicted there was a lineup of people waiting to get medical attention. Some people had minor injuries, while others there had obvious impairments. The medical staff had separated the influx of people into two lines; one for serious injuries, and another for minor bumps and abrasions.

"How many do you think are up here?" Sarah asked a medic as she was running by with some cotton swabs.

"I'd say at least half the crew is up here," the medic responded. "But I've got no time to talk; we're completely over run at this point with injuries. We're sending out two others to check up on others that might not have come up for their own reasons. But while you're here, you should get a checkup. Or if you don't want to wait, you can go back to the bridge and wait for the field medic to get there." The medic then ran off into the crowd to deliver the swabs to where they were needed.

"Might as well return to the bridge," Sarah sighed. "Looks like mechina and crew both took a beating from that last battle." On her way to the bridge, Sarah came across Sonluth and Jace talking to one of the field medics. "What's going on here?" Sarah asked.

"Oh, pardon me Commander, I'm making rounds. I'll be up to the bridge shortly," the field medic responded stiffly.

"At ease… I'm not angry at you or anything," Sarah responded. "No need to be stiff or anything, I was just asking what was going on for my own benefit."

"I just finished checking out the pilots, and I was here telling Sonluth and Jace the current situation with injuries," she reported.

"I feel like I failed as a captain when you say that," Sarah said with a sigh. "It seems like I did more harm than good to the crew."

"I wouldn't necessarily say that," Sonluth remarked. "I'll take a few broken bones over losing my life completely. Besides, I'm sure the crew is well aware of the circumstances we were in."

"I suppose you are right," Sarah responded despondently. "So how *are* you pilots doing?"

"We're doing fine," Jace responded. "It'll take more than a bit of turbulence to disrupt us. Even Rosita came out pretty much unscathed."

"Alright," Sarah said as her posture perked up a little. "Well, I'm not sure how bad the injuries and damage are. I'm waiting on reports to determine if we should return to Pluto or press forward to the Central Fleet."

"The Central Fleet. That is your only option." Sonluth said bluntly.

"What makes you say that?" Sarah asked.

"Sooner or later the Central Fleet will check in with the Saturn Fleet. With the lack of response will come an investigation. That investigation will bring them to us. The only difference your decision will make is the location of the battlefield. If we were to press on now, we might intercept them at the Asteroid Belt. Return to Pluto and we might be pinned down in Pluto when they reach us."

"Gee, I never thought of that," Sarah responded. She then sighed let out an exhale and looked down at the ground. "Sometimes I wonder if I'm really cut out for this amount of thinking and stress."

"*You* are doing fine," Jace responded. "*He* is a veteran. In a decade or so you *might* be able to measure up to him. But for now, he has greater experience, so don't feel intimidated when he thinks of something you may not have thought of."

"I'll keep that in mind," Sarah responded.

"While you are here Commander, what is the condition of the people on the bridge?" the medic asked.

"Exhausted, but in good shape otherwise," Sarah responded.

Alright, do you want to get your check up now or wait until I get to the bridge?"

"Might as well get it now," Sarah said with a shrug. "At least I can remain on the bridge when you deprive me of my crew."

"Okay, this way," the medic led Sarah to a side room away from Jace and Sonluth. She checked her over and in a short time gave her a clean bill of health. "I know this is a tall order, but don't forget to get some rest when you can," the medic said as she allowed Sarah to exit.

"Ha! Yeah right!" Sarah said with a laugh as she left the room. Once she had gone, Sonluth came in.

"Verdict?" Sonluth asked.

"It's not negative," the medic responded as she showed Sonluth a vial.

Sonluth looked at the red liquid in the vial. "Hmmm, this might help explain a few things. Sarah might be in more trouble then she even realizes. Run this test on the whole bridge crew save Marina. I need to confirm something among them."

"You got it," the medic said as she left the room.

"I see now; Operation Free Mind might have meant more than just collecting a few samples," Sonluth muttered.

As instructed the medic did the standard medical test on all members of the bridge. She also carried out the extra test that Sonluth had asked for. Other than a few small cases of hypertension, probably brought on by the stress of the last battle the bridge received a clean bill of health. The medic then returned back to Sonluth, who was talking to

Jace.

"Is now a good time?" she asked Sonluth as she approached the conversation.

"It's alright, Jace already knows," Sonluth responded. "What are the results?"

"You maybe onto something," she responded. "Sarah, Kazumi and Izumi all have lower tissue densities then normal Terrans. Sarah clearly has lower density then the rest. Only two people on this ship are lower, Qui Fen and Zee."

"I'm not even going to ask how you got your hands on that last bit of information, Aira." Sonluth remarked.

"I have my ways," Aira responded. "But, genetic material might have one other surprise left for us."

"Oh?" Jace asked, intrigued.

"Both of Sarah's parents may have been on this ship," Aira responded. "Initial testing carried out earlier in the voyage may suggest that Fen, Sarah and Commander Collins are all related."

"And you're just getting around to telling us this?" Jace asked.

"I didn't have a sample from Sarah. John went out of his way to prevent his daughter from being tested," Aira responded.

"But there were strict rules against, excuse my lack of a better word, but breeding with Silicians and Terrans," Jace responded.

"Which would explain Sarah's lack of being tested," Aira interrupted. "That aside, our dear captain will be facing not one, but two parents, however there is no way to confirm this as both suspected parents are not currently being tested. But judging from her stress level, I really wouldn't tell her this, because that would only… complicate things, especially if this hypothesis is correct."

"This confirms my suspicion that Operation Free Mind was a test to gather samples of people suspected of being mixed. To see if they had enhanced abilities when compared to the original parents," Sonluth said.

"What about the others?" Jace asked.

"Kazumi and Megumi are both partial Silician. We can also safely assume the same is true for Izumi. However, Izumi apparently has stronger psychic abilities that are more associated with the Silicians then her two siblings. I'm not sure if this is due to luck of the genetic lottery, or if she has different parents then her so called siblings," Aira reported.

"And you would conclude this because?" Jace asked.

"There has to be a reason why Izumi was selected over her two sisters," Aira shrugged. "Either way, something is not adding up and there has to be some other detail that we are missing as to why." She then started to walk off towards the Medical Wing, "But that is enough for you now Colonel, if I find anything else, I'll be sure to let you know. For now I better return to my duties before anyone gets suspicious."

"All personnel prepare to jump," Sarah's voice came over the intercom a short time later. "We are expecting to run into the Central Fleet shortly after our jumps towards the Meteor Belt, so we ask that you prepare yourselves accordingly. This mechina is now under Red Alert Status."

"That's our cue," Jace yelled out to Sonluth.

"I'll be right out," Sonluth said as Jace left. Jace acknowledged this and headed out ahead of Sonluth. Sonluth waited about five minutes before exiting the room. Instead of heading to the hanger, he took Aira's test results back down to his lab. Once down at the lab, Sonluth ran an additional test using the partial program he and Fae had gotten from the Nebulizer. He wanted to see how the samples reacted to the program, so he left them there and left the computer to monitor itself while he went to the hanger. He boarded the Fenix and then opened a link so he could monitor the computer's recording while he was on standby. Nothing seemed to be happening right away, but Sonluth kept the screen up as he had already figured it would take a while. Just before the jump ended there was a small heat reaction, but Sonluth couldn't monitor the test much longer as the jump was finished.

"No sign of the Central Fleet," Kazumi announced. "However we can not get any large confirmation beyond the Asteroid belt."

"Hold position," Sarah ordered. "We'll jump past the asteroid belt, since they maybe waiting for us in ambush."

"Unless you wanted to go through with full camouflage, and sensors off," Marina responded. "The only problem with that is we'd have to go through with just our own eyes to spot things and navigate."

"No, we'll sit it out," Sarah ordered. "We'll be a lot safer even if they come out to us then if we go in to them."

"You should probably know that intel suggests they might approach from within the asteroids, giving them a chance to pick up on us first." Marina responded. "Unless we used some of the outer rocks as a block to prevent us from being detected even if they were to come out from the Asteroids."

"Do that then," Sarah responded. "Do not activate the camouflage. We have to face them, and I'd rather do it now, then later with the Earth Defense Fleet."

Marina nodded her approval and piloted the RAINE towards the outskirts of the Asteroid belt and kept it behind a large asteroid that completely hid the mechina from anything approaching from the inner part of the belt.

"Very good crew of the RAINE," a voice came over the radio. "I see you have learned a few tricks on your voyage. You aren't the naïve crew that I left behind at Sector-J. You have survived both Generian and Osmerian Territory. You've apparently bested Visage from Pluto, and have managed to get across Jules at Saturn. However, this is the Central Fleet. I doubt you will get across us, especially not in the asteroid belt. But being the loving and caring father I am, I'm willing to give my daughter one last chance to redeem herself and surrender to the UTSF. I'll make sure to put in a good word so that your punishment wouldn't be too harsh."

Everyone on the bridge looked at Sarah as she prepared to respond. She was looking down at the ground and she was shaking a little as she flexed and extended her fingers in and out of a fist. After a few minutes of quiet, Sarah raised her head and despite wanting to cry, she fought back the tears and spoke with a small shake in her voice.

"Since I was small, all I ever wanted to do was follow my father's footsteps. I went to the academy, and they further instilled the ideals that I learned from home. Truth, justice and protection of the planet we call home. I believed in those ideals. I thought the UTSF top brass would follow the lessons they taught. This voyage has unclouded my sight. I can see clearly now. I see now, that my father died when he signed on with the Silicians. He was killed by the greed that has since killed millions of others who served in the UTSF. My mechina will *not* back down. Captain John Collins prepare yourself! The RAINE will uphold its oath even if it's through your fleet!"

"Such resolve," John said. "But it will get you nowhere. One ship can not take out a whole military force. If you will not surrender to the UTSF you pledged to, then you will die by them as I am judge, jury and executioner! Central Fleet advance! Our objective is to destroy the rogue mechina, the RAINE!"

"We are detecting numerous heat sources," Maiku commented. "It would appear the Central fleet was lying in ambush for us."

"Deploy the pilots," Sarah ordered. "And prepare the Gravitron Canon and the Vector Canon. Put energy fully into charging those canons and ignore shields for now. We'll blast them straight through this asteroid we're hiding behind. Or at the very least propel this asteroid forward to smash some of the ambushing units."

"Commander, you're not going to believe this, but we got mechina's approaching from Jupiter's shadow," Kazumi reported.

"What?" Sarah exclaimed. "How soon until they get here?"

"I don't know. I can't tell at this distance what mechina they are," Kazumi responded.

"I guess that means we missed the last bit of Jules fleet," Vladimir sighed. "I guess this is the rock and the hard place we were warned of avoiding."

"Everyone! Battlestations!" Sarah ordered over the intercom. "Pilots, shrink your perimeter. We got inbound units believed to be the remains of Jules' fleet coming from Jupiter."

"Aye, Commander!" they pilots all echoed.

"Both canons charged and ready to fire," Vladimir reported.

"Fire on the edges and then blast both canons straight through the formations in front of us!" Sarah ordered. Vlad pulled the trigger and fired the cannons at twenty second interval. The gravitron canon he shot along the right flank of the asteroid, and the Vector Canon he shot along the left flank of the asteroid. Marina had reversed the RAINE backwards a little so that a large part of the asteroid center did not get destroyed during this initial attack, but it had two large indents on the sides. Two minutes later, the weapons were recharged and Vladimir shot them both straight down the center, fully destroying the asteroid in front of them and taking out everything else in their direct path. There was now a clear path for the RAINE to fly through and a greater line of sight. The RAINE and all its support mechina then began advancing through the gap before the asteroids closed back up again. The pilots and the weapons aboard the RAINE kept the ship safe from most attacks as in order to attack the RAINE, enemy units were forced to come out into the open, giving the RAINE plenty of time to form countermeasures.

"I will *not* be mocked!" John yelled. "Helmsman, ascend into the gap. We shall hold our ground until reinforcements arrive!"

"Commander, the flagship Brahm is ascending to block

our pathway," Marina reported. "Orders?"

"Maintain speed and thrusters. Bring shields up full in the front. Don't bother shooting at them," Sarah responded.

"But Commander, our ships can't fit between this passage way without hitting some of the larger nearby asteroids," Kazumi said.

"She is correct commander, I know your father commands the opposing mechina, but we can't afford any haphazard plans now. We've got mechinas closing in from behind and only him really standing in our way between here and Martian Space," Maiku said as he readjusted the firing delays between of the interceptor guns.

"I agree with Maiku," Megumi said. "We're not going to have much of a choice but to shoot him down. Otherwise we might not be able to make it. You will *have* to put your feelings for family aside on this one."

"Quiet! All of you!" Sarah ordered. "He *wants* us to shoot him. The resulting explosion would probably take us both out in this asteroid field. Marina!"

"Commander?" Marina said with a small flinch.

"If we were to drop shields just before contact, would we be able to make it?"

"It would be close," Marina responded. "But on the plus side, we'd be too close for either of our weapon systems to accurately do anything."

"Are you serious?" Kazumi asked.

"Quite," Sarah responded. "Vlad, have both canons fully

charged once we pass over the Brahm. Marina, bring us about and Vlad shoot both canons. The Vector Canon to take out its shield, and the Gravitron Canon to take out the Brahm proper. Until then, Kazumi keep the shields full up front." Sarah then issued orders to the pilots. "Cover the rear of our ship until we pass the Brahm. After that, scatter, as fast as you can unless you guys want to be toast."

"Understood!" the pilots responded. They altered their sphere formation around the RAINE and changed it to more of a hemispherical formation at the rear of the RAINE.

"Captain Collins, the RAINE has not altered its course. At this rate they will collide with us!" the communication officer onboard the Brahm yelled at John.

"We hold our ground; just keep those shields up to prevent any damage. They will be stopped here, even if we have to play this giant game of chicken. They have too much on that ship to unwillingly sacrifice it."

"A-a-aye, sir," the helmsman stuttered and sighed. The crew onboard the Brahm maintained their position as the RAINE steadily approached. Both battlemechina's shields held up against their barrages as the distance had become too close for main canons to function efficiently.

"Distance to the Brahm, one hundred clicks… ninety clicks… eighty clicks… seventy clicks…" Kazumi slowly counted down the distance in increments of ten clicks. Sarah remained tense as she stood waiting for the right moment.

"Go up! Eighty degrees! Drop the shields and charge those weapons as fast as you can!" Sarah ordered at thirty clicks.

"Aye Captain!" the bridge echoed as they all scrambled to

follow orders.

"They're going around us sir!" the officer on the Brahm reported.

"Are they crazy! They'll never make it through that space," John remarked. "Fire weapons! Everything you got!"

"They are too close for the weapons to work effectively on their battlemechina," the weapon officer responded.

"And as long as they are above us we can not move or risk being knocked into one of the asteroids," the helmsman added. "We're going to have to hope they smash themselves into the asteroid above us, since behind us is open space, they'll be at a much better advantage to turn around and fire at us."

"I see..." John said as his posture dropped. "She made the calculation... that quickly..." John mumbled to himself.

Marina by now was maneuvering the RAINE above the Brahm. The move took all her focus as it was quite a feat getting the RAINE clear of the Brahm.

"Outcropping detected 20 meters ahead!" Kazumi exclaimed.

"Well hang on to something, there's no way we're avoiding it," Marina fired back. Before anyone had anytime to respond there was a loud grating sound as the RAINE ran into the outcropping. There was a small period of violent shaking, but it didn't last too long, as Marina made it past quickly once the RAINE was above the Brahm.

"Clearing the Brahm in 30 seconds," Kazumi reported as

Marina began leveling out the RAINE. "Preparing to re-engage shields."

"Canons fully charged," Vladimir reported.

"All other weapons remain on standby to come online once we enter optimum range," Maiku added.

"Pilots break formation in twenty five seconds," Sarah ordered. "Sweep the area and remain close to the mechina, I don't want any of you caught in the crossfire."

"You got it commander," Jace responded.

"As soon as we clear Marina I need you to turn about as fast as you can," Sarah said. "Even if you are drifting backwards while you turn, the turn is top priority in this maneuver."

"You got it commander," Marina responded. Her hand hovered over the controls, as Kazumi counted down the seconds.

The weapon officers and the helmsman aboard the Brahm did the same thing. All involved tensely waited for those final thirty seconds to tick by.

"We're clear!" Kazumi announced. She quickly raised all the shields as Marina punched in commands to cut the horizontal thrusters and put the full power into turning. The result was more of a power slide as Marina followed orders to put more energy into turning then creating distance.

"Little less spin sweetheart, we can't be expected to hit without a steady base," Vladmir commented as marina over rotated.

"Shove it you, my orders were to prioritize the spin and

spin we did, I can't help it if the response is a little slow stopping the spin," Marina fired back as she properly realigned to put the Brahm dead center in the RAINE's sights.

"Fire everything we can!" John ordered as the RAINE cleared the Brahm. "I don't care if it's only the mid weaponry we need to deter them from getting a good shot long enough for us to turn!" As the pilots swept around the RAINE, Sonluth released mines around the exits to the asteroid belt. This effectively blocked much of the support mechinas from being able to engage the RAINE once it emerged from the Asteroid Belt. They also blocked visual range of the mechina that could have shot at the RAINE or the pilots.

"Lock on confirmed and firing the Vector Canon," Vladimir reported. There was no need to fire the Gravitron Canon. The Vector Canon broke the shields into splinters and passed right through the middle of the Brahm.

"Sarah, my dear daughter. You have fought well. For one last time, I'll tell you how I've always loved and cared for you. But I have failed you as a parent, and for that there is no greater honour then being brought down by the person who you instilled those same beliefs that you betrayed. Farewell, my beloved daughter."

The Brahm then went up in one large explosion that Marina, even with shields up had to work hard to maintain control of the RAINE. The pilots didn't have enough time to get to the hanger they flew in close behind the RAINE. The explosion also sent debris all around and a great majority of the Brahm's support mechina was crushed by the asteroids that had been knocked around by the explosion.

"Phase Jump material detected," Megumi announced.

"What?" Sarah asked in confusion. "Where?"

"Behind us, approximately one point five kilometers," Megumi responded. "It appears to be the small fleet we saw approaching us. They've now jumped behind us."

"Turn us around Marina, and bring up those shields! Pilots, take up a defensive formation around the RAINE!" Sarah ordered. Everyone did as they were told, and watched as the ships came out of their jumps. They were facing away from the RAINE, but by the time they had come out fully, Vladimir already had a lock on the central ships.

"Hold on a second," Lucius interrupted Vladimir. "Open a comm link with them. They do not appear to be broadcasting the UTSF allied frequency."

"We'll open a communication link to them," Sarah said. "Just keep your weapons trained on them." She then spoke through the radio, "Ships that just jumped beyond the asteroid belt, this is the UTSF Battlemechina RAINE. Identify yourselves."

"Battlemechina RAINE, your reinforcements have arrived fresh from the Generian System," came a familiar voice over the radio in response.

"Gonsalves?" Sarah responded after a few seconds of pause.

"Good, you still remember us," Gonsalves responded. "We heard you were taking on the UTSF by yourself. Seeing as we owe the UTSF some payback, we decided to come out here and help you."

"Next time, a little warning would be nice," Sarah said with a sigh as she sat back down in her chair. "We were about to shoot you down as a hostile unit."

"I'll keep that in mind next time," Gonsalves responded. Then he added with a laugh, "especially since Mouse used to say 'anyone trained by the UTSF believes in shoot first ask later'."

"Not funny."

"So what is our next target? A direct attack on UTSF HQ on the Moon?"

"No," Sarah responded. "We need to take over Martian Space to secure supplies and a safe transport and launch point. We can also communicate with Pluto about any traffic that is out near the frontier of the Solar System."

"Sounds like a good plan. I will relay orders to my fleet and then re-establish contact with you at a later time."

"Roger that," Sarah said before ending the transmission. She leaned back in her chair, looking at the ceiling and letting out a long sigh.

"Prepare to move out to Martian Space," she finally ordered. "I'm going back to my quarters; call me when we get there."

"Aye captain." Vladimir responded as Sarah dejectedly walked out of the bridge.

"She's taking it rather hard," Maiku said after a few minutes of silence.

"Well, she did just essentially order her own parent's execution," Marina said solemnly. "Knowing that a parent is dead is one thing. Knowing you sent them there is completely different."

"I suppose…" Maiku responded. "Well, hopefully she get a handle enough to be back for Mars."

"Yeah…" Marina responded. "Back to where it all started…"

CHAPTER 5: MARS ATTACK

Sarah virtually confined herself to her quarters for the duration of the trip to Mars. She only really came out to eat a few meals, and even that was erratic. It was painfully obvious to everyone that she was taking the death of her father hard. Gonsalves wanted to meet with Sarah about discussing strategy before they began their attack on Mars, but Sarah was not present on the bridge.

"What! A commander not on the bridge?" Gonsalves remarked on the second day of travel.

Marina then relayed to Gonsalves everything that had happened since they had left Generian space, everything from initiating the syncer program right up until the death of John Collins.

"I see," Gonsalves responded. "You guys have been through a lot. Are you sure you can complete this mission as is?"

"We can, and we will," Marina responded.

"Forgive my rudeness, but your crew might be a little... overwhelmed at the moment. Real war is not like learning in an academy, and right now you guys have gone through much more on your first mission that saying trial by fire doesn't begin to explain what all you have faced. I admire and respect your courage and resolve, but going into battle in a broken state will only be detrimental if not kill you."

"We understand that Commander Gonsalves. But you also need to understand, for most of us this is our first major deployment. As you said before we might not all be used to seeing a lot of this, but we're dealing with it the best we can with each other. This most definitely isn't the most experienced crew, but I've seen others crack under less pressure," Vladimir added. "Our commander hasn't made it this far because of her weakness, but because of her will, and support from the crew. Would *you* be able to issue an order to kill your parent? Would you be willingly able to defy all orders and blindly go into enemy territory?"

"That depends on your orders. The Iron Wing is a defiance of UTSF orders." There was a small pause before he continued, "However, I do understand your plight. You guys are able to pull through because you aren't hardened soldiers. Being in touch with your emotions has both harmed and saved you. I will not further question the integrity of your ship or crew, but I do wish to speak to your commander before this operation starts."

"Speak to me about what?" Sarah asked sharply as she entered the bridge.

"Welcome back. I wanted to talk to you about strategy for the upcoming battle in Mars. As your home port, I expect you would know a lot more recent information about their military capabilities then I would have."

"Mars is more of a civilian center," Sarah said in a softer tone. "The tricky part about attacking Mars is that we can't use a blanket approach as that would only breed distrust amongst the local populous. Due to the UTSF's previously heavy handed tactics with Mars, if we were able to attack UTSF installments with blatant disregard to the civilians, we'd probably not help our cause much. On the other hand if we minimize civilian casualties, we'd gain a surge of support both on Mars and even on other colonies."

"So you'd incite a revolution."

"Not on heavily fortified UTSF areas. However, we'd get

support from others to hopefully assist us in having an incident free shot at the lunar base. However, it will also help our Mars Attack if we can get the support of civilians, as they'd be more willing to assist us in maintaining an order independent of the UTSF. I actually never thought all this would have such a large domino effect when Arianna first made the suggestion," Sarah added with a sigh.

"She always was very tactical minded, but it probably is the best course of action to take. That being said, I assume you have maps that indicate the location of military installations."

"That we do," Sarah responded. "We'll transmit the data to you, and I can't stress enough, avoid attacking civilian targets, especially those in the areas between Neovos and Taurus Sectors."

"Will do." Gonsalves responded. He then closed the communications link and Kazumi initiated the map schematics to Gonsalves and his fleet.

"If someone would have told me when this first started being commander on board the RAINE would be this stressful I would have laughed at them," Sarah said as she held her head in her hand. She then moved her hands upward to brush her hair back under her hat. "But I don't think I would ever trade in the experience for another crew. You guys have helped and supported me a lot. I heard how you guys handled Gonsalves, and for that I appreciate it."

"No need to get sentimental on us captain. We're just defending a friend who needed her space," Vladimir responded.

"But then again, if she didn't we'd think she was just another uppity military commander," Marina teased.

"You guys are something else," Sarah said with a weak smile. "If I die of stress, I'm going to write on my epitaph, 'It was the bridge, with their sarcasm onboard the RAINE'."

Commander Gonsalves then broke up the conversation with a radio communication. "We'll take our fleet and take out the far side closer to the main Martian HQ of the UTSF. We'll let you handle the civilian heavy areas since you seem more humanitarian oriented then my soldiers. Just be quick, as we don't know the strength of their defenses."

"You got it Gonsalves. Thanks for the help, and we'll be there as quick as we can."

"Understood. We'll prepare to jump to the far side in six hours. That should give you chance to get your operation underway in two hours. Bandpresto, and we'll see you on the far side."

Gonsalves then ended the communication and all was quiet on the bridge. Sarah broke the silence by moving from her chair as Marina held the RAINE's current position.

"Leaving again?" Kazumi asked.

"Yes, I need to make an announcement to the whole crew and I'm going to do it from my quarters."

"Ok..." Kazumi replied slowly as Sarah left the bridge. "You think she'll be alright?" Kazumi asked aloud once the bridge door closed.

"She'll be fine," Vladimir said without taking his eyes off his console. "We'll all be fine, just so long as we believe in each other."

"Crew members of the RAINE. It has been a long trip out and back to Mars. As your commander, you all have taught me a lot during this trip, and we've all had our ups and downs. In a few hours we will begin an assault on Mars, to give us one final launch point to bring down the corrupt UTSF. However, as you have all seen, war normally leads to what people in the military call collateral damage. But, I don't wish to fight with this mentality. You all have showed me how valuable life and friendship is. Knowing that I can't go into this battle and just disregard the lives that are down on Mars. This mission will not be a solo mission for the pilots. I know all of you onboard have had to have received some form of military training. I'm appointing Fae, Sonluth, Jace, and Ned to organize groups of mixed and balanced combatants to engage the enemy on the ground. We are not going in as Generians, Silicians, Terrans or Osmerians. This battle we are fighting for the safety of all those we hold dear to us. Those we don't want to lose, and those we may never meet. The four designates are free to each make four mini-battalions that will be covered by a corresponding pilot. The only person who is immune from this selection process is Marina and Vladimir as they are required to maintain the RAINE. As your commander, I ask for you all to put your faith and trust in each other, that we can successfully complete this mission with as little casualties. If those four can report to me concerning their squads within three hours, I would very much appreciate it. All four are now ordered to drop whatever they are currently doing and report to the main meeting hall to discuss groups, members and their roles in the upcoming battle. That is all."

"That was pretty impressive," Jace said to Sonluth as they gathered outside the pilot quarters. "She has most definitely matured in her role as mechina commander."

"That she has, and she isn't even showing a hint of stress while making the announcement."

Meanwhile down in the Generian Quarters, Ned was

lamenting to Fae who was dragging him off to the meeting "Why me?"

"Because the commander knows you are on good terms with people. You should feel honoured," Fae responded. "Now stop being a baby and let's go. A lot of Generians have died for the chance you are getting right now."

"Yeah Ned! Go up there and show those Terrans what we can do!" Justin cheered on Ned. "It is not often a Terran Commander will single us out for a big responsibility like this. You should take it, or I will beat you into submission to go."

"Okay, okay, I get the idea," Ned said as he exited with Fae amidst the cheers of the Generians. The quartet met with Sarah in the general meeting room a few minutes later.

"Okay guys, we are taking on a major operation in a few hours and I need all of your input," Sarah stated to open the meeting. "We're being charged with taking on the Martian General HQ. The same base we started at, but here is the catch," Sarah said as she brought up a map of the area. "The area is heavily populated by civilians. As a defender of Terrans, I really don't want to spill needless blood, and as such have ruled out a direct frontal assault or bombardment from the RAINE. So here is where you guys come in. Since most of you have knowledge of the base and the surrounding areas, do you think we can infiltrate the base keeping casualties to a minimum, or would it be safer to try evacuating the area and then applying a more offensive approach?"

"Well, this particular base is largely controlled by civilian contract workers. However, past the second defensive line, there are no civilians. If you want to spare the contract workers, you can infiltrate them by approaching them at around midnight, when they switch shifts," Jace explained. "Each station should have a booth, so incapacitate them and put them in the booths. Once past the second line, we should be able to use more force, and potentially use the mechinas to start fighting. Also, most of the booths are very durable, so as long as they remain inside, they should be safe from any shrapnel and stray bullets."

"So, we should approach this with our front liners being infiltrators, but have extract and backup nearby incase anything goes wrong," Ned responded. "But what about the main weapons on the base? I am sure they will be on high alert if Gonsalves goes in before we do."

"No, that might work in our favour," Jace interjected. "If the military were to put out its main artillery, they wouldn't want any civilians nearby, since; after all, it's marked as a research facility. Remember when we all left, there wasn't much sign of the civilian workers? They probably were sent home, or re-assigned to different areas. That being said, they'll probably have more soldiers on patrol. They will be expecting a battlemechina, so we would keep the RAINE out of range until we've at least started to secure their control rooms."

"Or maybe, you can just send the guys from security in advance," Fae suggested. "Think about it, they've been taught how to use all the security devices, and they probably know how to disable them. They would also rouse the least suspicion, because they know what the others are looking for and will act accordingly, even if they are held up for some reason."

"So get Julian and a few others to act as the advance guard," Sarah confirmed. "So who do we send in second?"

"Ned, do you remember your way around the Aqueducts?" Fae asked.

Ned hesitantly nodded. "I partially know my way around. I wouldn't say I know the place like the back of my hand. Why do you ask?"

"Well the underground aqueducts can lead one virtually unhindered deep into the base. The only resistance you might find is other Generians who maybe working down there. But if you were to secure that route you can probably get near the main control room quite quickly. The only problem is reinforcements might be a while in coming, and the group would have to be prepared to defend themselves for a long period of time. I'd suggest taking a few heavily armoured defenders and at least two mechanics to assist in hampering advances if you can gain control even one of the sub-control rooms," Fae explained. "The alternate route to that would be the air ducts, but that is a great deal riskier and the option of transporting heavy armoured people wouldn't be an option. They could be a strike team, but not a defensive team. In other words, the team in the shafts would need knowledge of the shaft so they can quickly move around to sabotage enemy movements."

"Well I can't take the shaft team," Ned responded. "I completely lack sufficient knowledge to lead a team through the airshafts; unless Jace and Sonluth have good knowledge about them."

Jace and Sonluth both shook their heads. "It would probably be better for Fae to lead that group. Although she isn't very experienced with strike tactics, it's more important to keep them safely in the shafts. Unless you want to put two of us present here into each team. Me and Fae can handle the strike team, while Jace and Ned can lead the aqueducts team," Sonluth suggested.

Sounds like a good plan infiltration wise, but how about a forward push? Or are we just going to try take them over from the inside out?" Sarah asked.

"If you don't mind switching out Marina for Kazumi as the helmswoman, deploy Marina and Vlad to lead a forward attacking force. Between Marina's sporadic tendencies and Vlad's trigger happiness, I think anyone opposing them will probably be mowed down rather quickly," Jace said with a small chuckle. "They also both have superior knowledge of firearms and explosives, giving the force an extra edge in knowing what they'd be dealing with."

"Is Marina combat ready?"

"Osmerians heal remarkably fast. Or rather their bodies quickly reach stability, but due to their inner workings and the complexity of Osmerians they take a while to fully heal," Sonluth explained.

"I'll take your word on it," Sarah frowned.

"She *is* back on duty on the bridge," Ned chipped in. "If she wasn't combat ready she couldn't have gotten us thus far. I mean it's the same with us mechanics. Even if we're the slightest bit sick or wounded, Fae will send us back to the barracks because an exhausted mechanic is no help to any of us."

"Well yes, I suppose you make a point. Ok, so Marina and Vladimir in a front push."

"How about deployment of the RAINE directly?" Ned inquired. "Or are we keeping the RAINE out of this completely?"

"We're keeping the RAINE out for the most part. Like I said before, we're trying to minimize casualties and the RAINE's weapons aren't all exactly precision weapons. That said, Kazumi has some experience with controlling the mechina. She should be able to manage on her own for a while and in the event we do need some type of response from the RAINE, be it covering fire or even to blockade the docks, her skills should be sufficient," Sarah answered.

"Final point is mechina deployment," Jace said.

"Well seeing as you and Sonluth will be deployed with teams that leave Forte, Saku and Rosita on standby with the RAINE."

"Or perhaps send Forte with the forward push to give covering fire and leave just Saku and Rosita on minuteman duty, because honestly speaking the front push is the only place mechina pilots would really be useful other than escorting and assisting the RAINE with blockading the docks," Jace said.

Sarah took a few minutes to ponder the plan that had just been thought up. She ran the scenario over in her mind, going over every detail that had been just suggested. She pictured the security division going in and scouting out ahead while the second group began their assault through the aqueducts. As they began their attack on the central defense areas, the third team would begin their sabotage runs through the air vents. As the UTSF soldiers became confused, one final group would push through the front.

"Alright, this mission plan has my approval," Sarah finally spoke. "All squad leaders debrief your teams on the difference between the civilian workers and the UTSF soldiers. While this is a military attack, I still wish to keep civilian casualties to a minimum. Although I won't be deployed with you all, I will still support you from the RAINE as best as I can. This meeting is dismissed, with the mission commencing at 0300 hours. Rest up and prepare your groups. This mission is only as strong as our weakest link, so make sure our weakest is better than their strongest."

"Aye Commander!" the others said with a salute and they all disbursed to form their squads. Sarah returned to the bridge and conveyed the details to the crew.

"Vladimir and Marina, you're going to be deployed as leaders of a frontal assault team. While it's called a frontal assault, you're not to go all gun-ho and shoot anything that moves. You're going to squeeze the last bit of resistance out of Martian HQ. Hopefully by the time you guys push through Sonluth and Jace's teams will have already shattered the Martian Resistance. Kazumi, you'll be in charge of moving the RAINE. Now before you object, it's mostly just a holding position as we don't intend to use the RAINE directly, and I'll be up here as well to help with direction."

"Ship controls again…" Kazumi sulked.

"At least you're not going on the front lines," Lucius said.

"That is true," Kazumi said as she perked up.

"Marina, tell Gonsalves we have a plan we're planning to start at 0300 hours, and we recommend he start his decoy tactics approximately ten minutes beforehand. I'm going down to Julian to inform him of his department's role in this attack."

"Commander Gonsalves, this is Marina of the RAINE, do you copy?"

"Loud and clear," came Gonsalves' response a few minutes later. "What is your status?"

"We've formulated a plan, and will proceed at 0300 hours. Our commander recommends that you should deploy approximately ten minutes before we do to put them on an alert status and reduce the number of civilian workers," Marina said.

"Intriguing strategy," Gonsalves responded. "But wouldn't it minimize your casualties if you attacked either simultaneously or earlier then we did?"

"The commander wishes to keep this a military fight. As such, she wishes to minimize civilian contact and keeping hostilities purely between military entities."

"I see. Well if that is your wish, then I have no objections. We will commence our attack ten minutes before you at 0250 hours. We will take up our positions and await the agreed time. Syncing timers and confirming it to be 1000 in five, four, three, two, one. Confirm that it is now 1200 hours."

"Timing sync confirmed, it is now 1000 hours."

"Iron Wing moving out. We will observe radio silence and stealth running. Bandpresto."

"RAINE over and out," Marina said as she ended the communication with Gonsalves. She took out her ear piece and let out a long sigh.

"Actually feeling the pressure?" Kazumi remarked.

"Sort of. I'd never thought I'd be part of something this drastic before. Even as an Osmerian, I know I'd be involved in some degree of fighting, but nothing like this."

Kazumi shrugged. "Life is like that I suppose, but it's still rather unusual to see you with the jitters like this. I feel nervous, but I'm always like this. Seeing you get them makes it feel like there's even more pressure."

"Don't let it get to you. We're all nervous, even if we never show it. Just don't let it get to you and you'll be fine." Marina smiled weakly as she continued, "This operation is bigger than all of us, hopefully we can see it through and be able to laugh at all these nerves in the years to come."

"I hope so, I really hope so," Kazumi said with a sigh. The bridge remained quiet as the crew took rotating shifts to rest for the coming operation. No one said anything, not a single word. Even when Sarah returned to the bridge, the crew looked up as she came through the door, but no one spoke to her and she spoke to no one. Sarah simply gazed out into the dark abyss of space as she sat down; the only sound heard was the ticking of the clock and the tapping on consoles.

At 0140, the squadrons began assembling and preparing for their assault.

"You think this'll work?" Ned asked Fae while they were checking over the gear.

"Of course it will," she responded with a smile. "All we have to do is trust the person next to you. Just as we've made it this far, we'll continue on until we're all safe and sound at home."

"Don't worry so much, it makes one grow old faster," Jace teased. "You don't look as good as me and Sonluth do at our ages by bogging yourself down with worry."

"I guess not," Ned responded.

"Watch Jace's back and he'll watch yours. No matter what happens, you fight shoulder to shoulder with the guy next to you. Small unified groups can triumph over unorganized masses."

"I guess so. We've made it this far."

"Precisely. Now stop worrying and put your mind in the game," Fae said as she slung her pack over her shoulder and moved off to meet up with her group.

The Aqueduct, Air Vent and Security Teams all departed on smaller stealth transport mechina and landed a little outside the Martian HQ complex perimeter. On the flight there, the squadron leaders went over one final debriefing and stressed the importance of the mission and the part they played in it.

They all landed at approximately 0230. The Security Team helped secure and temporarily disable the traps at the exhaust pipes for the air vents and aqueducts to allow those teams safe passage. They then made their way to the front gates. They waited in position just outside of camera range of the base's cameras until 0249. At exactly 0249, part of Julian's Team approached the front gates.

"Halt who goes there?" the guards demanded.

"Sharp as a knife I see," Julian responded as he produced his ID card.

"Oh, pardon me sir. We were not expecting any relief from outside of the complex."

"Yes, we're running a little… late."

"Let me radio in your---"

Julian tasered the guard as he lifted his radio to speak into it, at the same time the others with Julian pointed their side arms at the others on duty at the gate.

"Don't anyone make any sudden movements and no one

gets hurt."

The other guards complied and Julian's team herded them into the gatehouse. "How many of your men are on foot patrol?"

"You promise not to harm them?"

"I told you, no funny moves and no one gets hurt."

"Five of them…" he muttered.

Julian grabbed the radio and knelt down next to him. "Call them and tell them to report back to this station."

"What? So you can kill them too?"

"No. I told you I'm not here to harm; as a matter of fact I'm trying to help." Julian looked at his watch. "You only have a few more seconds. Call them before they really *will* be harmed." The man looked at Julian before slowly lifting the radio to his mouth.

"Foot Two this is Gate One come in over."

"Gate one this is Foot Two go ahead over."

"Report back to the front gate."

"Reasons?"

The man paused and one of the others on Julian's Team scribbled something down and passed the man the note. He then slowly read it out over the radio, "We have a faulty alarm and need to take a head count before the handover."

"On our way, over and out."

"Good," Julian said as he withdrew the radio. As Julian stood back up and was about to direct his men when the alarm sounded.

"Right on time." A few moments later the foot crew ran through the door.

"Sir! The alarm has--"

"Down on the ground. *Now!*" Julian ordered. The team put down their weapons and surrendered without a struggle.

"What are you planning on doing?" the team commander demanded as Julian and his team set about resetting some of the security devices.

"We're here to keep you safe in here. What's going on inside there is a military fight between the UTSF and the crew of the RAINE."

"There is no military presence here!"

"You ever thought about even with heavy handed tactics the UTSF would just leave you guys to your own devices? They have to keep a presence here to crush any uprising that would fester here."

"So why spare us?"

Julian paused what he was doing for a second before resuming and responding, "Our commander has asked us not to involve civilians in a military fight."

"I see... Well when you see your commander tell him Neuvo Securities thanks them for their compassion."

"Will do... will do."

Meanwhile inside the Martian HQ command center the room echoed with frantic messages from all around Mars. "HQ! The Generians have launched simultaneous attacks all across Mars!" Red lights lit up across the holomap in the center of the room.

"Calm yourselves!" the commander ordered

"But Admiral Adelaide, Mars is under heavy attack!" the communications officer exclaimed as he relayed the current situation.

"That might be so, but this is HQ! Even if they take over all the other bases, they won't accomplish anything until they take us over as well," Adelaide said. "Just tell them to calm down and sit tight until we can assess the situation. Panic and confusion is what the enemy wants."

"Yes Ma'am!" the officer echoed, and he turned back to his console and along with the others communication officers relayed Adelaide's message. Slowly, the communications became less cluttered and she was able to get a better grasp of the situation.

"This doesn't add up. How does a Generian Fleet get so far into our space without detection?" Adelaide thought aloud. "Where are the Central and Saturn Fleets, and even getting by Pluto without detection?"

"Admiral! We're under attack! From U-" a voice came over the intercom but was quickly quieted before he could finish.

"Lock us down *immediately*!" Adelaide ordered. "Get out the quick response team and repel those invaders!"

"Aye ma'am!" the room echoed. The room became filled

with the noise of people typing on their consoles and issuing of orders. Adelaide crossed her arms and intensely stared at the holomap in front of her.

"The Generians couldn't have gotten this far by themselves. And even for them, this is far too tactically sound. Why would they systematically attack various bases but not use a major force here. Even if they are trying to attack on all fronts, this would in practice be the place you use the biggest force."

"Damage increasing in the second quadrant. Team Charlie is reporting traps and sporadic gun fire throughout their section. A military force is preparing to storm the front!"

"What! Bring it up on screen," Adelaide ordered.

"The security cameras aren't working. They have been disabled!" a soldier responded.

"How?" Adelaide wondered a loud. "Even with knowledge of our technology no Generian Force should be able to disable our equipment in that short span of time."

"More fighting has broken out in the third quadrant," a report came in. "Sergeant Kish has been wounded in battle and his squad is withdrawing. They are reporting facing fellow UTSF soldiers."

"Facing… what!" Adelaide exclaimed.

"The front gate fell with next to no resistance! We're losing control of the security systems! The third and first quadrants have fallen!" the communications officer began rapidly updating the situation as it unfolded.

"Dammit, this is quickly spiraling out of control. How did the Generians locate this base so easily? Or how have they secured so many uniforms to fool security."

"There is a communications from an unknown battlemechina, we are patching it through." With a few swift strokes the Communications Officer put up a large screen and as it became focused Adelaide's eyes opened up very wide.

"No... way..." Adelaide said as Sarah's face focused into view.

Sarah hesitated for a moment as the image focused before speaking. "Commander of the Martian HQ, this is Commander Sarah Collins of the UTSF Battlemechina RAINE. I suggest you and your remaining forces surrender peacefully to us to avoid any more unnecessary conflict."

"It's been a while Sarah. Who'd have ever thought those years as mock enemies would actually occur in a real combat situation," Adelaide spoke. "But life is full of surprises, and being dealt this hand, I've sworn to uphold my duty to this post. Even if I believe you to be right, even as a friend, I can not simply surrender this base to you. Even you I'm sure are aware of the oath we took. Does it mean that little that you simply are turning your back on us?"

"Adelaide, think it over carefully." Sarah responded. "You have no idea what I've been through, how hard this is on me. Turn my back on you? No, you know I've never had the ability to do that. I know you like to fight to the last, but do you really want to sacrifice that many people? Think Adelaide. Think about our days at the academy."

"Those days don't matter at this current time. We are on opposite sides of the battlefield. You have your orders and I have mine. This base will not be yours until I draw my last breath. So come if you dare, your advance ends here and now with me." Adelaide said as she cut off the communication.

"Admiral, perhaps now would be a time to use Operation Caduceus," a voice suggested over the radio.

"But what good would it do for us Supreme Commander?" Adelaide snapped.

"Even if we lose here, the civilians will believe the Generians are at fault for attack. You will be known as the heroes who stood up to a major uprising on Mars. You may lose a few good men and women, but your base would remain a symbol of our strength."

"A win or loss does not give reason to turn weapons on our *own* people!"

"Morale is the most important objective in a war. With it we can build momentum and resolve to rally against anything."

"No! This is our fight, if they want to bring it to us, then we'll take it to them." She then spoke to those around her, "Gather up, we're going to fight a strike team with another strike team."

"As expected," the voice spoke as she left the room with a few others. "Then we shall initiate the sequence from here."

"What is that buzzer?" Sonluth asked as he paused for a moment.

"Put on your air masks and grab onto something! *Now!*" Fae ordered.

"But why?" Fae did not allow him to finish and grabbed a mask and put it on his face. A few moments later a large suction came through the vents. The group held on, but Sonluth saw Fae's grasp slipping. He grabbed onto her shirt and held it down just as her grip was about to release. After the longest few minutes of their lives the suction subsided and everyone fell back to the ground.

"Thanks," Fae said in between gasps of air.

"I'm pretty sure that's why they say put your mask on first."

"Sure, whatever," Fae wheezed. The group medic gave Fae some oxygen and they waited a few minutes for her breathing to return to normal ranges. The ground rumbled a few times as they waited.

"I thought you weren't deploying the RAINE?" Sonluth radioed.

"We weren't," Sarah responded. "However, the UTSF has turned their weapons on the civilian populous, so we're moving to intercept as much of the firepower we can. I'd advise you all to get out of there as there is no telling what means they might employ within the base."

"Roger that commander. Where shall we rendezvous?"

"The front gate, we'll have Marina and Vladimir pull back and hold to give you and the other teams time to extract yourselves. It would also be easier for Kazumi to put the RAINE down for a pick up."

"Roger, Shaft Group over and out." Sonluth then turned to his group. "Alright sounds like its getting hairy around here, you able to move Fae?" Fae nodded her head and Sonluth helped her to her feet. "Alright let's move out."

Jace and Ned's group left a time bomb in the security room before pulling out and returning to the aqueducts. Marina and Vladimir pulled back to near an exit for the ducts and vents near the front gate and held until the two teams confirmed all their members were present at the gate. The RAINE descended to extract the groups and as they were loading Adelaide and an attack squad emerged from the Mars HQ.

"I demand to speak with your commander!" she yelled as the battle groups faced off.

"I don't think you're in any position to negotiate," Sonluth responded. "Even if you were to open fire, your outside weapons have been disabled and destroyed while we have the force of a BA-Class battlemechina behind us."

"You think that matters now? My base is in ruins; I have *nothing* to lose. We can just take as many with you as we go down fighting."

"You know you don't have to go through with this," Sarah said as she walked up past Sonluth.

"I just want to know why," Adelaide demanded. "Why throw away all this that you have worked so hard for."

"It's not real; the rules, the treaty, even the people. It's not real."

"What do you mean by that?" Adelaide demanded.

"I've lost two pilots to the Silicians. Both forcibly removed with assistance from the UTSF. I've been shot at, threatened and nearly killed by the UTSF. I've watched Silicians murder defenseless civilians, and I've seen the hatred bred by the UTSF." Sarah took a few steps towards Adelaide.

"Stay your distance!" Adelaide said as she drew her gun and pointed it at Sarah.

"Brash as you are Adelaide, killing in cold blood isn't your style," Sarah said as she continued to advance.

"You are an enemy. Even if we were room mates at one time… no, we were never room mates. The Sarah Collins I was with was kind and gentle. Never would she turn her back on the UTSF like this."

"I have not turned my back on the UTSF," Sarah said. "They have turned their back to me. And I still am kind and gentle. Check you logs after the invasion. There are no civilian casualties. Even so, think about this situation, isn't it eerily familiar?"

Adelaide's eyes soon opened wide, "No! Say it is not so Sarah. Say it isn't so."

"I wish I could. But you and I both know your brother faced a similar situation, and we both know what happened to him."

"No! I won't believe it! We were always taught to never leave each other behind! There's no way that you will make me believe that Sydney was killed because he knew the truth about the UTSF! We all lived for the UTSF, and we all hold dear those tenants that had been instilled in us. This organization exists to defend humans, not to control them as they see fit!" she trained her gun at Sarah. "I refuse to believe that's what happened! Tell me Sarah! Why are you doing this!"

"Because it's the right thing to do." Sarah said. "Shoot me. The UTSF already has me recorded as MIA. You'd just be giving them a valid reason." Adelaide was fighting back tears and shot one round. Sarah didn't try to avoid it as it grazed her hair above her left ear. A quick succession of shots rang out afterwards and Adelaide fell to the ground. The gathered UTSF forced quickly apprehended the shooter and dog piled him to the ground.

"Adelaide!" Sarah yelled as she saw Adelaide fell to the ground. Fae held back Marina and Vladmir from shooting as they prepared to return fire. "Adelaide! Adelaide! Come on! Are you okay?"

Adelaide smiled weakly as she tried to raise a hand up to Sarah. "That's her... Sarah Collins... my roommate. Looking... with such... a concerned... face. I'm sorry... this time... it's not a prank..."

"Sarah, we need to get you back inside the RAINE before more UTSF soldiers decide to shoot you," Jace said as he knelt down next to Sarah.

"He's... right. I'm... sorry I doubted you." Adelaide said. "I have... one last request."

"Anything."

"Kill me."

"No, I couldn't... why would you even make such a request."

"Think... if they did that to Sydney... it will probably be just as bad for me," Adelaide responded. She struggled to pick up her gun and placed it into Sarah's hand. She then guided the point to the center of her head. "Don't think of it as killing me. Think of it as releasing me."

"We need to move!" Sonluth yelled.

"My room mate... that I protected all those years at the academy... if you see her... tell her... Adelaide gives her... her best regards," Adelaide struggled to speak. "As for you... you're a great... commander. It... was nice... getting to know you... and an honour to die at your hand."

"I will..." Sarah said as closed her eyes and pulled the trigger.

One of the Martian soldiers stepped forward and put down his weapon and raised his hand. The others followed suit, except for the ones that were still restraining the soldier who shot Adelaide. "Admiral Adelaide has been killed in battle. Mars surrenders to the battlemechina RAINE and her crew."

"We accept your surrender," Jace said. "Inform the rest of your troops on the planet to cease hostilities." He then signaled to Sonluth, "With me, we'll take a communications officer to notify the rest of Mars." Sonluth nodded to Jace and the two lead away a communications officer while the other UTSF soldiers were disarmed and rounded up.

Fae knelt down next to Sarah.

"Why does it always end like this Fae?" she sobbed.

"Because everyone interprets things differently, and war is one of those things where people hold on to what they believe in. Unfortunately this means that when people see things differently it puts us on a collision course."

Sarah fell into Fae's arms and continued crying. "Still why is it so painful why can't we all just get along, why wouldn't anyone listen to reason?"

"Because everyone believes they are right," Fae responded as she embraced Sarah. "Just as you fight for what you believe in, so do they; just remember this pain and use it as incentive to never fight more than you have to. Fight only to defend what you believe in."

Sarah broke away from Fae and stalked over to the Martian soldier that shot Adelaide and pointed her fire arm at him.

"Why! Why would you shoot your *own* commander," she yelled between her tears.

"Because it's better to kill the traitor than to follow one," he scowled. "You kill innocents and then try to play mind tricks in an effort to undermine our own race. Go ahead, shoot me. Just like you've done the thousands of others here."

"Sarah, I know how you feel, but now is not the time for this. Don't throw away all your hard work on this guy," Fae spoke to her as she held Sarah's arm. Sarah remained motionless as she tried stemming the flow of tears before lowering her weapon and turning back to Fae who helped her away.

"Be lucky it was her and not me," Sonluth growled. "I wouldn't have hesitated to kill you." Julian and a few members of security secured him and carried him off to the brig.

"Gonsalves reports that all hostilities have ceased," Kazumi reported to Sonluth. She then looked out in the distance, "But at what price is a totally different matter."

"I wouldn't say the price was too high. Fortunately for us, even with the obvious implications, it would be hard sell for the UTSF to blame an outside force for attacking the *most* despised Terran colony. Besides, unlike other times this time there are plenty of survivors who saw the attacks first hand."

"Commander and crew of the RAINE, this is Fleet Admiral Gatrie Masa. You have fought brilliantly to get this far, but your game ends here. Surrender to us peacefully or we will begin to plummet your home colonies into the planet Earth below. You have two days to fulfill this order or we will begin dropping colonies." The communication was ended as abrupt as it was started.

"What! More! No... way..." Sarah said in tears. "All that, and they still threaten innocents to get to us."

"Tch, more dirty tricks," Sonluth muttered.

"Do you want for us to support an attack on the home planet?" Gonsalves asked.

"Can we?" Sarah asked.

"No," Fae responded. "There are too many variables. Although I hate to admit it, unless you are willing to play Russian Roulette with a whole lot of people and colonies, not to mention those on the planet it would be best at least for now to surrender and try work on a plan if it presents itself later."

"Are you sure?" Sarah asked. "We have the Generians and each other."

"No," Fae cut her off. "Don't go Silician Military Commander on me now. Think about how many civilians would *easily* slip through your hands if they start dropping colonies. Yes, it's possible to reach Lunar HQ and perhaps even beat the Earth Sphere Defense Fleet but we'd lose so much more in terms of human life that all this humanitarian work would all be for naught."

Sarah's posture dropped and she spoke in between her

tears, "Fine, tell Gonsalves to not involve himself in anymore fighting. We're going to surrender to the UTSF in exchange for no colony drops."

CHAPTER 6: CAPTURE

Sarah let out a huge sigh as the first outpost colonies began to appear on radar.

"Don't worry, we'll find a way through this as well," Vladimir said, to Sarah.

"Rogue Mechina RAINE, you are to disable your weapons and approach colony one-three-three-seven. Any suspect of your non-compliance will result in your immediate termination."

"Roger that sir," Vladimir responded, "Weapons are disabled and off line. We are approaching the target colony completely disarmed." As if to test their compliance a missile was fired at the RAINE. It wasn't a large missile, but it still did some minor damage as it hit the RAINE without being intercepted. The Earth Defense Fleet closed in ranks around the RAINE as it slowly proceeded forward.

"Is there no way out of this?" Kazumi asked quietly.

"Not unless we can secure the colony control rooms," Marina responded wistfully. "Not to mention avoid a whole fleet that has us surrounded."

Kazumi sighed heavily. "So this really is the end. I never expected to be remembered for anything other than an experimental crew."

"We still will be," Sarah said despondently. "A failed experiment or maybe not at all."

"Docking is now complete," Marina announced. "The UTSF has begun boarding, and will be up here shortly." A dead silence fell over the bridge and was broken a few minutes later when armed soldiers entered the bridge. All of the members were searched and then handcuffed and lead out. As they were lead out onto the docks, Sarah looked back at the RAINE one last time.

"Good bye friends. Although our time was short, it was a great run," Sarah whispered to herself. She was then lead off to a holding cell with Marina. The two sat quietly in the cell as neither had anything to say to each other. A few minutes later, another guard came and escorted them to a military court. The panel present was made up of what appeared to be three high ranking generals.

"Commander Collins and Helmswoman Welsh, my name is Brigadier General Milos, next to me is Rear Admiral Mithos, and lastly is General Kratos. We are convened here to discuss your mechina's renegade actions. Before we start is there anything you would like to say?"

"Sir, I believe I acted in the best capacity as commander of the RAINE. My crew was also obedient and followed orders to the letter. As such, I believe these allegations are unfounded," Sarah spoke.

"Well, I have a pretty long list of things," Milos spoke. He looked at a sheet and called off the items to Sarah and Marina. "Interfering with an active investigation on Pluto, freeing a military prisoner, insubordination, entering and aiding Osmerian Forces, attacking the Pluto Garrison and subsequently killing their commanding officer, attacking and destroying the Saturn Fleet, attacking and destroying the Central Fleet as well as killing their commander who was your father, and taking aggressive actions in Mars planetary space." He put the sheet of paper down and leaned back in his chair. "The record speaks for itself Commander, or are you going to tell me you didn't do any of this?"

"What good will denying any of that do, besides humiliate my crew and mechina," Sarah responded. "I did all of those actions, but I acted according to what I deemed best in the given situation that would allow my crew to survive."

"Well you're confession is very good and it saves us time and energy. However, these crimes are normally punishable by death, and as such I'm obligated to hand the punishment down to you and your crew. But, your family has good standing within the UTSF and as such I'm willing to overlook this situation on one condition. You will be the one that executes your crew and destroys the RAINE."

Sarah flinched back and let out an audible gasp. "Why kill crew and destroy the ship? They were following orders, just like they were trained to do."

"Does it matter? Those are the terms. We will give you twenty four hours to think about it. At which time we expect a response. You are dismissed for now." Sarah wanted to protest, but the armed guards firmly held her and Marina and moved them back to their cell.

Once back in their cell Sarah began to cry and then yelled at Marina, "Why didn't you *say* anything! Do you *want* me to kill you all?"

Marina crossed her arms and fired back. "No, but even if I said something would it have changed anything? At least they are giving you a chance to live. We're all dead no matter what you choose! So shut up and think about your choice."

"A choice to live eh?" they heard a voice in the adjacent cell.

"Sonluth?" Sarah asked.

"Yes ma'am, but tell me, what is this choice they are giving you?" Sonluth asked. Sarah recounted the events of the short court martial session to Jace. After she finished there was a brief pause before Jace responded. "So those reports were probably true."

"What reports?" Sarah asked.

"Apparently, within UTSF controlled areas, our ship has become an iconic symbol even greater than the UTSF. Civilians and especially rebel factions were willing to take up arms and fight with us."

"I never heard any of this," Sarah said. "Or at least never had it confirmed."

"There are spies everywhere," Sonluth responded. "There is no safe place they can't see. But if you want direct proof, think about this. Even with the destruction at Mars, the civilians never approached us in a hostile way."

"Good point. I suppose they would have had time to bog us down like they did in Osmeria, but they didn't."

"Speaking of spies, I haven't seen ours in a while."

"Ours?" Sarah yelled.

"Shhh, keep it quiet," Sonluth responded sharply, "you can't just yell out things like that, people might hear you."

"For real," Marina responded as she leaned on the cell wall. They then heard footsteps approaching and fell quiet.

"You prisoners sure are a tame bunch without your fancy ship," the guard spoke as he walked by. "You all don't look any better than any other crew. Mind you I've never seen a whole crew locked up before either."

"So we're all in this same block?" Sarah asked the guard.

The guard laughed. "Heck no. The Generians will be assigned to heavy labour until they are executed with you. The security and medics are being held in another block from you guys."

"That's enough Ricky. There is no need to divulge information to these traitors," A voice boomed as another person approached the cell block.

"Supreme Commander Hunter!" Ricky said with a salute.

"At ease," Commander Hunter said as he came into view of Sonluth and Jace. "I'm impressed you two got caught without a fight," he said to Jace and Sonluth.

"Our commander's orders were to keep casualties to a minimum," Jace responded.

"You mean ex-commander. By the time they finish with her the only way she'll be back in any good standing with the military is being a consort to an officer," Hunter smirked. "You on the other hand Sonluth are still of great use to us."

"For the Nebula Project?" Sonluth responded.

"Obviously. The Silicians have asked us to hand you over ASAP. You and your fellow pilot Saku."

"And you have a way of getting me out of here without resisting?" Sonluth asked. "Like you said my ex-commander's orders are no longer in effect and if you want casualties I have no qualms about giving them to you."

"Of course I do," Hunter said. He quickly drew something out of his pocket and quickly fired off two shots, causing

Sonluth and Jace to fall to the ground. "Not even you can stand up to one thousand volts of electricity." He smirked to himself, and then faced Ricky. "Now quickly get Sonluth out of there before he recovers. The quicker the Silicians activate the Nebuliser the sooner we can gain control of things!"

"Yes sir!" Ricky exclaimed with a salute.

"Good," Hunter said as he saluted back and walked off. Sarah and Marina had heard the whole conversation and were still quietly sitting in their cell as they heard Ricky walk in and gather Sonluth's body. Just as he was about to exit the cell, Marina and Sarah saw a second shadow jump down onto Ricky's shadow. A short struggle followed, but the victor was the mysterious shadow. The mysterious shadow then went inside Sonluth's cell and they heard a small electrical zap followed by Sonluth's growling.

"Damn woman you can't do things easier?" the heard Sonluth mutter.

"Well genius I wasn't the one who was hit with a jolt of electricity," a woman's voice responded. "Either way, there are your keys, if I were you I'd roll over your pal there and make a dash for the docks. The rest of the crew is already out there, albeit in temporary execution cages."

"Already!" Sarah exclaimed at this remark.

"Oh, you're here too," the woman replied nonchallantly. "You're gonna have the honour of pushing a big red button to destroy the RAINE and kill off her crew. These two here should be on a shuttle to Silicia, but will probably see the ship and crew go up in flames."

"No need to be so sarcastic," Sonluth's sharp reply came. "I'm sure you've thought of a plan."

"Not quite," The woman admitted. "But here's what I do know. The crew has been placed inside the areas of the ship where they work. In other words, the crew will die when the ship goes up in flames. There are two hundred charges spread around the ship. My plan would be for you to sneak onboard now and begin dislodging the explosives. Do *not* dispose of them. Let them go off around the ship. That should give you a smoke screen to begin an offensive before the Defense Fleet can react. The force of the explosion should disable the manual stabilizers of this colony, and as a domino effect the others would follow suit."

"So there couldn't be a colony drop," Sonluth mused.

"Precisely. Your only hurdle would be keeping your commander alive long enough for her to be deemed the Supreme Commander of the UTSF. But I've said enough. Time's a ticking, and I need to get back before they miss me. You have three hours to find and locate all two hundred charges. Good luck!" The woman then bid Sonluth farewell and disappeared into the shadows she had appeared from.

"Who was that?" Sarah asked Sonluth. "The voice sounds a little familiar."

"Someone you never want to get on the wrong side of." Sonluth responded. He grabbed Ricky's keys and bound and restrained him, as well as switched clothes with him. "You heard the plan, but act as if you never heard it. By the looks of things, no matter what I do; you will still hold the crew's fate in your hands." Sonluth said as he threw Ricky's unconscious body into the cell. There was another 'pip' sound and Jace jumped up.

"Oh, it's just you," Jace said as he relaxed his posture. "I assume you need me to babysit your body to make sure no one notices?"

"Indeed," Sonluth nodded.

"Consider it done. Better yet, help me drag it over to this corner," Jace motioned behind the cot. "That way I'll sit on the cot and if they assume you're gone I can pretend you are, whilst if they know you aren't I can just motion to your 'body' back here. They all know we can sleep anywhere."

"Good idea," Sonluth said and the duo quickly moved Ricky's body behind the cot. Sonluth then exited the cell and closed the door behind him.

"Good luck on your side," Sarah said.

"Thanks, good luck to you as well," Sonluth said as he quietly ran off.

Meanwhile, Generals Hunter, Milos, Mithos, and Kratos were having a video conference with their Silician counterparts.

"We have the RAINE and her crew captured and are in the process of sending pilots Mistral and Eclipse to you so you can begin activating the Nebula. How are things on your end?"

"Things are proceeding as planned on our end. The two pilots we have are almost fully synced with the program, despite the run aways. The tests are also almost complete, and we are in the process of finding a suitable and stable genetic balance that will allow us to make the perfect soldiers."

"Excellent," Hunter responded. "We shall begin the broadcast of the execution in 3 hours. That should quiet down any hatred towards us, until we activate the Nebuliser. Then we will crush anything that stands in our way."

"Very well. Just keep up your end and you will be rewarded," the Silician General responded as they cut off the communications.

"Round up everyone. We will not allow anymore hindrances," Hunter ordered. "This little game ends here and now."

"Yes sir!" the others echoed. As they were about to exit the room, another person walked in dressed in a medic uniform.

"Major Aira of the Scientific Intel Division, we're about to give your department a large work load," Milos spoke to her.

"Oh, really, that makes me feel all warm and fuzzy inside knowing you're giving my department a gracious amount of work," Aira responded. "What exactly does this job entail?"

"As you know, we are killing off the traitors that were onboard the RAINE. However we need some... biological materials extracted afterwards as some of the crew members have mixed genetics, and we can still use them for testing, to see how stable the genes are."

"Yes sir!" Aira said as she saluted. "I will have my team on standby." Aira exited the room and made her way to her office. She closed the door behind her and let out a sigh. "So their project failed. Guess that's why you need a foolproof plan." She then began issuing orders to prepare her unit for gathering information after the executions.

Meanwhile, Sonluth had made it to the docks where the RAINE was located. As he had been told, there was a light guard present as most of the crew had already been moved onto the ship already. His first stop was Julian and the Security Division. He figured they'd be able to pinpoint things faster as they knew how to operate the security system onboard the RAINE. He got there without much trouble and his presence greatly surprised the Security Division.

"How'd you get out?" Julian asked as Sonluth released him.

"Special Ops and then a mercenary, I'm trained to escape things like this," Sonluth responded. "But that aside, we need to locate and release everyone else as well as throw out two hundred explosive charges."

Just then an alarm went off and the RAINE began to move.

"That doesn't sound like a security alarm," Julian said.

"No, it's probably them starting to move us into position, so don't worry about that. Just help me find where all the charges and crew are," Sonluth said.

"You got it," Julian said. He quickly brought up the security systems for the RAINE. The cameras were able to provide locations of the crew, while the sensors were able to locate the detonation charges. "Initial scans only indicate one hundred and sixty charges. I am also not able to locate the medics, pilots and Sarah."

"Marina and Sarah are the ones pushing the detonator. The pilots I'm assuming they are keeping for... future reference." Sonluth began to explain, but was interrupted by Julian.

"What! Marina and Sarah are going to kill us?"

"No, calm down. The UTSF wants them to kill us, but I doubt they will do it willingly. Just get me a location of the charges so I can start releasing them. You get your department to start releasing the crew and locate those last forty charges. The plan is we make our move when the charges go off."

"Got it. But you better be right about Marina and Sarah," Julian remarked as he gave Sonluth a print off indicating the location of the charges.

"I know I am." Sonluth said as he accepted the map and left the room. He then muttered to himself. "Dammit Aira, what are you doing with your division. I knew having you on board was a bad sign."

Meanwhile, back at the prison cells, the guards had come down to collect Marina and Sarah. "They've already gathered the pilot I assume?" the guards asked Marina and Sarah. The two just nodded in agreement. "Don't worry, at least you two won't be blown to bits like the rest of your crew."

"Is that supposed to make us feel better?" Marina remarked.

"Of course it does, not that you can do anything about it," the guard sneered.

"Watch me," Marina said as she prepared to fly into the guards when Sarah restrained her.

"Let it go. While you might be able to handle a four v one, I cannot and I doubt you can handle an eight v one. Marina seethed for a few moments before putting up her hands and walking out of the cell. Marina nor Sarah said anything else for the rest of their escort. They were lead out to one of the observation points of the colony from there they could see the RAINE being held in place six hundred meters away.

The platform they were led to was full of media cameras that turned towards them as they entered the platform. Both were then led to a table, where Sarah was seated and Marina stood a little behind her. Supreme Commander Hunter then approached them followed by a major whom Sarah instantly recognized as one of the medics from onboard the RAINE.

"I'd like to thank all those who have come out on this most auspicious of days," Hunter spoke to the cameras as he reached the table. "The terror faction that is the commander and crew of the RAINE has been subdued after causing us much pain and suffering. We of the UTSF are a united front against the dark tyranny that exists in this universe. Despite that, these members had all decided to try dividing us, and have all been sentenced to death."

"The 'ceremony' as it were has started," Julian radioed to Sonluth. "We've located the last ten that you need, but they are down below the hanger."

"Got it," Sonluth responded. "Don't worry I'll get them. Send Fae and Mandy down, they should be able to help me get this last leg done quickly."

"Aye sir!" Julian responded. He then forwarded Sonluth's request to the people closest to Mandy and Fae, and the two raced down to the hanger to assist Sonluth.

"The UTSF will now pass on the responsibility of this execution to the former commander of the RAINE," Supreme Commander Hunter said after he finished off listing all the crew of the RAINE. Aira then presented a small remote detonator to Sarah.

"Special Instructions, push the green button first, and then push the red one. If all goes well, your ship and crew will be safe. The green button is to activate the explosives on this platform. Grab Marina and run down to the emergency lift. There will be allies waiting to assist you. Once you get there, don't look back. If all goes well, all of the corrupted officers will go down with this colony," Aira spoke quickly and quietly.

"What about you?" Sarah asked.

"I said, don't look back. Just run," Aira said harshly as she forced the controller into Sarah's hand and walked away to take her position behind Hunter.

"Ex-Commander Sarah Collins of the UTSF!" Hunter yelled and Sarah stood up as she was addressed. "You have committed a great crime against our organization, and as such your crew has been sentenced to death. Although we should give you the same sentence, because of your good record and compliance with us, we're giving you the chance to redeem yourself. To prove that you are with us and not against us. In your hand you control your own fate. The remote to detonate the explosives onboard the RAINE. Should you carry out this duty, then you will have your sentence reduced and not be stripped completely of your rank. Refuse and you will be killed along with your crew. Do you understand?"

"Yes sir, I do," Sarah responded. "My decision is already made; I will execute the crew of the RAINE as per my orders." While she stood at attention, she was able to push the green button without much notice.

Marina stood at attention as well and took a side glance at Sarah. "Don't do it," she said to herself.

"Very good young Sarah Collins," Hunter said with a grin. "Now take a salute as the RAINE and her crew is blown into the abyss of space." All military personnel that were present saluted as Sarah prepared to push the detonator. Marina closed her eyes began to tear up as she saluted and Sarah brought her finger to rest on the red button.

"Get ready to run." Sarah said to Marina a split second before she pushed the button. Marina didn't even get time to react. Sarah pushed the button and a large chain explosion occurred around the RAINE. Simultaneously large explosions occurred in and around the platform.

"What?" Marina gasped as she looked around for the source of the colony explosions. As she had been told, Sarah didn't hesitate and grabbed a stunned Marina and ran towards the emergency lift.

"We've been set up! Kill them! Kill them all!" Hunter ordered as Sarah and Marina ran off. By now the smoke had started to clear around the RAINE. "What! The RAINE survived!" Hunter gasped as he looked out the observation window. "Destroy *everything* leave not a trace!" Hunter bellowed. He looked around and saw that most of his conspiring partners were dead and his eyes fell on Aira. "Major Aira! Order your squads to assist and kill!"

"I'm sorry Hunter I can't do that. My orders are to collect information after they are dead," she said as she uncapped the tip of a syringe.

Hunter pulled out his side arm. "Do it now or I'll shoot!"

"It will probably be what I deserve," Aira remarked. "After all, I did do a lot of dirty work for you all." Hunter's shot interrupted her sentence.

"I don't care if you have moral second thoughts now. I want them and that mechina destroyed and its crew subjugated. That's why I put you on there in the first place."

"Have it your way," Aira said. She lunged at Hunter and stabbed him with the syringe and injected its contents in response he shot at Aira. She staggered back from the gunshot and held her wounded shoulder with her right hand.

"You make this hard on yourself Aira. But since you want to go down with the ship, then down you will go. At least I will have the joy of seeing you go with me," he sneered as he removed Aira's syringe and shot at her again. His first shot grazed past her hips and the second shot went between her legs.

"Can't shoot?" Aira jeered Hunter. "I do work for the SID but while we maybe medics, we are also trained in stealth and infiltration operations. That solution you were hit with will see to it that you won't live to see the UTSF change hands. Well, that was probably sealed when I loaded the extra explosives."

"You were in on this deal too Aira. You're just as guilty as I am," Hunter yelled as collapsed down on one knee.

"That maybe so... but I have at least tried to amend my ways," Aira said as she slowly backed away from Hunter. "I saw the error after forcing the issue with Saku and Zee. I also owed it to Leo as my mentor when I failed to warn him about your impending assassination. But it all doesn't matter now... even if I go to down with you... the RAINE now has a clear and unhindered pathway to UTSF HQ. Even with the Earth Sphere Defense Fleet, Commander Collins and her crew should be able to take back the UTSF. And do what we couldn't... lead it and hold it to the ideals that the UTSF was established on."

"That's all well and good, but the Silicians will not stand for it," Hunter said as he began sweating profusely and struggled to maintain his balance.

"It doesn't matter. The Silicians were bound to cross you sooner or later. They passed the RAINE at Pluto… its possible they suspected this from back then. Who can say for sure… all I know is… it no longer matters to me," Aira said with a weak grin.

By now Sarah had literally dragged Marina down to the Emergency Elevator. There they found Sonluth waiting for them with the Fenix.

"Quickly! This colony is collapsing in on itself," Sonluth yelled as they came within earshot.

Marina and Sarah quickly crossed the last bit of distance between them and the Fenix. Marina quickly got into her space suit and got into Fenix's hand.

"Hurry up Sarah!" Marina yelled to her as she hesitated to board Fenix. There were a few tense seconds before Sarah began to move. However, she was moving away from the Fenix. "Where are you going?" Marina asked through the radio.

"You two go on ahead, I have to retrieve a crew member." Sarah responded back. Sonluth was going to try stop her, but a large piece of debris fell between the Fenix and Sarah, forcing Sonluth to abandon his attempt.

"I'm going after her!" Marina said to Sonluth.

"No!" Sonluth yelled as Fenix closed its hand on Marina. "Let's get out of here; it will be too dangerous for us to stay here much longer."

"But our commander is in there!"

"It doesn't matter now," Sonluth said. "We need to get out of here. I'm sure she has a plan to escape herself." Sonluth then engaged the engines on the Fenix and began moving away with Marina in hand.

"Be quick..." Marina whispered as the elevator entrance collapsed on itself.

Sarah had a little tough going running back up to the Observation Deck. Debris was falling all around as the colony started to crumble. The colony was also violently shaking as it struggled to maintain its own structure. A run that took five minutes to get down took close to twenty minutes to go back up. As she passed through the door, nearby she saw who she was looking for; face down on the ground was Aira. Blood was everywhere, but she couldn't tell if it was Aira's or someone else's. Aira had her hand holding fabric close to her wound, but her eyes were closed. Sarah turned over Aira and knelt down to check her pulse and breathing. Both were very faint and shallow. Sarah rapidly scanned the room, but nothing else seemed to be moving except the rapidly deteriorating colony. She refocused back on Aira and lifted the fabric from around the wound to see if it was still bleeding. As she did, some of the droplets began to be suspended in mid air.

"Not good, not good," Sarah muttered as she stood up and looked around for a way to get Aira out. "Hang in there Aira..." Sarah said as she began looking around for a space suit. She then remembered something from colony construction that she had been taught in the academy. Every Observation Deck has a small closet. In the closet there are four space suits as well as a detachment device that was made for emergency situations such as invasions to kill invaders from within the colony. Sarah quickly located this closet and took out one of the suits and began trying to stuff Aira in it. Midway through the process Aira winced and opened her eyes.

"Commander… you're supposed to be on your mechina… taking back the UTSF."

"Yeah, but not before I take back my full complement of crew since I refuse to leave anyone behind."

"I don't deserve to be picked up. Just leave me and go."

"No, you're coming with me. Now if you want to do something help me put this space suit on you."

Aira smiled weakly and complied. Within a few more minutes Aira had her spacesuit on. Sarah then quickly ran over to the closet to press the release button. It did not respond. She pressed it again and again at a gradually increasing frequency, but it still did not release. As she was about switch hands a bullet hit the wall beside her, and she whirled around to see who shot at her.

"Aira what are you doing! I'm trying to help you, why are you doing this?" Sarah demanded.

"Let me shoot the button. It will apply more concentrated pressure then your finger pressing," Aira responded. Her aim was a little unsteady and she was still lying on her back.

"Let me take the shot. You are in no condition to shoot properly."

Aira lowered the gun and threw it towards Sarah. The gun didn't quite make it to Sarah, but she quickly retrieved it and held the muzzle directly in front of the button. "Now let me out!" Sarah remarked as she fired off the first shot. The button did not respond on the first shot, but by the third shot the system engaged. Sarah heard chain explosions going off in the colony's interior and Aira smiled a little as she too heard the same sounds. However, the Observation Deck had become unstable from the previous blasts and it imploded before the colony proper did. Sarah was deafened and disoriented immediately following the blast. Once she fully became aware of everything, she frantically looked around for Aira. However, the debris was not making it easy, and the colony was still exploding, and every new charge that went off was adding new debris and propelling other debris further out.

After a few minutes, she spotted a floating space suit and she pushed off a nearby chunk of debris to faster propel herself towards the suit. However, it was not being used and she had to discard it. Her search continued for a few more minutes and then she heard a small crackle on the radio.

"Co... Ra... In..." It sounded like random rhetoric on the radio. Sarah stopped her search and tried to tune her radio to a better frequency. After a few minutes of tweaking, she clearly heard who was on the other side of the radio.

"Commander Sarah, come in. This is the RAINE. Give us your status. Over." Megumi said over the radio. There was approximately a thirty second pause before Megumi repeated the message.

"I'm here and I read you loud and clear," Sarah responded. "But I'm looking for Aira, over."

"Well I'm glad you are safe Commander, but you might have to put off looking for Aira, over."

"Why is that?" Sarah asked.

"The Earth Sphere Defense Fleet is mobilizing."

Okay, I'm at point two three Beta Alpha Foxtrott, over and out." Sarah finished off the communication. Then she muttered to herself. "Dammit Aira, where did you go?"

CHAPTER 7: LAST STAND

Sonluth quickly flew out to the co-ordinates and retrieved Sarah. Once safely back on the RAINE Kazumi quickly brought her up to speed on the current situation.

"After our fancy escape, the Earth Sphere Defense Fleet decided to remobilize themselves. They apparently didn't expect us to foil their plans and had stood down. One of the more interesting things is that there were quite a number of feeds open to Silician Space. We are not sure why, but the medics claim that the Silicians were somewhat interested in our crew. The medics, by the way, were not on board initially. They boarded shortly after our break away, which I find suspicious."

"We can deal with them later," Sarah responded. "Their commander seemed to be working a side job as well. But until we find her or get out of this situation, we have to get into HQ."

"Commander, the systems are all back on line, we are ready to advance," Vladimir reported, interrupting Sarah's conversation.

"Marina, how is the route looking?" Sarah asked.

Marina responded by bringing up a holographic map. "We are here." Marina said highlighting an area in the bottom right hand corner. "The ESDF is mobilizing over here near the lunar base. However, it will take them two more hours to fully mobilize. That being said, most of the battlemechina in our class size are already there. It's mostly the larger ones and a few of the command ones that have not yet gathered."

"Who is commander of the fleet?" Sarah asked.

"I don't know. They aren't saying. Hunter and at least the top four commanders were all inside the colony when it blew, so there is no way for us to deduce either," Marina responded. "Either way, they are steadily gathering the fleet to defend the Lunar base. Now here is the trouble we are facing. We have to either decimate the fleet and force a surrender, or we will have to forcefully take over HQ and kill the commander inside; both options without the element of surprise like we had on Mars."

"Which path do you suggest?" Sarah asked the bridge in general.

"Both will be difficult, but if we move now, we might be able to deal a heavy blow to the fleet. But even with our firepower, it's still a small chance of victory that way. This fleet is much larger than the Central Fleet, and unlikely to be taken out with a few shots," Vladimir responded.

"Which means our best chance would be an infiltration team?" Sarah asked more than remarked.

"With heavy diversionary tactics," Marina responded.

"Summon Jace, and Sonluth," Sarah ordered. "We might need their input on this."

"Yes, ma'am!" Kazumi responded. She then delivered the message over the intercom and within minutes both Sonluth and Jace were up on the bridge. Once there Sarah briefed them on the situation.

"It would seem that an infiltration would probably be best," Jace concluded. "However, I'm sure they have some fairly high level soldiers in there. Additionally, you'd have to cover any craft that is going down into all that mayhem."

"But can it be done?" Sarah asked.

"It will be difficult, but it may be possible," Sonluth said as he walked over to the holographic map. "The Lunar Base is here," he said pointing to a large green dot. "The Fleet will probably form a large layered blanket over the base. While most of their focus will be set to us approaching from this direction, if we flew in a small team from the opposite direction below the radar, we might be able to take over the base. Or at least cause enough of a diversion to send the fleet into some form of disarray."

"But do we have enough time to organize an infiltration team?" Sarah asked.

"Of course we do," Sonluth responded with a small smirk. "Isn't that what this ship is built around."

"I don't get..." Sarah started to say before getting the full gist of Sonluth's statement. "Infiltration and deception. But by our estimates it would take the fleet two hours to fully amass at which point resistance would be pretty much futile."

"We could make this very much a pyrrhic victory for them," Vladimir interjected. "I don't intend to just roll over, even in the face of terrible odds. All we have to do is hold out until a hostile take over is complete yes?"

"Fine, Sonluth, do you want the Diversion Team or the Infiltration Team?" she asked abruptly.

"I'll take the infiltration team," Sonluth responded. "Jace is probably better than me at Diversionary tactics." There was a short pause before Sonluth continued. "Actually, I'll solo infiltration."

"Are you sure?" Sarah asked as she raised an eyebrow at Sonluth's suggestion.

"Quite." Sonluth responded. "Besides, it's easier to infiltrate with lower numbers. And I have been a solo mercenary all this time. I received all the training if not more then what awaits me in there. Just keep the outside occupied and I'll do my job on the inside. This ship's operation has gotten by so far with small numbers; this mission will operate the same." He took a brief reprieve to look at the holo map. "Besides, they don't look like they're gonna let us by easily with a large group."

"Alright Sonluth, solo infiltration it is. That leaves you me in charge of a Diversionary Team. Well it's not going to be much of a Diversionary Team; we won't have any time to plan. It's more like minutemen team dedicated to drawing enemy fire away from Sonluth."

"Actually, that might not be accurate either," Sarah said a she moved her finger along the map. "They will probably be expecting us to move forward as a defensive block, ship and pilots. So if we drop Sonluth down here in basic space gear, he should be able to get in below the radar. He'd also avoid detection from any larger forces approaching from that direction."

"And how do you propose we get him down that far without being detected?" Jace asked. "We don't have time nor the resources to plan out anything spectacular."

"We can just fire him with a missile. With all the commotion going on, they won't take note of a missile failing to detonate or impacting the ground nearby."

"And we have unarmed missiles just lying around this ship?" Jace asked.

"We did when we left Mars. In the hanger armoury, we are always stocked with blanks, so that we know what to order if we are involved in any military exercises."

"Makes sense," Jace mused.

"So, with this infiltration being successful, I assume we are just taking over leadership and declaring ourselves in charge?" Sarah asked, more as a confirmation of the plan then as an actual question.

"That is the plan," Sonluth responded. "But we better get going. We don't know exactly how much time we have, or how fast these guys can reorganize."

"Understood." Sarah responded. "Alright, you all know your missions. Failure is not an option. Just come back alive."

"Aye Captain!" all present echoed and saluted before disbursing to their stations."

"Communications Line from HQ," Kazumi announced as the others left.

"Put it through," Sarah responded as she stood in front of her commander chair.

Kazumi opened the channel, but there was no video, only audio was used. "Members of the UTSF Vessel RAINE, your current course of action is not befitting of a vessel belonging to the UTSF. Why rebel against the very organization that was created to protect everything you hold dear?"

"Because the organization I once knew is no longer protecting the things it was intended to protect. The UTSF sold itself out to the Silicians in an attempt to gain strength and power. When they signed a treaty without even researching or seeking advice from other Terrans, it became clear that they no longer had the people in their best interest."

"So you believe, and perhaps may even be correct. However, we cannot allow you to simply incite rebellion and leave. You must serve as an example to others who may want to mutiny against us. This is your last chance to surrender and avoid needless bloodshed."

"Never! I refuse to sell out on my ideals and will see them through until the end."

"Hmph, very well, you were warned. One mechina against a fleet, if that's the odds you want then those are the odds you'll get." The communication was then cut off.

"At least now we know for sure the commander is still inside Lunar HQ, which would obviously make sense," Sarah said to herself as she leaned forward in her chair. "One against the many maybe the odds, but all we need to do is either cut off the head or cut off the body. This is no longer a physical confrontation, but a mental one."

"Why don't we just shoot at the top floor of the Lunar Base?" Lucius asked as he loaded up some of the peripheral weapons system.

Vladimir slapped Lucius in the back of the head. I'm sure even you know that is not possible. There is an eye shield to nullify beam damage and a gravitational field to cancel out gravity weapons and ballistic weapons. The area is also littered with radar and sonar jammers to prevent any automated shooting and it kills the lock on system."

"Oh, right, I knew that," Lucius commented as he rubbed his head. "I was just… testing you."

"Right. Now, mind your Ps and Qs, we're in for a long day," Vladimir said as he prepared his console.

"Marina, honestly, how much time do you think we have once the fighting starts?" Sarah asked quietly.

"Thirty minutes," Marina responded without taking her eyes off the growing mass of mechina forming in front of them. "This is a main defense fleet, and we are just one mechina. Voluntary Suicide seems to be what this mission is if you want my honest opinion. But that is neither here nor there. It's what we have to do to survive."

"Yes, survival," Sarah sighed. "But even a slim chance is better than no chance at all."

"Agreed," Marina nodded. Sarah continued watching the assembling fleet and the formations being employed when a few moments later Fae radioed that Sonluth was loaded into missile shaft ten and was ready to go.

"Military Convention says we should wait until we are fired upon," Maiku remarked.

"But this isn't a conventional battle," Vladimir finished off the comment. "We begin firing dispersed volleys in thirty seconds at ten second intervals. Do not shoot off Sonluth until at least the third volley. By then the automated defense systems should be sufficiently busy to start letting a few missiles through."

"Understood," Lucius and Maiku echoed.

Sarah had listened to the plan and nodded her approval without taking her eyes off the fleet. She then blinked and stood up to address the crew. "We are now beginning our take over of the UTSF. All crew to stations, and prepare to engage!" Shortly after issuing the order to attack, the weapons crew began their volleys on the UTSF fleet as they began completing their formations. The initial volleys began disrupting the formations and they began either breaking up or not forming correctly. Sarah then noticed a change in tactics.

"The UTSF fleet is employing multiple V-formations, allowing them to be less susceptible to linear shots. Adjust your firing to ballistic and spread shots," Sarah ordered. The weapons crew adjusted their shooting accordingly, relying less on optical shots and using more ballistic type ammunition. The pilots were all deployed to take care of any advancing small units, and told not to stray too far from the RAINE. Eventually the UTSF began advancing small portions of the fleet that had formed up unto the RAINE's position.

"Front fringes of the Earth Sphere Defense Fleet fully mobilized and advancing," Kazumi announced. "Approximate speed is ten clicks per second."

"Taking their time are they?" Sarah mused. "Although, I suppose, all they really need to do is buy time since it is a rather large fleet and a battle of attrition would favour them over us."

"Graviton Canon online and fully charged." Vladmir announced. "Vector Canon on standby due to shield outputs. Your orders Captain?"

"Fire the Graviton Canon, then fire Sonluth. Hopefully the Graviton Canon will clear a path for Sonluth and he'd be able to land with minimal chance of interception," Sarah responded. "Aim it at the lower altitude support mechinas. Continue to slowly charge the Vector Canon, because by the looks of things, we're in for a long day."

"Yes Ma'am." Vladmir responded. He initiated the firing sequence for the Vector Canon and informed Sonluth about his impending departure.

"Good, I was getting claustrophobic in here," Sonluth responded as he fixed his earpiece. He armed and cocked his side arm and put on the safety. "All right, here goes nothing," Sonluth said to himself as he felt an increase in pressure as his missile was fired off from the RAINE. Sonluth's missile was not targeted by the automated defense system of the lunar base as the Graviton Canon caused a small lag in the electrical systems of the UTSF. He landed a little short of his desired destination, but as he peered out of the missile shaft, he saw there were not many ground forces near his area. The entrance to HQ was still quite a distance away, and from what he could see, there were quite a few ground forces stationed at the entrance.

"Tch, just my luck. They say we're not a threat, yet they put up so much ground units to prevent an attack which by their own words shouldn't happen. Ah well, time to go locate one of the automated defense systems," Sonluth muttered as he made his initial observations. He then tried to locate one of the automated canons and soon found one a little to his right. Since he was wearing a black space suit, he easily remained hidden as he quickly made his way to the canon. As he suspected, there was a small cavity he could climb through were the builders had made room for the canon. He put his back to the wall and prepared to jump around the corner with his weapon trained on whatever might be around the corner. He took one last deep breath as he prepared to leave the chaos of the space fight behind and prepared to infiltrate the organization that taught him all he knew about infiltrating.

After a few seconds of gathering his thoughts, Sonluth quickly came around the corner, but found no one in the control room. "Fully automated with no human intervention?

I suppose with Izumi gone they didn't have to worry too much about hackings, but still it is rather dumb to have such an advance position without any manned monitoring." He brought up the console controls and typed in a few commands before running into sections he knew nothing about. "Guess I can't sabotage them from here," he frowned as he shut back down the console. Instead he followed the wiring and piping to a small grate in a concealed corner of the room.

"You'd think they'd hide these things a little better," Sonluth chuckled to himself. "But oh well, it's their loss." He opened the grate and climbed into the vent. He then carefully replaced the vent so that it would appear that it had not been disturbed should someone come by at a later time to investigate.

The pathway was fairly straight forward, as the pathway became larger and larger as Sonluth got closer to HQ as the wiring and piping for other outlaying batteries converged into a larger grouping. He noticed the lack of personnel in the hallways, although he assumed most had manned stations to take on the approaching RAINE outside. However, he did still make a serious attempt at moving quietly through the vents incase there was someone of a noise detector in the hallways below.

Meanwhile, back on the RAINE, the crew had successfully held out against the first advancing wave of the Earth Sphere Defense Fleet. However, the fleet was getting more organized in their formation, and began attacking in a proper united unit. The RAINE was also soon facing another problem.

"Commander, we are running dangerously low on ammunition," Lucius reported. "While not completely disarmed, the UTSF did remove a good portion of our ammunition before the scheduled execution."

"Ration the ammunition as best as you can," Sarah ordered. "Concentrate ballistics on V-formations and general disruption. We have enough optical weapons that we should still be able to hold our own, even with reduced ballistic firepower." She then spoke to the pilots, "This probably means we'll need to depend on you a little more, especially for the smaller targets or those who break formations early."

"Aye Captain." The pilots echoed. "We got the mechina covered," Jace added. They rearranged themselves into a square formation around the RAINE, and also began intercepting some of the small arms fire, as well as taking out more of the automated units on the ground that fell into their defensive perimeter around the RAINE.

"Sarah! We have unconfirmed contacts coming from Earth," Kazumi exclaimed as a swarm of contacts suddenly appeared on her detection console.

"From *Earth*?!?!" Sarah said as she jumped out of her chair. "I thought they dismantled all the installations on Earth?"

"Practice and theory are sometimes two *very* separate things," Vladmir responded. "However, none of them seemed to be pinging us."

"Unguided? That's a little risky isn't it?" Kazumi asked.

Sarah bit her lip as she thought on the situation. In front of her was the massive Earth Sphere Defense Fleet, and behind her appeared to be a large volley of missiles. She closed her eyes and crossed her arms as she tried to figure the logic of the missile volley coming from Earth.

"The missiles appear to be in waves. Contact with the first wave of missiles in ten minutes." Kazumi reported as the calculations for the missiles came up on the console. "Missiles are clustered in 5 groups at one minute intervals."

Sarah opened her eyes. "One minute intervals you say?"

Kazumi nodded. "That's what the console says. I take it that means something to you?"

"It does. Those are Earth military tactics that were used in conventional warfare before the move to space. The minute was required to adjust and recalibrate weapons systems for wind and such things," Sarah explained.

"But what does that have to do with our current situation?" Kazumi inquired.

"If I'm deducing right, those missiles aren't for us. They are for the fleet."

"What makes you say that?"

"While we were held captive and even the tone of the CO at the start of this battle, it would appear that our rebellion against the UTSF had sort of sparked an overall rebellion within the Earth and some of the colonies. Seeing as these missiles are not being fired according to normal UTSF intervals, I'd say the missiles are being fired off by rebel factions on the Earth; probably in protest of their general poor care over the last century or so." Sarah explained.

"But if those missiles are really for the fleet, why fire them so that they hit the fleet head on? Do they expect the fleet to not have up their shields while fighting us? Not to mention how are they going to *hit* a fleet they have no site of from Earth."

"The how is easy, they will be caught in the Moon's gravity and sling shot around the moon and hit the fleet head on. While it would make more sense to hit the fleet from behind where one would suspect the shields would be lowered, there is one other advantage to hitting from the front.

"Expound?" Lucius asked.

"This is space, so there is no friction. Which ever force is greater will be the direction that debris will fall. In this case the missile velocity is the strongest force, so by launching them from behind us, the missiles will push debris away from us. I'm sure they have enough energy to just raise rear shields if the volley came from behind them. Additionally, and you can correct me if I'm wrong, they'd get more of a warning if the missiles came from behind to shift up their rear shields."

Kazumi typed in a few calculations in her console before responding. "They would have approximately five more minutes notice. But still, *why* shoot past us without telling us?"

"We are in the tracking range. They have probably accounted for us being here. If a missile misses its target, it doesn't just die out you know. It keeps going. If they were coming from behind, 'keep going' would be hitting us. And we don't know the type of tracking is being used, so it's very well possible that we'd be seen as a viable target if a missile were to fly straight through the fleet," Sarah explained.

"You worked that all out marvelously fast," Vladimir commented.

"We haven't all survived this long by being slow on our feet."

"Touche."

"Fully charge the Vector Cannon; we will fire it just before the missiles pass, to put their shields under maximum pressure." Sarah then spoke to the pilots, "Guys you have eight minutes before a missile barrage heads past us. We are expecting the missiles to bypass us and head into the fleet, but we need you back here or as close to the RAINE as possible to avoid being hit."

"Aye Cap'n," the pilots echoed. The pilots slowly retreated back towards the RAINE as they shrunk their perimeter. The UTSF fleet made no visible attempts at defending against the missiles, and instead pressed their attack further on the RAINE..

"Sarah, we might not be able to shrink this perimeter," Jace radioed to the bridge. "The UTSF are taking advantage of our retreat and increasing the offensive pressure on us."

"Fine, retain current formations," Sarah ordered. "We'll hold out until the last minute, and then you guys have to dash back here to avoid the missiles. Got that?"

"Aye, Cap'n," the pilots echoed. They pushed back out to their previous perimeter and fought to maintain it for the current time."

"Anything from Sonluth?" Sarah asked Kazumi.

"Nothing yet," Kazumi responded. "But I haven't heard any chatter from HQ yet, so I assume he hasn't been caught yet."

"That's good." Sarah responded. She remained standing, and silently watched as the battle continued to unfold in front of her.

Sonluth by now had made it very close to the command

room. He noticed there were not many guards posted outside of the doorway. The grate of course was fairly secure, and not wanting to make any noise, he bypassed the grate after tempering for a while with it. Instead, he moved forward to see if there was a grate in the command room proper. Sure enough, there was one there, but as he approached it, he noticed it looked unsecured, almost like the one he had found when he entered the vent system.

"This is too good to be true," Sonluth muttered. "Are they really not expecting anyone to use vent infiltration?" He was about to reach out for the vent when a thought occurred to him. Despite being at the command room, where in theory the UTSF Commander was waiting, there was no noise. No constant chatter or panicked orders. It was quiet; hear a pin drop quiet. He readied his sidearm and slid off the safety. He received his answer to the eerie quiet as he reached out to move the grate.

Pew-pew. Two silenced shots went off and Sonluth quickly withdrew his hand. Judging from the sound of the shots and the holes in the vent, he gathered the person outside was using a ballistic weapon. However, the silencer prevented him from being able to determine exactly where the sound was coming from.

"Damn," he muttered as he checked his hand to make sure he hadn't been shot. A quick glance confirmed his hand was not hit with either initial shot. He then took out a mirror he had in a camouflage compact he had with him. Carefully, he leaned forward to use the mirror to scan the area. With his initial search, he couldn't find anything, and neither did the mirror get shot at. He did another slow scan to better look around the room to locate the shooter. After not finding anything for the second time, he decided he'd have to take his chances and rush into the room. He took a few minutes to clear his mind and get control of his breathing. He also prepared a flash grenade to give him an edge if someone was watching from a location he couldn't see with the mirror.

In one swift motion he kicked open the grate and rushed out into the room. As he was about to detonate his flash grenade when he heard the bouncing of something metal behind him and he instinctively dove away from the grate. In the process his flash grenade slipped out of his hand and went off simultaneously with the grenade that had been thrown into the vent that he had just emerged from. The deafening explosion and the brilliant flash caused Sonluth to become disoriented momentarily. While his sight still remained a little blurry, his hearing recovered markedly quicker and he was able to hear movement off to his left and he quickly shot over in the general direction he had heard the sound. Again he heard the sound of something heavy hit the ground, but there was no return fire. A few moments later, Sonluth heard the sound of a shots once again being fired by the same silenced weapon, but the shots were still aimed at the vent.

"I guess you're as blind as I am, or you are a programmed AI," Sonluth remarked. There was no initial response, but Sonluth heard the very faint sound of someone trying to move away from his position. He listened carefully and tried to take another aimed shot at were the noise was coming from, but heard it ricochet off a metallic sounding obstacle. Sonluth cursed his luck at dropping the flash grenade, but continued to strain his hearing to locate the sound of movement. He had figured due to the lack of return fire, that his opponent was still just as blind as he was, and that this would be the better opportunity to get them before both of them had their full vision back. He closed his eyes once more to better focus on his hearing. Slowly he listened around the room, panning his ears and gun around as he turned. For the first few seconds it was quiet, and all Sonluth heard was his own shallow breathing. But as

Sonluth expected, his opponent eventually moved, creating a small shuffling noise. Sonluth turned to the sound, and picturing what he remembered the command room as, he took aim in the direction of the noise. He inhaled one last time, and held his breath as he made an adjustment to his aim in case the target had moved further and then double tapped his trigger. This time there was no sound of ricocheting off any object and he heard a groan.

"Well I know where you ar…" Sonluth's thought was cut short as he was forced to duck for cover as he heard gunshots ring out all around him. After a few tense moments, the shots stopped firing and Sonluth heard the weapon click. The click gave Sonluth an exact location of the weapon, and presumably its owner. He took two more shots at the presumed direction, and this time he heard a thud and rattle on the floor.

"Blast it, I don't understand how one mechina and her crew could cause us so much trouble," the person finally spoke.

"You should know, you assembled a force of classified projects, and didn't expect us to cause you trouble?" Sonluth responded. His eyesight was now blurry, and he could see the shadowy outline of his opponent. The man was clutching his chest from what Sonluth assumed was a gunshot wound, and nearby to him off to the side was his firearm. Sonluth approached him, keeping his gun trained on him, even without his full eyesight. Sonluth kicked the gun away from the man and put the nozzle of his gun on the man's head.

"Hmph, so it ends here huh? Even if you do kill me, the Silicians will not stand by. We were the only ones keeping them away, but killing us will incite them to attack, unless you take the same approach we did."

""Are you done?" Sonluth asked. "We don't care about what you or the Silicians think. Underhanded tactics are never appreciated. I'd rather die knowing I at least didn't sell out my own people." As Sonluth finished speaking a large flash occurred outside. The man also felt the flash, although all he noticed was a large brightening as his eyesight was just as bad as Sonluth's.

"Well it still looks like you have no mechina to go back to," the man said.

"I wouldn't count on that," Sonluth responded as his eyesight came back into focus. "That would be your fleet going up in flames."
"What? How?"

"It doesn't matter; your time as is your organization here is at an end," Sonluth said as he shot the man in his head and then spoke as the light died down. "I guess that takes care of the corruption in the UTSF. Good job guys."

CHAPTER 8: REBIRTH

"Jump material, detected!" Kazumi jumped up before sitting back down, "oh it appears to be the Generians."

"Reinforcements?" Sarah asked.

"Sorry we're late, but reinforcements have arrived!" Gonsalves radioed as the Iron Wing completed its jump.

"Commander, we have incoming transmission from HQ," Kazumi reported.

"Patch it through," Sarah responded as she snapped back to reality.

"Commander of the UTSF RAINE, this is Fleet Commander Ray of the Earth Sphere Defense Fleet. Since our hierarchy was killed during your attack, I am now the highest ranking member of the UTSF and de facto leader. After learning of the demolition of both Saturn and Central Fleets, as well as the crippling of our own Defense Fleet, the UTSF formally surrenders to Commander Sarah Collins and her allies."

"We accept your surrender," Sarah responded. "Please ensure all remaining UTSF Personnel stand down, and have a report detailing their locations to me ASAP." She terminated the transmission and leaned back in her commander's chair and let out a long hard sigh. She looked up at the ceiling and pushed her hair back with her hands.

"Relieved?" Kazumi asked as she pushed away from her console and flexed her hands.

"Very…" Sarah said with a long breath out. She leaned back in her chair and closed her eyes. "Nothing at the academy could have *ever* prepared me for the past few days. It's still all hard to believe we actually made it this far."

"It is, but we made it..." Marina echoed as she maneuvered the RAINE towards the docks at the Lunar Base. An honour guard was present when they landed, and Sonluth was at the head and lead the salute as Sarah and the others disembarked.

"Mission Completed Successful," Sarah spoke to Sonluth as she returned his salute, and afforded herself a small smile.

"Indeed," Sonluth replied as he too broke a little smile. "Now all that's left is the formality of installing you as the official leader," Sonluth added as he dropped his smile. "They have set up an impromptu ceremony for you in the main hall so we can make this official ASAP before the Silicians get any funny ideas."

"Alright, lead the way," Sarah replied. Sarah and most of the crew from the RAINE were then escorted to a large open hall.

"Following decisive defeats of all major Solar System based Fleets as well as the deaths of a series of high level commanders the UTSF promotes Commander Sarah Collins to the rank of Commander of the Fleet with immediate effect," an adjutant announced as the crew of the RAINE looked on. "Can she please step forward and accept her new insignia and all the responsibilities and powers that go along with them."

Sarah approached the adjutant and they both saluted each other. "Commander of the Fleet, do you solemnly swear to protect Terra during times of war, and safeguard her safety and prosperity in times of peace that she may always be the envy of the universe and galaxy at large?"

"I do."

"Then by the powers vested in me I announce you the new leader of the United Terran Space Forces. May your judgments be sound, your actions be decisive, and your representation of this organization and its people always be of the best caliber."

"They will be," Sarah replied without any emotion on her face or voice. She then turned around as the soldier placed the new insignia on her shoulders. Once completed he took a step back and ordered everyone present to salute. "I will do my best to never let you all or Terra down." Sarah said as she took the salute.

"Sir we have an urgent message coming in from the Silician Capital. They wish to speak to the new Commander of the Fleet," a communications officer said as he burst into the hall.

"Can we patch it through here?" Sarah asked the adjutant.

"Yes Sir we can," he boomed loudly.

"Patch it through to this room, we'll take it here," Sarah ordered the communication officer.

"Right away sir!" he said with a salute. He ran back out of the room and a few moments later a hologram appeared in the middle of the room.

"Oh, well this is unexpected my dear," Fen spoke as he image came into proper focus. "You have become quite a thorn in my side Commander Collins, or should I say Commander of the Fleet Collins. You have bested many on your way to the top, some I would have never thought possible. But you've left your system in ruins. Your infighting has left precious little defenses of your planet and system. Had you gone along with the plan you would have been a simple innocent bystander, but now I will have to bring you in line just as I did the Osmerians. You too shall learn to fear the intellect of the Silicians."

"I'm sorry you feel that way Fen, but we do technically still have a treaty, do we not?" Sarah asked without blinking an eye.

"We do, but you have been fighting amongst yourselves, I figure you need an authoritative figure to stop your bickering, much like a parent to a child. As such the senate is on their way to nulling the treaty, and intervening on behalf of the late Commander of the Fleet Hunter to rein in the ones who usurped power from him in a bloody coupe. So to avoid more bloodshed, I am offering you a peaceful surrender now and transfer all your power to us until you reorganize. There would be a small price to pay of course, but you and your people would be safely under our wing and you'd not have to face any sort of aggression from us or anyone else."

Sarah straightened up a little as she prepared her response, "With all due respect Qui Fen, we decline your offer. We have seen for ourselves that even as allies you kept many secrets from us, and stole whenever the opportunity arose. As a matter of fact, you even still have two of my crew members which you haven't even seen fit to return to me. We Terrans may fight amongst each other, but we fight shoulder to shoulder with the hope and burning desire to see ourselves through anything. War is not new to us, and even with your posturing, should you invade our system you are not the first and you certainly will not be the last. So as Commander of the Fleet I reject your offer as it does not benefit us in anyway."

"Very well," Fen said with a sigh. "It is in your blood, we tried. If it's a dare you want, it's a dare you'll get. Our Senate is expected to approve the nullification within three days, and we can have our troops organized to invade within the next two days. So you have four days to stew in the knowledge that you just condemned your civilization to a harsh fate." The transmission ended and the room went deathly quiet.

Sarah exhaled and closed her eyes as she turned around to the troops that had been gathered in the hall. After a few moments she opened her eyes back up and looked at the troops in front of her. Directly in front of her when she opened her eyes was Marina. "This war isn't about just Terrans and Silicians; it never was," she said in a quiet voice. "This war was about control of the galaxy on a larger scale." She raised her voice and paced a little as she continued, "Osmerians, Generians, Terrans, Silicians, all onboard my ship, all have helped me, all have hurt me. I look at the soldiers here and while we've all sacrificed a lot, some more than others, we've all held onto the belief that we can win this. Allies come in the most unlikely of places, so before we give up, before we give in, I'd like to call on those allies that have helped me." She stood back in place as she gave her next command, "Midshipwoman Marina Welsch, Ensign Fae Kirin, Colonel Jace Falcon and Commander Gonsalves step forward."

The four all stepped forward and presented themselves before Sarah with a salute. "Welsch, Kirin, Falcon and Gonsalves reporting sir!" Gonsalves barked once everyone was in place. "What are your orders?"

"At ease you four," Sarah responded as she relaxed her stance a little as well. "I've asked for your assistance many times over the course of this mission, and as such even with my new rank, I ask for your assistance and support yet again. Firstly Colonel Jace Falcon, I do not know all your history, but I do know you have served our ship and crew to your utmost ability. You have also led the pilots admirably during the sorties that they have undertaken. I hereby promote you to Admiral, and you are to help me find and organize troops from Terra proper who may have suffered from the long forgotten wars."

"Yes Sir, I can accomplish that. Four days is more than enough time to rally troops from Terra proper. I will not let you or the UTSF down," Jace said with a salute.

"Good," Sarah replied. She then moved to face Fae. "Ensign Kirin, yours is a struggle we all know about. Due to your race you've been held back from promotion, yet you still work tirelessly to keep our mechina running as well as hold the mechanics in order and good standing with our crew. As a result of your actions I am promoting you to Vice Admiral, and you are to serve in the capacity as Chief Engineer. I expect you to continue training mechanics to their highest standard, as well as to continue fostering Generian - Terran relations."

"Yes Sir," Fae responded stiffly. "I will do my best."

Sarah then moved to Commander Gonsalves. "Commander Gonsalves your assistance has been invaluable since we first met in Generian Space in what seemed so long ago. Although your rank is was not recognized by the UTSF, I now place the rank of Rear Admiral on you, with the duties of assisting Vice Admiral Kirin with unifying the Terran and Generian Forces as well as your continued duties to the Iron Wing."

"I will strive to work with Vice Admiral Kirin in furthering Generaian – Terran Relations and offer the assistance of the Iron Wing to the UTSF," Gonsalves barked in his usual tone and saluted Sarah.

Lastly Sarah moved to face Marina. "Midshipwoman Welsch…" Sarah said with a sigh, as her voice trailed off.

"Commander?" Marina replied a little apprehensively as her eyes met Sarah's.

"Marina, I don't even know what to address you as anymore. In terms of this whole assignment yours is by far the most complicated. Knowing your actual title and rank makes this seem almost trivial. That being said, I know no designation I give you can ever fully make up what happened to you, but should you be the last remaining Osmerian, I offer you the rank of Vice Admiral with the hopes that you aren't the last of your kind and should we ever be able to locate them we can work together to better both races in the greater universe."

"We'll find them," Marina whispered as she began to tear up. "And they'll help us make the universe a safer place."

"That they will, that they will," Sarah whispered back as she fought back her own tears. She then took a step back from her newly promoted officers and addressed everyone in the room. "Well you have heard the Silician's threat. They wish to nullify the treaty and attack us directly. I know this is a rough time, and we've all lost many during the course of this war, but I ask you to all band together, not just as Terran, Generian or Osmerian, but as one unified force; a force capable of pushing back the threat posed by the Silicians. As a unified front, it would be improper of me to refer to this as the United Terran Space Forces. This is a unified fighting force. Since the Silicians aim to undermine us, we shall rename this group the United Planetary Alliance." A loud cheer rang out as Sarah finished her speech. She stood there, smiling at the seemingly renewed vigor among those present. "We're coming Zee and Izumi, we're coming." She whispered.

As everyone disbursed, Gonsalves approached Sarah and saluted her. "Never in my life would I have thought we'd be siding with the Terrans and joining forces with them against the Silicians. But as proud as I am of this moment, I will depart immediately for Generian Space to rally troops. I hope that my fellow Generians can put aside their differences and rally to our cause in a rapid fashion, as I would assume the Silicians would not wait to let this rebellion as they see it grow."

"No, probably not," Sarah replied. "I wish you the best of luck in gathering troops. We are going to try gather allies from the planet proper and try to fill in some of the numbers lost during this coupe. Godspeed, and report back in three days regardless of your status. I fear that is all the time we'll have at most to get prepared before the Silicians can prepare and authorize an attack. This is one time I'm grateful for red tape, because right now that is all that is slowing them down."

"Indeed it is," Gonsolves replied. "I will report back in three days as per your request, I wish you and your flagship crew the best of luck in gathering forces for the upcoming fight."

"Thank you and I wish you the best of luck as well," Sarah said with a salute. Gonsalves then turned and left the room. Sarah then walked out of the hall and turned right. She wondered around for a time, watching the crews get to repairing the damage done by the earlier assault.

"Never been to HQ before?" a voice spoke up behind Sarah. She snapped up and whirled around to face who was talking to her.

"Oh! It's you, you startled me," Sarah exclaimed. "No I haven't been to HQ before, we just get told about it and its defenses at the academy."

"Well seeing as you're lost and needing something to do, would you like to join Sonluth, Kazumi and I in going down to Earth to negotiate some troops and supplies?"

"Sure," Sarah said with a nod, "But is it really that obvious I'm lost?"

"Not going to lie commander, but you are pretty easy to read," Jace replied as he shook his head. "You definitely don't have a poker face like Sonluth or I do. And when you're not in your captain's chair you do wonder around a lot."

"I suppose not," Sarah replied with a sigh. "But if you're going down to Earth, I'll be happy to come along. I've never been down to our home planet before, only pictures of what it looked like in times passed."

"How far in the past? Depending on how far back the images were you will probably be sorely disappointed."

"Turn of the millennia?" Sarah replied with a shrug. "I don't remember, most were just file photos used in text."

"I'll assume you've seen the old images of what Earth looked like before the Exploration Era. That means don't keep your expectations too high; Earth was far more beautiful back then. Back before humanity became too concerned with things beyond their own backyards."

"You almost sound saddened by that," Sarah replied giving Jace an odd look. "You don't seem like the reminiscent type."

"Well it certainly was a much better place before the Space Era, when people still cared about their home planet.

But now, compared to the advancement of the space colonies and planetary bases, Earth itself is in shambles."

Sarah shrugged, "Well I've never been so I don't have an opinion either way. So I suppose it would be an interesting visit. More so since we want to be working with them, it would be kind of silly to ask for aid of a place you've never been."

"There is that too," Jace mused before continuing. "Well we are shipping out soon, because there is no telling how long negotiations would take. Even though someone on the planet clearly likes us, there is not telling how deep the Earthborns' hate for us Spaceborn is."

"And my presence would go a ways to at least settle down any potential doubters," Sarah finished off Jace's thought.

"Exactly," he nodded. "See you're catching on to these things quickly."

Sarah laughed, "When you're thrown into the deep end like what we've been through, you tend to learn rather quickly.

"Yeah, sure," Jace said with a slight laugh, "So shall I head to the shuttles and head for Paris?"

"Where?" Sarah said with a blank look before slowly nodding her head, "Oh, yes, head for Paris."

"We're leaving within the hour sir," Jace said with a salute.

"I will be down within the hour to check on your preparations," Sarah replied as she saluted back with a smile. Jace then turned and headed towards the docks, while Sarah went back to her office.

"Sir, excuse me for asking, but should you really be wondering around unguarded?" a soldier asked as he saluted Sarah in the halls.

"Why?" Sarah replied with a frown.

"Well it's just that you're the leader of the UTSF, I mean UPA, what would happen if someone where to attack you? Shouldn't you have a detail or something?" the soldier said as he stiffened up.

Sarah let out a small laugh, "Oh I'll be fine. While I appreciate your concern, I do not mind putting myself in similar dangers as my fellow soldiers. Just because I'm a commander doesn't mean I should receive special treatment. Besides, I have to be tough to survive most things my crew will throw at me," she added with an extra chuckle.

"You mean you're not staying here at Lunar HQ?" the soldier asked wide eyed.

"Heavens no," she said trying to stifle a laugh. "I'd get bored of here within the year. I know the leader is expected to stay tied down to a place and command from the back lines, but a leader on the front lines inspires more courage and morale from their troops."

"I-I suppose you're right," the soldier stammered. "I never thought of that. I apologize for doubting your course of action."

"Don't worry about it," Sarah replied, "Just return to your post and never forget what you have learned today."

"Yes, sir!" the soldier replied with a salute and then walked off.

"Geez, I know the higher ups were kind of stuffy, but I hope I don't make things seem too relaxed," Sarah muttered to herself before sighing, "Probably best not to think about it too hard. My crew has killed whatever remnant of military rigidness I had prior to starting off with them." She shook the thought off and continued walking. Instead of going to the office, she wound up at the shuttle docks.

"Oh Commander, you're early," Sonluth said as he spotted Sarah walking towards the shuttle.

"Yeah, I guess I've been on the docks for so long, I can't remember what its like to be in a base for a long period of time," Sarah replied as she looked towards the RAINE.

"Don't worry commander, you'll be used to base operations soon enough, but since you're here, we're almost ready to go." Sonluth then yelled back into the shuttle, "Are we almost ready to go?"

"We sure are," the pilot replied back. "Not much to prep, just some old navigation routes down to Earth proper without burning up in the atmosphere."

"Guess you're right on time then commander welcome aboard," Sonluth spoke to Sarah as she reached the doorway proper.

"Well I'm glad I didn't stop by my office then," Sarah said with a grin as she saluted back. "I wouldn't want to hold up your emissary mission."

"Oh hey Commander, didn't think they'd let you out so soon to come join us," Kazumi said from her seat.

"To be fair, I was stopped by a soldier on the way here and he asked if I needed a detail and I should be in the office," Sarah said with a chuckle. "Unfortunately for him, I think you guys are more than enough of a security detail, and as for sticking in the office. My office has been the RAINE's bridge for the past little while, and it feels most like my office."

"Aww, that's so nice of you to say," Kazumi replied as Sarah sat down next to her.

"I'm serious!" Sarah protested. "It seems so quiet and tranquil without you guys all buzzing around me. And I don't know the layout of HQ, so how could it feel like home?" she said as she shrugged.

"You have a point," Kazumi said with a laugh.

"This is your captain speaking, can all passengers please take their seats and buckle up as we prepare for take off," the pilot said over the intercom. There was the unified sound of seatbelts being buckled.

"Geez, I wish I could get you all to buckle down to seats like that in one go," Sarah remarked as she adjusted her buckle.

"You can," Jace replied from across the aisle. "You just don't do it because tying anyone down on the ship causes it to stop running."

"He makes a good point commander," Kazumi said with a laugh. "Although most of us on the bridge stay put most of the time, unless you command us to move elsewhere."

"I do not order you to stay there," Sarah said as she crossed her arms. "You guys rotate in and out unless there is an emergency and all hands are on deck."

"We're trying to help you here commander, at least play

along with us," Kazumi remarked.

"I should make sure you stay buckled to your seat next time we're on the RAINE," Sarah said as she sat back in her chair, and then smiled to herself. "These guys have worn on me; I guess it would be rather dull to stay in HQ without these guys." She said to herself. She closed her eyes and relaxed as the shuttle launched from the docking area and headed towards Earth.

A few moments after take off she opened one eye to see what everyone around her was doing. Sonluth seemed content to sit in his chair with his eyes closed and his hands clasped, resting in his lap. Jace had gotten up from his seat, and she had no idea where he had gone. Kazumi was engrossed with her personal handheld device. Sarah was not sure if it was a game or something related to the UTSF, but what ever it was, she was rapidly using her pointer to input commands. She then closed her eyes again and just enjoyed the quietness of the moment.

CHAPTER 9: DOWN TO EARTH

The next thing Sarah remembered was Kazumi nudging her, "Commander, wake up! We're in Paris!"

"Huh... already?" Sarah replied as she slowly opened her eyes. She rubbed her eyes and then stretched, "I must have been sleep longer than I thought."

"You sure did," Jace replied. "In any case, welcome to Paris, we're currently at one of the few old UTSF outposts left on the planet proper."

"Is that why there is so much concrete and walls around here?" Sarah asked as she looked out the window.

"Not exactly," Jace replied. "Sadly, most places on Earth have been a concrete dump for a while. People on the planet felt abandoned, why do you think there have been rebellions over the years?"

"I suppose you make a point," Sarah replied. She got up out of her seat and followed the others out of the shuttle. "Oh God that's bright," she said as she squinted her eyes upon reaching the doorway of the shuttle.

"Oh, forgot, take these," Jace said as he handed Sarah a pair of sunglasses. Sarah took them and put them on.

"Much better," she said as she adjusted the arm over her ears and hair.

"Yeah, our lights have never been able to reproduce the brightness and intensity of the natural sunlight. I don't remember the science behind it, but part of the reason it's brighter is also due to general neglect of the planet," Jace added as they walked down the ramp.

"Welcome to Paris, my name is Lt Curie and I'm in command of this outpost," he spoke with a salute as the group reached the bottom of the ramp.

"At ease Lieutenant," Sarah spoke as she gave a salute.

"You are the first sitting commanding officer that has visited the planet in quite some time, to what do we owe this auspicious occasion?" Curie asked.

"We've come down here to look for allies and to seek out who fired the volley of missiles that saved us much trouble over Lunar HQ."

"I see," Curie replied slowly. "Well there aren't many people stationed here, and I wouldn't trust too many of the Earth Borns. They are quite rebellious."

"They're still just as Terran as we are," Sarah interjected.

"Terrans they maybe, but allies is another matter. You would do well to not take them lightly. They are like roaming pirates most days, they like to steal, plunder and pillage, even from us behind this heavily fortified area."

"I guess Terrans act the same all over," Sarah replied with a smile.

"Don't make light of this situation," Curie said sternly. "They would have you endure hours of pain and torture before killing you as a sign to us behind these walls."

"Well like I said, I intend to try meet with some of them, and these guys here have proven to be a pretty good security detail," Sarah replied motioning to the others with her. "Besides, it doesn't look like you can spare the manpower or resources to help us out."

"Not really, no," Curie admitted in a low voice.

"Sir we have a situation!" a soldier ran up to the group and interrupted the conversation.

"Speak," Curie ordered.

The soldier stiffened up and began talking, "Some Earth Borns are gathering outside our gates. They demand entrance and wish to speak to those who just arrived on the shuttle they saw coming down."

"Guess we won't have to go anywhere after all," Sarah said. "Sounds like they came here looking for us."

"It could still be a trap," Curie growled as he dismissed the soldier and he ran back to his post.

"A trap where they are in sight of our heaviest and most powerful armaments?" Jace questioned Curie. "That would indicate they are either willing to put that much belief in whomever came off the shuttle or your armaments don't really scare them."

"Just lets go see what they want, we can debate here all day the merits of whether or not it's a trap. Just you guys watch my back and I'll keep my eyes and ears peeled for anything as well," Sarah ordered.

"Yes ma'am," the group echoed. They then moved off in the same direction as the soldier ran, leaving Curie lagging behind a little muttering various obscene phrases under his breath.

"We wish to meet with the people who just landed in the shuttle!" Sarah and the others heard as they drew close to the gatehouse. There were two snipers positioned on the wall as well as two turrets that were aimed at those gathered outside.

"So force and intimidation to handle this situation?" Sarah asked Curie with a frown as he came along side the group.

"Yes," Curie nodded. "It seems the only way the Earth Born understand anything is using force."

"But I don't even see any weapons on them!" Sarah exclaimed. "Two snipers and two anti personnel turrets are excessive force for a group of what looks like fifteen people!"

"Better too much power than not enough."

"I can't *believe* you!" Sarah yelled. "Order your people to stand down!" she demanded of Curie.

"But sir, what if they retaliate?" Curie protested.

"*Now!*" Sarah yelled at Curie.

"Yes, sir," Curie spoke slowly to Sarah before yelling out, "Decroche!"

The snipers on the wall looked down at Curie and he nodded to them. They seemed to remain on the wall for a bit before they put the safety on their rifles and backed away from their positions on the wall.

Sarah then walked up to the gate and spoke through it, "Whom may I ask is looking for the people that flew in on the shuttle and for what purposes do they wish to talk."

A man stepped forward and replied, "I am Olaf Samuelsson formerly of the Swedish Ski Resistance, but have since moved her to Paris to join the stronger rebel faction here."

"What's a Swedish?" Sarah whispered as she leaned over to Jace.

"It's one of the former political countries down here on Earth," Jace replied. "Before the jump to colonies, there were around three hundred of them, but once we moved to the colonies, their names became nothing more than words as we kind of neglected them once the United Nations dissolved and reformed to the UTSF."

"Ouch, harsh," Sarah replied.

"We wish to speak to those who just landed in the shuttle in the hopes that after recent events that we might finally be heard by members of our space born brethren," Olaf announced once Sarah refocused back on the conversation at hand.

"Very well, I came off the shuttle, but I also have a question for you. Are you the group that fired off the missile volley that severely damaged the Earth Defense Fleet?" Sarah asked.

There was a small pause before Olaf replied, "Are you trying to use that as an excuse to kill us?"

"No, not at all," Sarah said. "As a matter of fact, I'd sooner thank you than kill you."

"Sir you can't be serious about that?" Curie demanded. "These people have killed many of our comrades."

Sarah raised her hand to silence Curie, "And I'm sure we've killed plenty of theirs too. Not that it makes it right either way, but credit must be given where credit is due."

"I can't believe what I'm hearing! You are obviously too soft on these cretins!" Curie yelled as he drew his side arm.

"I wouldn't do that if I were you," Sonluth and Jace had their firearms pointed at Curie's head before he could completely get his to Sarah's.

"I told you they were a good security detail," Sarah said to Curie without turning to face him. "Now do you want to work with us or shall I relieve you of your duties?"

Curie remained in place for a few moments before he lowered and holstered his firearm again. "I just don't see how talking will help..." he muttered.

"Have you ever tried it?" Sarah asked as she looked over her shoulder at Curie. "Killing each other certainly hasn't gotten us anywhere. And right now, we need to unite as much as we can. Fighting amongst ourselves will kill us in the long run. Now stand down, and let us work."

"As you wish," Curie sulked as he took a few steps back.

Sarah nodded to Sonluth and Jace and they lowered their weapons as well. She then returned her attention to Olaf. "If you are unarmed and wish to talk, then we are also willing to talk with you."

There was a small pause before Olaf took a side arm out of his pocket and handed it off to someone next to him. He then stepped forwards towards the gate with his hands raised. "As you can see I'm unarmed, and trust that you will do the same."

Jace opened the gate and gave Olaf a pat down. "He's clean," Jace announced after a few moments. Sarah nodded and stepped outside the gate, looking over her shoulders at the walls to note if the snipers had returned.

"I'm Supreme Commander Sarah Collins of the United

Planetary Forces," Sarah said as she extended her hand to Olaf.

"Well I'll be damned," Olaf replied as he shook Sarah's hand. "A complete overhaul of the old system? I knew there was a small band of rebels, but I didn't expect you to have a separate name."

"Let's just say we needed to take the UTSF in a new direction," Sarah said with a smile. "After all, this isn't just about the Terrans; this war is about everyone living in the whole galaxy. Besides, we can't call ourselves United Terrans, if we aren't really all that united."

"Ha-ha!" Olaf let out a hearty laugh that caused Sarah to flinch. "You're a special one aren't you? I'd never have thought I'd hear those words come out of an ex-UTSF officer." He then broke off the handshake and continued talking, "But I assume you did not just come down here to visit and shoot the breeze, so what business do you have with us?"

Sarah took in a deep breath before talking, "Well the Silicians are in the process of declaring war on us. Considering the amount of damage we had to inflict on our own to get this far, we were wondering if you guy were willing and able to send some people to fight alongside us."

"In exchange for what?" Olaf asked.

"Nothing," Sarah replied with a straight face.

"Nothing?" Olaf repeated as he raised an eyebrow.

"Absolutely nothing."

"Not even any of the soldiers or officers we have captured recently?" Olaf asked.

"Well, to be fair on that point, I've only been in charge for twenty four hours, and I haven't had a chance to see if we've lost anyone down here," she said sheepishly.

Olaf blinked twice and then let out another loud laugh, "Lady you are definitely showing your novice skills at this. I'm not sure if I should feel sorry for you or take advantage of you."

"I am not *that* green," Sarah said with a frown. She then turned to Sonluth and Jace, "Am I that green?" They both nodded their heads, and Sarah sighed.

"I do say though, it is probably that small degree of child-like naivety that got you this far. You weren't weighed down by the external pressures and politics of the others, so as you have come down here in what is obviously good will, I will entertain your request. If you wish, I will allow you and a few others to come to one of our meeting areas to make your pitch in front of more of our people."

"They won't shoot me on the spot will they?" Sarah asked.

"Kidnap you yes, but we don't tend to shoot UTSF personnel on sight, so as not to give away our positions," Olaf reassured her. "You can even bring a security detail with you if you feel insecure."

"Can I discuss it with my security detail first?" Sarah asked.

"By all means. I'll be over here with my boys and wait for your response."

"Thank you." Sarah then turned around and gathered in a huddle with Kazumi, Jace and Sonluth. "So what do you guys think? Should we go or should we stay?"

"Last time you ventured into so called allied territory you came back with a broken nose," Kazumi replied. "So can we really trust them? Curie said they do horrible things to UTSF personnel, and I don't want to be tortured."

"I see your point, but Curie is also a hardliner," Sarah said with a sigh. "Sure they'll probably despise us either way, but if we go, at least it'll be showing signs of some trust right?"

"That maybe so, but I still would feel uncomfortable unarmed," Sonluth replied. "Even if they do assure us no one will be armed, there is always someone who breaks that rule. There's also the task of hard liners, just like we have Curie, I'm sure they have their own versions of Curie. And believe me when I tell you, it's been bad blood for years down here."

"I agree with Sonluth," Jace nodded, "If we are to go with them, we need to be allowed our weapons."

"Alright, I'll ask if we can bring our weapons along for security reason, and your three are all coming with me." Sarah reiterated. Jace and Sonluth nodded immediately, while Kazumi nod came a little later and very slowly. "You don't have to come Kazumi if you don't want. I'm sure you can stay here at the base until we get back."

"No, that's okay. I've been out on other somewhat 'safe' excursions; I suppose one more won't hurt. That and I'd rather be with you guys than Curie and the others. They will probably give me an earful while you guys are out."

"Good then its settled," Sarah said as she left the huddle. She approached Olaf and his group. They stopped chatting and Olaf met Sarah halfway. "We've decided to go with you, under the condition we are allowed to carry our weapons incase an unfavourable situation may arise."

"Sounds reasonable enough," Olaf replied. "We'll make you feel as comfortable as possible, but we'll not press the issue of complete disarmament."

"Thank you," Sarah replied. "We'll be ready to go within a few minutes."

"That soon?"

"Yes," Sarah replied. "We've worked together for a long time, so we don't need to draw out any plans, or get our weapons. We already have them and know what to expect of each other. Also considering our main goal was to meet with you, we have no reason to draw out any longer than we need to."

"I see," Olaf said with another laugh. "Well let us know when you are ready to go, and we'll transport you to our humble abode."

"You got it," Sarah replied and then turned around to go back to her group.

"Judging by your smile I assume they agreed," Jace said as Sarah drew near to where they were standing.

"Indeed they did," Sarah replied with a nod. "I told them we'd be ready in a few minutes, since I assume you all have your weapons on you and we don't really need to form any new contingent plan other than the ones we already have from our travels."

"Sounds fair to me," Jace replied. "You do all the talking and we'll watch your back. If something bad happens, I'm sure they have vehicles or something we could hotwire and get back here."

"And where exactly is... here?" Sarah asked as she looked around. "The area seems like a warzone, with no distinct landmarks around."

"Remember how I said the place looks really bad compared to what it looked like before the Space Exploration Era?" Jace waited for Sarah to nod her head before continuing. "Well this base is in an area called La Defense. It's at the end of what used to be a ten kilometer pathway of historical monuments and buildings. Most of which have become ruins, but if you know what you are looking for, you can see the remnants and find your way back."

"Uh-huh," Sarah replied, "Well if we have to flee, I guess I'm leaving navigation up to you." She then reached into her pocket and pulled out a small package. "Here take these. They are beacons incase we do get split up and are forced to scatter. Jace, I'll give you the extra transponder to track us down after we scatter."

"Yes Ma'am," he replied as he accepted the transponder.

"Now we're all clear on what's going on in an emergency?" Sarah asked and everyone nodded their agreement. "Good, now let's go and not keep our hosts waiting." The group then walked out the gates and approached Olaf and his men.

"All ready?" he asked.

"Ready as we'll ever be," Sarah replied.

"Alright, this way to the transport trucks," Olaf motioned behind him. Sarah and her group stuck close together as they followed Olaf to his trucks. Olaf stopped at three large transport trucks and then looked back at Sarah and her group. "I assume you all want to stick together, but are the ladies alright with being piled in with a group of guys?" Olaf asked with a bit of hesitation.

"I think we'll be fine," Sarah replied. "The academy was mostly guys, and we got transported all the time in groups, regardless of gender ratios."

"Suit yourself," Olaf said with a shrug. "You all can hop into that truck over there," Olaf said pointing to a truck that appeared to be in the middle of the convoy. "Arrange yourselves as you wish."

"Man this brings back memories," Sonluth replied as he hopped in the back of the truck. Jace helped up Kazumi, but Sarah decided to jump in on her own power, and after a failed attempt made it into the truck.

"I suggest you not sit in the corner," Sonluth told Sarah.

"Want the safest spot to yourself? You don't have to worry about dropping the soap in a truck Sonluth, you'll be fine," Sarah said with a slight laugh.

"Not what I meant," Sonluth sighed. "But just don't say I never warned you."

"Everyone hurry up and sit down," the driver yelled out as he started the truck and it rattled to life. The group sat in the inside right of the truck; Sarah was against the back followed by Jace, Sonluth and Kazumi on the outside. A short time later the truck lurched forward and they were off. Between the bumpy roads and the lack of suspension made for a very bumpy ride, and the people near the outside of the truck kept bouncing inwards, causing Sarah to be squashed against the inside wall for most of the trip. Sonluth kept a wary eye on the others in the truck, although most of the rebel soldiers seemed content with watching Kazumi struggle to keep her skirt down every time they bounced a few inches off their seats. After what seemed like an eternity, the trucks finally came to a stop.

"We're here!" the driver yelled out. All the others quickly disembarked from the truck.

"I feel like I just came out of a blender," Sarah said as she leaned heavily on the cab back to gain her footing.

"And that is why I told you not to sit on the inside," Sonluth commented.

"Are you coming out anytime soon?" they heard Olaf ask.

"Yeah, we just got a greenhorn here with shaky leg syndrome," Sonluth yelled back.

"Ha-ha, I guess we can let her ride in the cab on the return trip," Olaf laughed.

"I can handle it just fine!" Sarah yelled as she tried to stand up straight. She took a few more minutes before she was able to regain proper feeling in her legs and was able to exit the back of the truck.

"Never been in the back of these old diesel trucks eh?" Olaf asked to Sarah as she jumped down out of the truck.

"No, definitely not what I was expecting," Sarah replied. "Never felt so shaken up in my life."

"You get used to it," Olaf said with a laugh. "At least you didn't throw up," he said as he slapped her on the back, causing her to take a step forward. "Some of your captured soldiers are so used to smooth rides they get motion sickness on these here trucks. We have to put them up front with the drivers when we transport them! My men also say you were doing well to keep your modesty."

"You don't say," Sarah said with a frown as she tried to rub near to the spot where Olaf had hit her.

"Sir, members the council is still in the main hall. Are you sure you want to bring them along?" A nearby soldier asked Olaf.

"Yes, besides if Miss Commander here can show the same mettle she just did by not throwing up in the back of your truck to the council she might be able to get more allies faster than she ever imagined." Olaf replied.

"Aye sir," the soldier said with what seemed to be a sigh.

"This way," Olaf motioned to Sarah and the others as the soldier moved off. "If you can catch the council maybe you can hasten your request for aid."

"Sounds good to me," Sarah replied with a weak smile and some support from Jace. They followed Olaf into a nearby door. The pathway wasn't very well lit, not that Sarah took much note. However, something caught Sarah's peripheral vision that made her stop walking.

"Aira?" Sarah asked as she altered her direction towards the cell.

"You know her?" Olaf asked as he looked over his shoulder to Sarah.

"Yes, she was our head medic onboard the RAINE. She went missing after helping to release us from UTSF custody," Sarah replied as she slowly nodded her head.

"Trying to get on the good side of the new leader incase they won the fight?" Olaf remarked to Aira. "I must say you always were a rather crafty one."

"How so? She's only a medic. I've never had any issues with her," Sarah said

"Oh? So trying not to air your dirty laundry now? Or simply biding your time to properly inject her with some lethal virus?" Olaf jeered at Aira.

"Look Olaf, if I wanted to save myself, why would I have ever returned down to Earth?" Aira asked as she looked away from Olaf and Sarah. "Yeah, sure I've been involved in a lot of underhandedness, but I do have a conscience. But after you witness so much, and after you are taught that sacrifices must be made, sometimes it gets suppressed. Sometimes you learn to ignore it, like a fly that buzzes around your ear, you just swat it away. But after a while, you realize that your conscience never fully goes away. Those sacrificed had families and homes that would miss them. Eventually your conscience would surface as an unshakable force. That's why I came down here. It wasn't so that Sarah would hear a sob story. It was so that I could face up to my actions by my own peers." She stood up in her holding cell before continuing, "It does matter to me what happens. You could kill me now; I was already convinced that would be my end the moment you guys saw me climb out of that escape pod."

"But what have you done? I don't understand," Sarah remarked. She turned to face Olaf, "How is it that she's been pretty helpful to keeping our ship running, even helping us escape, yet she's really been our enemy all this time?"

"Aira smiled weakly at Sarah, "Commander Sarah, while I appreciate your vote of confidence, I can't even stand here and say I was always completely loyal to you and your crew. My directives largely came from your dad and Fen." She sighed and turned her back to Sarah and looked at the roof of her cell. "Truth be told Sarah, there was a lot you don't know. Yes I'm trained as a medic, but I'm also trained as a covert agent. Almost everything that went wrong or seemed to be an ambush I was already well aware of. I'm not asking for your forgiveness, but I only saved you, because of things that occurred in Osmeria. After that, I was sure you could turn things around. But for everything else, it's probably just better if you simply leave and pretend you never saw me here."

"So that's it Aira? You're just going to give up and take the coward's way out?" Sonluth asked.

"Funny, coming from the man who ran away from the UTSF after Operation Free Mind," Aira said as she shifted her head lower. "Coward's way? Maybe. But I do owe these guys down here some form of atonement. One life can never equate to the thousands lost, but at least they'll know that justice and some form of satisfactory closure could be reached."

"And do you think I can just leave you here? After all you did save us from execution. I don't know what you did before joining our crew, I don't know what a lot of us done before joining our crew, but you are now one of us. If you feel bad for events in the past, imagine what I'd feel like knowing I left behind a crew member to die. Did you learn nothing from Izumi at Pluto? She was under twenty four hour surveillance because she was considered a threat to ship and crew, but we still did everything we could to keep her onboard, perhaps even bending some rules in the process. This is the same, except I don't know what you're being accused of. You can't just expect me to leave you here and do nothing?"

"Are we really talking about the same person? What mind control have you subjected these people to Aira, because as far as I'm concerned you could never be worthy of such large amounts of loyalty," Olaf remarked as a forrow ran across his brow.

"I guess there is no point in beating around the bush," Aira said as she slowly turned around to face the others outside her cell. "How long has it been Olaf? Ten years?"

"About that," Olaf replied.

"On that day ten years ago; the day this war was initiated. The final results of Operation Free Mind came available. The data showed that children of mixed heritage possessed the abilities of both parental species without possessing their inherent weaknesses. It was further deduced that Terrans were the perfect mediums. An offspring that included a Terran could leave abilities dormant until called upon much later in life. A Terran mixed with either an Osmerian or a Silician was superior to the original as well as a mixture of Osmerian and Silician. The Osmerians were still rather impartial to it all, but the Silicians saw it as a way to gain an edge of the Osmerians. Recall the Silicians and Osmerians have had on again and off again wars. The last major confrontation between the two ended when the Terrans forced an armistice as there would have been a second front for both planets and neither was willing to risk that. Either way, the Silicians approached the UTSF High Command with a proposition. Give them breeders and the Silicians would allow the Terrans to invade, capture and control Osmerian space without any interference. Seeing the new resources and possible cheap labour of Osmerians, the UTSF thought of the idea as a good one. However, the Terran People were opposed to another long war. Although the Generian Conquest had been fifty years in the past, people could not shake off the atrocities of another interspace war. So what did the UTSF do? They arranged for some fake Osmerian strikes and raids. One of those fake raids was a chemical attack on heavily populated centers on Earth and some minor ones on the colonies. I wrote up the plans, developed the chemical agent and oversaw the execution of the plan. At first we thought of using an explosive, but it was deemed that would cause too much infrastructure damage. We then settled on Osmium Tetroxide. Only a little bit needed to be inhaled for it to be toxic, and since Osmium was rare on both Earth and Silicia, the subsequent scientific probes would fine Osmium as the culprit and thus Osmeria would be blamed. With that plan, all that was left was to send out the taxation forms laced with the chemical and wait for the people to start dropping."

"That sounds cold coming from a medic," Kazumi interjected.

"I know it does," Aira said with a sigh, "but all I could think about was the science. I like most others knew the overall populous wouldn't go ahead with another war without first being agitated. All I could see was that the Terrans would forever avoid a war with the Silicians, and being allied with the Silicians we could soon have all the science and technology afforded by the Osmerians at our own whim. In hindsight it was a bad move, but all we could think of was the scientific and military advancements that could be made. We were always told that science requires sacrifice, but a conscience doesn't always agree. That's why I became a medic. Even now I can hear the millions of people coughing and gasping for air, some may have even been blinded when they died. So I thought that in exchange for killing thousands, maybe if I saved a few thousand the guilt would go away. It never did, because even as a medic, there are some that are beyond your saving. When they take their last breaths, all I do is wonder, is this what it was like for those who died from the Osmium? And the longer the war drew out, the less valuable it seemed the operation was, since people were still dying, and there was no quick victory as had been originally thought."

"So wait, this is the Mail Massacre we're talking about

right?" Sarah interjected. "We learned that the Osmerians were responsible for that at the academy. That's why we now have chemical steamers that mail goes through, to prevent such an incident from happening again. But if what you are saying is true, how did anyone outside of High Command find out?"

Aira turned away from Sarah and took in a deep breath before replying, "Izumi Maehara."

"But how? She was our Sonar Technician. Did she defect and come back?"

"Not hardly," Aira said with a sigh. "Izumi was a member of Terran Intelligence, and was a trained IT specialist. Her high level of IT training and knowledge was why she was assigned to the RAINE. However, the UTSF had learned that she needed to be kept restrained, and that's why she came with the twenty four hour surveillance order. Fen and John suspected she had gained access to the data stored on the RAINE, and needed an excuse to seize both her and her equipment while drawing as little suspicion as possible. So I agreed to shoot Zee and then have Izumi walk in on the crime scene. That way Pluto would have an excuse to remove both of them from the RAINE and transport them to Silicia without anyone suspecting anything. However, as you know, Sonluth rescued Izumi and his producing of the Periodic Pendant distracted Fen long enough that she never put in the paperwork for Zee's transfer. The Silician raid and subsequent capture of Zee, the Silician Fleet locating us in Osmeria, the Pluto Garrison finding out about Arianna's Base, the capture at Sector J, and the ambush in the Meteor Belt by the Central Fleet all were caused by my actions." Aira then turned back around to face Sarah, "So you see dear captain, I'm not really worth your time saving. I've killed and sabotaged my own people and crew mates. I'm beyond redemption. If there was some way to do it all over again, I would do it differently, but there are no second chances in life. Olaf's anger is justified, and even though your pity is welcome, it is gravely misplaced."

"No, you're wrong," Sarah said softly.

"Huh?" Aira perked her head up, not quite able to hear what Sarah had just said.

"You're wrong!" Sarah said louder. "Sonluth is right; killing you would be the easy way out. Yeah, you'd free your mind from being able to think about what you've done, but what about us? We killed an unarmed, defenseless fellow Terran who had given up on life in cold blood. Sure she killed a few thousand of us, sure she even tried to stab me and my crew behind our backs, but like I said before, I could never convince myself that killing one in exchange for another is a worthwhile cause. Your death will not bring back those you betrayed or killed. It may ease you're pain, but it will never fully ease ours. You became a medic to redeem yourself for one crime, now I'm ordering you back to our ship to redeem yourself for your others."

"Hmph, naïve as always. Yet I can't say that I detest that about you."

"You can't just take her like that," Olaf objected. "The people will not stand for it, and will see it as favouritism. She is one of the last who will face judgment, and bailing her out like this will only infuriate those she left maimed and destroyed."

"Well tell me Olaf; has the death of all the others made you sleep better at night? Has the judgment you passed on the others made you feel any better? Will killing her right now bring peace and happiness to the people of this planet?" Sarah asked Olaf as she looked over her shoulder towards him.

"No…" Olaf muttered, "But at least the people will hold onto the belief that there is some shred of justice left in the world."

"Look at it this way Olaf, if it wasn't for her, we wouldn't even be having this debate right now." She again faced Aira, "I'm not saying we should forgive and forget everything she's done, after all it sounds like she has a deadly track record, but killing her at this point will accomplish nothing. For the moment at least, I owe her my life and the life of my crew." Sarah then turned around to face Olaf, "So if I may at the very least ask for a stay of execution. We need every able body to fight the Silicians, and even if its just one, its one soldier we can't afford to lose."

"As much as I see your point, the choice is not mine alone to make," Olaf responded. "Fortunately or unfortunately the members of the Roundtable Council are all here from discussing the plan to assist you with the missiles and thus will convene again tomorrow to determine Aira's fate, which is likely to be a public execution. You are more than welcome to attend that meeting once you finish your pitch for allies, but I would not get my hopes up too high if I were you."

"That's alright," Sarah replied. "As long as I have a chance to speak on behalf of Aira."

"Well if that is your decision do you want to make your pitch today and come back tomorrow, or do everything tomorrow?" Olaf asked.

"Tomorrow to do everything might be better. I'm not sure I could make a proper pitch today knowing now what I do about Aira," Sarah said despondently. Everyone then moved off towards the exit except Sonluth.

"So do you think we should tell them?" Sonluth asked

once everyone was out of earshot.

"About what?"

"Everything, but more so what really happened with Operation Free Mind and Operation Osmerian Raiders."

"I'm sure you know the answer to that," Aira said with a frown. "On those topics, there is no need to burden them with that. We're the last in the military from that era, its probably best we take that back home with us that these younger ones in the next generation can correct things without being held back. They'll soon have a *lot* to worry about, so it's probably best we leave the past in the past and let them deal with the present and future." Then she added after a small pause, "Even if fate is conspiring against us."

"Heh, I suppose so," Sonluth said with a small laugh. He then leaned his back on Aira's cell door before speaking again. "We all make mistakes, sometimes we're able to correct them, and sometimes we never live to do so. Regardless of what happens tomorrow, the commander is right, to a large degree, you've tried to redeem yourself. Don't sell yourself short. We're both spent time running, but don't give up just yet. You owe it to yourself, and Sarah to see this completed. Even if you don't tell her the full truth, stick it out if you can at least that way, for sure, you can rest completely in peace."

"You make a point, but like Olaf said I guess we'll find out for sure tomorrow," Aira replied. She walked over to a corner of her cell and sat down. "Tomorrow..." she added with a sigh. Sonluth started to walk away when Aira called out to him, "Before you go, I have a question for you."

"Sure," he replied as he came to a halt, but did not turn to face Aira.

"Is it better to live a lie in happiness or be forced to face a sad truth?" Aira asked from her spot on the ground.

Sonluth took one step forward before responding, "I'm sure you can answer that yourself." He then walked a few more steps before saying one last thing to Aira, "Remember a lie ends eventually, the truth is forever." He then walked off before Aira could form any reply.

CHAPTER 10: THE COUNCIL OF PARIS

Sonluth got outside to find Sarah already sitting in the cab of the truck. Her eyes were glazed over as she leaned on the door panel. Jace was standing behind the truck waiting for Sonluth.

"Last minute advice for Aira?" Jace asked as Sonluth jumped into the back of the truck.

"Not really, there isn't much to tell her that she doesn't already know," Sonluth replied as he took his seat.

"An assassin medic," Kazumi said with a sigh. "I don't know what to think about that." Jace banged on the back of the cab and the truck engine roared to life and started the journey back to the outpost.

"Don't think too hard on it Kazumi," Sonluth spoke as the truck jerked forward. "Believe me, its complicated."

"Still, she helped us escape and taken care of us all, yet she's responsible for things like framing my sister and the Mail Massacre. I just don't get it. How can a person swing so far on the morality scales," Kazumi said as she stared out the back of the truck.

"And even those tests were for ulterior motives," Sonluth said to no one in particular.

"What do you mean?" Kazumi asked as she glanced towards Sonluth.

"Some of those tests were for an old assignment," he brought his eyes up to meet Kazumi's. "They confirmed what had been suspected, and were used to keep track of some of our crew." He then broke off his gaze and looked out the back of the truck, "In a way I suppose she still did protect the crew from some awful truths."

"Like the Silician Tests?" Jace replied.

Sonluth nodded, "Yeah that was part of it," Sonluth shifted his seat and looked at the ground. "Silicians, Osmerians and Generian, she had a test kit for them all, yet none were more important than the GBA."

"GBA?"

"Genetic Background Assessment. It takes chemical markers on genes and helps determines ancestry."

"But what good would that do?" Kazumi asked as she looked at Sonluth with a frown. "We all know everyone's background. Who would have been impacted by it?"

"Was it?" Sonluth said as he closed his eyes a grinned. "Knowing now that there was an Osmerian Princess onboard without our knowing, how can you be so sure about there not being any more connections or subversions without knowing the facts?"

"I suppose I don't," Kazumi said with a shrug, "but I'm pretty sure we're all around the same age except you two, John Collins and maybe Fae?"

"There are others," Sonluth replied as he opened his eyes again. "Fen believe it or not is older than us." A grin spread across his face as he finished the sentence. "Yeah, Fen."

"What's with that smirk?" Kazumi asked.

"Nothing, nothing at all," Sonluth replied still smiling. "Just thinking of something that had happened last time I was in the army."

"Okay," Kazumi replied as she leaned back in her seat with her arms folded and looking at Sonluth. She kept her eye on Sonluth for the rest of the trip, but could not get anymore out of him as he closed his eyes and grinned to himself.

"Give it up Kazumi, he's not going to say anything more," Jace said.

"I figured as much," she replied with a sigh. "Still it would be nice to know what he's thinking," she said to herself as she stared out the back of the truck. "What all this is all really about." The rest of the ride was quiet, and they arrived back at the outpost a short time later.

"Disappointed that they didn't agree to your terms?" Curie asked as he noticed Sarah's feet dragging as she walked back to the compound from the truck.

"Huh? No." Sarah replied as she snapped her head up momentarily. "They haven't really heard the argument yet," her voice trailed off as she walked past Curie.

"Hard day at the office?" Curie asked Sonluth as he approached the gate.

"You could say that," he replied without breaking his stride.

"Are you *sure* she's fit for a leadership role if a minor thing like this breaks her?" Curie asked.

Sonluth stopped walking and spoke without turning to Curie. "To you it might be minor, but to her it means a lot. Don't mistake her humaneness for weakness. She is a more than capable leader who has seen her crew through more than you could ever imagine." He then resumed his walk, "Also we're going back out tomorrow to officially propose the alliance. So unless you want a repeat of earlier today, I suggest you inform your men otherwise you may find out just how strong willed Sarah and her crew really are."

"Yes sir," Curie replied with a half hearted salute and sigh.

As there were not any spare rooms, Sonluth and Jace split a room while Sarah and Kazumi split another. Kazumi had no problems falling asleep, but Sarah was unable to sleep. Her mind raced as she tried to figure the best course of action for the following day. One task seemed like a mountain, two seemed insurmountable. She looked over at Kazumi who was soundly asleep. "Maybe a walk outside might help out." She got up and quietly exited the room and went out the front door. "The moon really does look different from down here," she mused to herself as she got out the front door. "I can see why Arianna took Saku to the roof to see the night sky, it's so beautiful."

"Pardon my intrusion Commander but outside is perhaps not the best place to be, especially with the moon so bright," Curie spoke as he came out the door behind Sarah.

"Curie, why do we have outposts down here?" Sarah asked ignoring his comment.

"To keep the Earthborn in line," he quickly responded.

She held her hand up to the moon until it nicely fit within its sphere before continuing, "I've only been down here a few hours and I already envy you."

"How so?"

"Look at the sky; the stars, the moon a real sunrise and

sunset. In space we only get a fabricated version of these. Or if on the other planets a poor substitute."

"There is nothing to be jealous of. Fighting the Earthborns does not make up for the celestial views. Nothing does because they've destroyed even the good things that were down here."

"Then why fight? Why not just leave them here?"

"You underestimate the ingenuity of the Earthborns," he frowned. "Even if we took everything with us to space they'd eventually find a way up."

"But they'd still be… human, just like us."

"Well a little less civil, but there is nothing a few good months of training couldn't fix."

She brought her hand down, looked at it and smiled weakly before turning to Curie and speaking, "But they'd still be human. They'd bleed red, their hands, their hair, their body shape would still be like ours. Even if you tested their genome, it would be the same as ours."

"What are you getting at?" Curie growled.

"We're both the same, yet we have taken it upon ourselves to divide each other. Isn't there a saying united we stand, divided we fall? Why have we so readily accepted division? Are we so lacking in self belief that we divide ourselves simply to get a few rungs higher on the social ladder?"

"Are you trying to undermine us from the UTSF?"

"No, not hardly. I'm just trying to put my thoughts in order and thinking aloud. Are we as Spaceborn really more intelligent and less brutish than Earthborns? If not, why are we so divided? Why did we take it upon ourselves to kill each other to get our way."

"Humans have been doing it for years," Curie responded. "For as far back as the books go, they all make mention of how our ancestors conquered and divided people. When we made the leap to space, the idea was that we'd leave all the wars and petty disputed back on the planet, while intellectuals lead us into a brave new world."

"So if people had been doing it for years, what made them think they could stop it dead simply by changing the scenery?"

Curie shrugged, "That I cannot answer. Ideally as we moved to space we lost direct control of raw materials, political affiliations, and direct borders with others which lead to wars."

"So you left behind what made us Terrans."

"Well yes, but Earth is not in the best shape. It was sacrificed a long time ago from constant wars and diseases and natural disasters."

"See, there it is again. That word… sacrifice. That's the second time I've heard it today. What is with us that we are so willing to sacrifice the very thing that makes us… Terran."

"It would have never lasted," Curie said as he walked past Sarah and looked out the gate. "First there was the war, then came the famine, then came the diseases. Our ancestors who initially made the jump to space had sacrificed so much for their victory that there was nothing more they could do for Earth, so we moved to space. Truth be told it was fairly balanced arrangement until the Generian

Wars. That's when it really headed south. Space colonies are nice and all, but they couldn't provide one thing; raw materials. We drained the planet of all its materials, in exchange it was as if Earth itself began to rise up against us. The disasters that followed during and shortly after the Generian War rendered large swaths of landmass unlivable. That was when space truly became the envied place to live. In an attempt to not overload the colonies the UTSF imposed the immigration laws that to this day are still in effect, preventing people from moving between colonies and the planet. The UTSF sent them some supplies. We didn't abandon them completely but then the Mail Massacre happened. That was the tipping point. That lead to loud public outcry and uprisings sprang up all around the planet. The UTSF then did what they do best... crush things. Overkill? Perhaps. But from that point on the Earth was never the same. The Earthborn forever resented the Spaceborn for not assisting them during the massacre, while the Spaceborn despised the Earthborn for acting brutish and what was perceived as throwing a tantrum because they needed something to blame."

"And all this time you've never tried to correct it?"

"No. There is no need to. You cannot reason with that which will not listen to reason. There have been others before you who have tried to reason with the Earthborn and have never comeback. They have devolved back into a primitive human whilst us in space have moved forward."

Sarah let out a small chuckle, "Perhaps you and them have a lot more in common than you are willing to admit."

"I beg your pardon?"

"Sorry, just thinking aloud again. I'm going back to my room, my roommate would be most terrified if she was to wake up and I not be there." Sarah gave a small wave and then re-entered the compound. She went back to her room and sat down in a corner of the room and looked up out the window, "At the end of the day no matter how we look at it, we're all really Earthborns. Our ancestors came from the same place and to that same place we shall all return."

The next day, a Resistance Truck picked up Sarah, Sonluth, and Jace from the outpost and drove them back to Resistance HQ. Sarah borrowed a pair of pants for the trip this time and opted to sit in the back with Jace and Sonluth. No one exchanged any words, but Sarah spent a lot of time with her head buried in her hands. Once at the compound the trio were escorted by four soldiers to the main hall and seated near the front. In the center was a round table that six people and Olaf were currently sitting at. The members were all talking amongst themselves in groups of two or three and the hall in general was fairly noisy. Eventually, a woman walked in with some files and folders and sat down at a vacant seat next to Olaf. She said something to him and he nodded.

"Order, order," Olaf said as he banged a wooden mallet on the table, "The Paris Council is now in session." He waited for a few seconds for the noise to quiet down before continuing. "Today's meeting will cover three things. Firstly, our missile barrage was successful in destroying the morale of the UTSF, and allowing for the rebel mechina to successfully take over UTSF Lunar HQ. They are currently undergoing a rebranding, which will be addressed on a later point when their new leader addresses the council with a proposition."

"What type of proposition?" one of the members asked.

"You will find out later," Olaf replied, "but first, we must deal with our second bit of business." He signaled to someone on the side and Aira was lead out in hand cuffs to stand in front of the council. She kept her head down, and didn't look at or acknowledge anyone on the council as she stood there. "Aira you are charged with war crimes involving premeditated mass murder of Terrans in an attempt to turn the Terran People against their at the time Osmerian allies. How do you plea?"

"Guilt as charged," she replied without lifting her head.

"Her guilt has never been in doubt!" a woman remarked as she jumped up from her seat. "We all saw the reports that she had formulated and executed the Mail Massacre. Why is she even wasting council time going through this?"

"To show that we are still capable of that which she is not, fairness." Olaf replied.

"Whatever," the woman said as she sat back down, "Just let me know when we can pass her sentence on her."

"There is nothing fair about this at all!" Sarah exclaimed out loud. Everyone turned towards Sarah as she made the outburst. "How is this fair? Everyone just wants to tear her to pieces!"

"Justifiably so," the woman replied. "She certainly didn't care when she gave the order to put toxins in our mail. Additionally, she even tried to pin it on someone else and incite a war. What's so fair about that?"

"I told you commander, it's pointless," Aira spoke. "I have committed atrocities beyond any form of forgiveness, and if they want me dead, they have every right to it."

"Look, I've heard about everything Aira is done wrong, but hear me out for a second, to let you know what she's done right."

"Why should we?" the woman asked with a glare and a collective murmur emanated from the crowd.

"The natives are restless," Jace commented to Sonluth as the murmur seemed to grow with each passing moment.

Olaf banged his little mallet on the table, "Order, order everyone! We said we want this to be fair, and fair it shall be. Let the woman present a defense for Aira." The murmur seemed to die down a little after Olaf's announcement. Sarah looked around and it was as if all eyes were on her. She made a glance at Jace and he just nodded at Sarah. She then turned to face the council, closing her eyes and taking in a deep breath before exhaling and opening them again.

"Major Aira is the head medic onboard a mechina I command, known formerly as the UTSF RAINE. Just like the UTSF she worked for, her actions were flawed, but unlike the UTSF before her, she has tried to amend her ways. Without her, our medics may not have been as organized as they were. Most importantly though, she released us from the UTSF, and saved us from execution. Without her intervention there wouldn't have been a battle at Lunar HQ. I searched for her in the aftermath of the escape, but she was no where to be found. She has changed over the course of this placement and at the very least give her a chance to redeem herself. Everyone talks about fairness and justice, but killing each other will accomplish nothing but dividing us. I can't bring back the people Aira killed, and neither can I reverse the subsequent paranoia and orders that came down afterwards, but with Aira's help we've started to turn things around. I know she hasn't been the best during the course of her life, but as her commanding officer, I'd at least like her to see her current assignment through. Give her a chance at life, to redeem herself." There were a few moments of silence after Sarah completed her speech and she glanced around before quickly sitting down.

"We will... consider... your defense," Olaf said slowly. He then rose from his chair, "the council will adjourn temporarily on this matter and discuss it in private. We shall endeavour to be back in short order." The other members of the council got up from their chairs and followed Olaf out of the room.

"You think that was enough?" Sarah asked quietly to the others as she leaned forward in her chair and rubbed her upper arms with her hands.

"Enough is never enough," Jace said, and then he added as he rested his hand on Sarah's shoulder, "but you done well, relax a little its out of your hands now."

"But what if I could have done more?" Sarah asked as she stopped rubbing her arms and looked at Jace. "What then?"

"Sarah, like Jace said it's out of your hands now. No matter the outcome, we're grateful for you trying," Sonluth looked at Aira as she remained standing stone faced near the council table. "Even Aira."

A short time later, the council members filed back into the hall and all except Olaf took their seats. A silence fell upon the hall as Olaf looked down at the table and slowly stood up straight and erect. Placing his hands behind his back he looked at Aira and addressed her, "Aira, you have caused the deaths of millions of people, deceived millions more, and destroyed the lives of countless others. For these deeds you have offered no defense and you willingly admit. According to the law of the land you should be executed for treason against your fellow Terrans. Even with this knowledge you still have not offered a defense nor have you denied the claims. However, having heard testimony from your commanding officer, and the circumstances that we find ourselves in, we will offer you a stay of execution."

A collective gasp could be heard in the hall as this announcement was made, and even the stone-faced Aira lifted her head and dropped her jaw. "Just like that?" Aira thought aloud.

Olaf turned and looked directly at Sarah, "Your commanding officer speaks highly of you, and you do show some remorse for your actions." A loud murmur arose from the crowd and Olaf raised his hand to quiet them. "This is not an easy case to pass judgment on. The guilty party has been proven and admits to everything well beyond a reasonable doubt, but as we were blinded by the rage of having lost our loved ones, it never occurred to us that there are some who care for Aira. Thus we are presented with a moral dilemma, one that cannot be resolved so quickly and easily right here and now. Guards take her back to her holding cell, and we will deal with her at a later date." The murmur grew once again as Aira was lead back out, and Sarah hugged her nearest ally, Jace.

"I'm glad for you too," Jace said at the sudden outburst from Sarah.

Olaf then took his seat and hammered his mallet on the table again. "We also have another bit of business." He clasped his hands and rested his elbows on the table. "The UTSF… I'm sorry, the United Planetary Alliance has asked for our co-operation with attacking the Silicians. Commander of the Fleet Sarah Collins come forward and presents your case to the council and the people of Paris."

"Again?" Sarah sighed as she stood up from her seat.

"We're right behind you fearless leader," Jace said with a quick salute.

"Gee thanks," Sarah replied with a scowl. She slowly walked over next to the table and with a nod from Olaf began her proposal.

"As you have heard, I am Commander of the Fleet for the newly established United Planetary Alliance. I have come down to Earth proper to ask for your assistance with repelling a Silician Invasion." Sarah spoke with a slight quiver in her voice and her hands rubbing against the seam of her pants.

"And what are you asking in return?" an audience member yelled out. "You may have a fancy new name, but how do we know you're not just using us like the old UTSF before you did?"

"You have my word," Sarah replied. "I don't want anything in return but your co-operation.

"Your word isn't good enough," one of the council members interjected. "The UTSF promised much, but never did anything to help us. All they've really ever done is killing us." This comment caused the crowd to boo and yell at Sarah. What ever she said for the next few minutes was lost in the din of the crowd.

"She's going to need some help," Sonluth said to Jace as he got up from his seat. Jace followed suit, and while Jace walked over to Sarah, Sonluth walked over to Olaf. Sonluth grabbed Olaf's mallet and smashed it hard enough on the table for it to break, which instantly quieted both the crowd and the council.

"Look people, a fellow Terran is offering you a chance to do something and you are rejecting the idea before it even takes flight. All of you talk about how the UTSF abused and persecuted you, yet when someone offers you a chance to change all that you laugh and mock her. You guys are no different than the UTSF that you so despise, all for yourself and no thought for the guy sitting next to you. Think about it, you can mock her all you want right now, but if you don't consider everything you maybe suffering a far worse fate then what you did under the UTSF."

As Sonluth made his talk, Jace walked over to Sarah and rested his hand on her shoulder, "Relax, don't be so nervous, they feed off your fear. See how Sonluth just took control? Talk like that, like it's your last. Don't worry about diplomacy and political correctness. There is a time and place for that, but not now. Not when our civilization's fate hangs in the balance. Speak from your heart and make them listen to you. Now start again, and know that although I'm right here supporting you, you have the backing of the *zaniest* crew I have ever served with."

"Thank you, Jace," Sarah said as she touched his hand and smiled a little. She closed her eyes and took in a deep breath before removing her hand from his with a long exhale. She looked up into the crowd and began speaking as Jace took his hand off her shoulder and stepped back.

"People of Paris, I know it's hard to believe in something, least of all from one who formerly persecuted you, but as a fellow Terran I hope that we can all work together, not as Spaceborn and Earthborns, but as a unified Terran Race," she spoke in a stronger tone and used hand motions as she continued. "I've been called naive and inexperienced, but there are at least some of you who have faith in my abilities as you helped us to take the Lunar HQ of the former UTSF. Now I know we can't change everything overnight, Rome was not built in three days, so I ask you to give us a chance. If we don't fight as a unified front, then we'll be crushed underfoot by someone who does. I have recruited Generians as well as the Osmerians for our cause. They stand united, as do the Silicians. Why can't we do the same?" There was a brief pause before she continued. "You also ask what I want in return. Can you not believe that I don't want anything? Maybe there is something you want? If there is, no one has told me. Everyone just seems so much more eager to keep us divided and killing each other than working to make things right." She stopped and looked around, and everyone was still silent. Sonluth coughed at Sarah and she turned around to see Olaf had stood up from his chair. His hands were on the table and he was looking down at the ground as he leaned on his hands.

"You have spoken many truths just now. I can see how your naivety has helped you shed the past. Yet for many of us we simply cannot shake the past as we live in it every day. The UTSF always made promises that they'd clean up and take care of us on the planet; that we'd be able to be promoted through the ranks and bring recognition to those of us born on the planet. But all they did was take our best; be it people, resources or manufactured goods and use them to their own means and then throw them away like they were refuse. Paris was once a beautiful city with such landmarks as the Eiffel Tower, Notre Dame, and the Arc De Triomphe. And not just Paris; across the whole globe, things fell into a state of disrepair, people lost hope and the economy collapsed. All that remained for us was to fight against what we saw as the source of our problems, the UTSF. Now someone comes before us who sounds like them, talks like them and even dresses like them and tells us they want better? It is a rather difficult sell. However, I would at least to voice my opinion, even if the council does not agree." He lifted his head up and looked at Sarah as he continued, "I for one do wish to believe in you and your cause. We know that you had allied with the Generian Resistance, something no Terran has ever done on such a large scale willingly of the Generians. You've also come willingly to us, without any conceitedness. You trusted us to bring you here unharmed, and I suppose the obvious gesture would be to return your trust." He then stood up straight. "Council, prepare to vote on the Request for Allegiance to the UPA. You must answer Yea, Nay or Abstain when asked and your vote can not be retracted. It takes four votes to pass or reject. Should there be a tie or the threshold not met due to abstained votes, then I will cast the deciding vote." The council members all nodded in silence. "Councilman Bird." Olaf said as he started to go clockwise around the table from his position.

"Yea."

"Councilwoman Uhl."

"Nay."

"Councilman Sienna."

"Nay."

"Councilman Lloris."

"Yea."

"Councilwoman LeBlanc."

"Yea."

"Councilman Avignon."

"Nay."

"Councilman Mani."

"Abstain."

"We have a tie vote of three yeas and three nay. As per regulation I will cast the deciding vote. However, before I do, I have one final question for you Sarah Collins. Aside from fostering good relations, is your organization able to allow us promotions without biased regardless of our place of origin?"

Sarah nodded, "Yes, I can. We are all Terrans, there will be no distinction made between those born on the planet or those born in the colonies. Just as I've included Generians in my hierarchy I would also include some of you as I know that like you said before, it's hard to believe in something if you never see it happen. And there is a lot I don't know about Earth proper. As with the Generians, I would immediately place a planet born Terran in a high rank to assist with overseeing and helping those from the planet integrate into the forces of the UPA."

"Very well," Olaf said with a grin. "With my vote, I will end this deadlock, and thus make this result binding before all those present here today." He closed his eyes for a moment and then reopened them, still grinning to himself. "I vote yea on this resolution, with the hope that this will indeed move Terrans to becoming a more unified civilization." As Olaf finished talking, there was a solitary clap from the audience. A second one came soon after, followed by a third, and soon the whole hall was applauding and cheering, "United!"

"Well chalk up another hard fought win for us," Sonluth said with a grin as he came over to Sarah and Jace.

"Indeed good sir, indeed," Jace replied with a nod as the council members filed out of the hall.

"Thanks you two," Sarah added as she hugged both of them. After a few moments, Sarah released the two from her embrace and went to locate Olaf.

"Thank you Olaf," she said when she caught up with him in a nearby room. "You won't regret making this decision. I'd promote you here and now, but I didn't bring any spare stars with me," she added without holding eye contact. "Maybe when you come up to space I can give them to you," she said as she resumed eye contact with a smile. "I will alert all the outposts to begin ferrying you guys up to the training facilities. Assuming you know more about the people here than I do, you can feel free to also pick four officers and present them to me when you come up. That should be able to both ease tension during the transition and set up a hierarchy that the Earthborns can believe in until we're able to fully prove ourselves."

"You have really thought this through," Olaf said as he rubbed his chin. "Very well, the new recruits should be heading up late tonight or at first light tomorrow."

"And Aira?" Sarah asked as she shuffled in her spot.

"She will come when I appoint my officers. I will also release other captive former UTSF personnel back to your outposts. Whether or not others will unite, I don't know, but like you said, united we stand, divided we fall, and hopefully they will follow our lead."

"I sure hope so," Sarah replied. "I guess this is goodbye for now, but I'll see you in a few days to give you your stars?" she asked as she extended her hand.

"You got it," Olaf said with a hearty laugh as he shook Sarah's hand. Olaf then excused himself and Jace and Sonluth came alongside Sarah.

"Well, we ready to go back?" Jace asked. "You've made yet another ally out of a former foe."

"Mmhmm," Sarah nodded. "It was close, but we did it."

Olaf then returned, "I take it you wish to return immediately?" he asked. The trio all nodded. "Alright, I'll get the driver to take you back, as well as three immediate recruits for you." Olaf then indicated the two men and one woman next to him, "Misha Trotski, Alex Rose, and Benjamin Shmitt. Misha is a mechanic, while Benjamin is one of our munitions specialis, and Alex is a communications officer."

"Pleased to meet you Commander," they all echoed with a salute.

"Welcome aboard," Sarah replied with a smile. All six soon piled into the back of a truck and drove back to the outpost.

"Halt, these others will need security clearance to get by," the gate guard told Sarah as she led the new recruits to the gate.

"You are *not* going to irritate me with protocol are you?" Sarah growled. She then put her hands on her hips and continued, "Why can't you just take my word that they are with me and let them pass?"

"Sorry, even if you are the Commander of the Fleet, we can not let anyone else through without expressed permission from Lt. Curie." Sarah wanted to say something, but covered her own mouth and walked away from him.

"Protocol needs to go in a corner and *die*." Sarah said with a slight twitch once the gate guard had gone out of earshot to call Lt Curie.

"But aren't all those protocols in place to keep things orderly and secure?" Alex asked. Sarah glared at her and returned to covering her mouth.

"She's a little special," Jace said with a slight chuckle.

"She has had very free reign for a military commander for the past little bit, and I think its getting to that point she may have forgotten some of it." Sarah was about to say something when the gate guard emerged with Lt Curie.

"I see you brought prisoners for us to exchange?" Lt Curie asked.

"No, there are new recruits for the UPA, and you are going to let us through to take a shuttle back to HQ," Sarah said with crossed arms.

"Rules are rules," Curie said with a smirk. "Nothing I can do about them."

Sarah shook her head and covered her face with her hands and let a muffled scream. "What," she muttered as Jace tapped her on the shoulder.

"You do realize as the Commander of the Fleet you could just make up a reason to let them by and change the rules on the spot," Jace whispered. Sarah's features softened as Jace's words sunk in. Her frown became a grin as she walked over to Curie.

"I *order* you to let these three through the gates so we can bring them to Lunar HQ."

"What? You can't just order me to break protocol," Curie said taken aback by the sudden order.

"I just did," Sarah said with a smirk, "And if you don't follow *those* orders I suppose I can charge you with insubordination, which will lead to a court martial, and a dishonourable discharge. Which means you'll *never* find work ever again, and we wouldn't want that now would we?"

"I-I… no, you can pass through," Curie said as he hung

his head down and sighed.

"See, that wasn't so hard now, was it?" Sarah said with a smile. "I promise next time I'll have a list for you," she added as she walked past Curie.

"Yes sir," Curie sulked.

"Excuse me, but a list is still pretty useless since most of us don't have any form of ID," Alex said as they entered the compound.

"Well I had to tell the poor guy *something*," Sarah said with a shrug. "I guess we can just have the new recruits register and get photo ID when they arrive at the outposts," Sarah said as she looked at Jace and Sonluth.

"Which also means they'd be frisked and searched for security reasons," Jace added. "I can't see everyone here just going all opened arms because of what happened in one city."

"Why can't we all just get along," Sarah said with a sigh. She then added as she fixed her hat, "I'll notify the outposts when we get back to HQ. For now, let's get these three back so we can start their processing and hopefully start replacing our lost numbers." Jace and Sonluth nodded and the group soon departed on a shuttle for the moon.

CHAPTER 11: THE FINAL PIECES

Once they got back to space, Sarah immediately sent a message back Curie and the various other outposts still on Earth that anyone wanting to join the UPA should be allowed in through security checks and a photo ID issued before sending them on a shuttle to Lunar HQ. Once she finished sending the message she walked back outside her door and found Alex, Benjamin and Misha waiting for her outside.

"Jace and Sonluth didn't help you guys?" she asked as she leaned her head to the side.

"Nay, they said they were pilots and thus were unable to help us, so they told us to wait for you to assign us somewhere," Benjamin replied.

"Those bums," Sarah mumbled as she looked down the hall. She then refocused on the trio before her, "well let's get you all sorted out." She assigned Misha to shadow Ned, Benjamin was assigned to Vladmir and Alex was assigned to Kazumi. Once those assignments had been completed, a soldier arrived with two boxes of personal effects.

"Sorry to bother you, but since you are the next of kin, these boxes contain the personal effects of the late Commander Collins. Do you wish me place them in here or would you rather I have them destroyed?"

Sarah sat down in her chair and motioned to a place near the doorway, "Just rest them there, I'll look at them when I have time. Thank you."

"Very well," the soldier replied and rested the boxes down. "And I'm sorry for your loss," he added with a salute.

"Thank you," Sarah replied as she saluted back. The

soldier left the room and Sarah looked at the boxes. Resting on top was a folded flag of the UTSF and a commander's hat. She was about to refocus on some paperwork when she noticed a yellow stain on the hat and went over to pick it up. She ran her fingers over it, and tears began to form in her eyes.

"Sorry dad, I put your hat in the dryer…" she recalled when she was younger, her head hung low, shoulders hunched over and sniffling a little as her dad stood over her examining the stain. She remembered his stern look as he squatted down to her height and brought her face up.

"There are many hats like this, but now, I know which one is mine," he said with a kiss on her forehead. "My dear, don't ever be afraid of making mistakes. Be afraid of making the same mistake because you are too afraid or proud to admit it in the first place."

She clutched the hat close to her chest as she recalled this memory, "I'm so sorry dad, I'm so, very sorry," she cried. As she clutched the hat, something fell out. She bent down to pick it up. On the side that was facing her was written 'John, Sarah and F' on one line and below it 'Together ag'. She flipped it over and it was a picture similar to the one she kept on her desk when she was little with her dad. But this picture had a crooked edge with a slightly jagged cut. Sarah's closed her still teary eyes, "So you missed mom after all too. What was she like dad? I guess she was nice and loving too," Sarah sighed as she put the picture down.

There was a knock on the door, "Come in," Sarah said as she stood back up and wiped away her tears.

Marina walked through the door, "Captain, I wanted to…" she was holding a clipboard in her hand but stopped as she saw Sarah, "Are you okay?" Marina said as she stopped short. "Your eyes are all red and bloodshot."

"I'm fine," Sarah said wiping away the last of her tears. "I was just looking through some of my dad's personal effects."

"Oh," Marina said as she looked at her clipboard, and then back to Sarah, "I can... come back later," she spoke without maintaining eye contact. "I know it must be... hard... for you."

Sarah shook her head, "No it's alright Marina. This can wait," she said as she rubbed her eyes.

"Okay," Marina said as she leaned her clipboard back away from her. She took in a deep breath before reading what was on the board. "Fae reported back that Osmerians were found scattered about in Generian Space. The Generians and Terrans there have put them under arrest and by the sounds of Fae's report their treatment hasn't been the best." She handed Sarah the clipboard and continued as Sarah flipped through the pages, "Those are some of the names that Fae has returned."

"Some?" Sarah said as she looked up from the paper at Marina.

Marina nodded, "Yes, Fae says there are many more, but the former UTSF forces have set up another planet to become a makeshift prison for the Osmerians. Fae says the Prison Warden is preventing any of the Generians from going down to investigate, but reports are that the conditions are not optimal."

"So what do you want? An Order of Reversal?" Sarah asked. "You certainly have enough names here to start over again."

Marina shook her head, "Not just that, although I'd really

appreciate it, but I want to be able to go and assure my people that everything will be alright. And maybe convert the planet into a new planet for the Osmerians." She continued as her eyes began to tear up, "I know it's a really big favour to ask, and the Generians would have to give up one of their own system planets, but at least for now, could you do this for me, for my people just so that they have a place to call home until we can figure something out?"

Sarah rested her hands on Marina's shoulders, "Vice Admiral, Princess, Queen, like I've said before, I don't know what I should call you. But I did promise you, if we found any surviving Osmerians, I'd do everything I could to help you. If you want to go to your people, go. Rest assured everyone here will be behind you. I will write up the order to release the captured Osmerians. We can discuss a new home for your people probably after all this is done."

"Thank you," Marina said as she embraced Sarah.

"You're very welcome," Sarah replied back. After a few moments the two stepped away from each other, and Sarah smiled at the still sniffling Marina as she wiped away her tears.

"Thank you again," Marina whispered and bolted out of the room.

"Wow, I don't even know what to think about that," Sarah said as she walked towards the window and looked outside. "Even with so many losses, we've managed to somehow find hope and survivors," she said as she looked down at the shuttles taking off and landing at the spaceport. She looked then at Marina's clipboard, "And a queen has found her people, when we were so sure they were all dead." She smiled to herself as she turned back around to her desk, "I guess it's that determination and hope that makes us all so dangerous. Maybe that's what the Silicians have always been afraid of someone growing up and beating them through sheer determination and will. Maybe that's why they go through great lengths to completely annihilate their opponents." She sighed and plopped down in her chair. "Three days isn't optimal training time, but that's the time we know we have; at the end of which we will go into a final confrontation with nothing more than grit, determination and the hope of a better tomorrow."

Sarah returned to her paperwork that finalized the rebranding and current hierarchy. "Now I see why things used to take so long to come back from HQ," she muttered as she looked at her stack of paperwork.

"You've got mail!" Sarah's computer dinged. Sarah sighed and opened the new email.

"Distribution of mechina, supplies and personnel," she read the email title as she scanned through the message. As she was scanning that message she got a similar message from Gonsalves. "Thank God they're not trying to launch an invasion," Sarah whistled as she looked over the Generian numbers.

"We are keeping Generian training in Generian Space so as not to overwhelm your training facilities. Additionally we have informed Vice Admiral Welsch of the Osmerians within our system. We are assessing their capabilities and should be able to update you by tomorrow."

"Good to know," Sarah said as she erased the message. Sarah felt her head getting heavy and leaned heavily on her left hand as she continued to screen through her paperwork. She felt her eyes slowly closing when someone banged on the door causing her to jerk wide awake.

"Sir some of the outposts are reporting that the

Earthborns are trying to storm the outposts. They are requesting immediate reinforcements to be sent."

"Whoa, whoa, storming outposts? Like attacking them?"

"I don't know, the wording used in the message is what I delivered to you."

Sarah rubbed her temples and closed her eyes. "I doubt they're attacking," Sarah muttered to herself. "They are probably all just trying to get up to space."

"Your orders?"

Sarah shook her head and looked up at the soldier to respond. "Send down some people to assist with the processing."

"Yes sir," the soldier said. He then turned around and left the room.

"So much to do, so little time," she mumbled as she rested her head in her hands.

"You look like you could use a rest," a voice said from the hall.

"I could, but I want to get all this squared away first then I can rest easier knowing that everything is running smoothly."

"I'm sure you do, but you ever heard the saying a last minute chore never lasts a minute." With that comment Sarah looked up to see Fae standing in the doorway.

"Oh Fae, I wasn't expecting you back so soon."

"Well I figured you'd let Marina out when you got the

message so I decided to come back and help you out." She then added as she proceeded to walk into the office, "And I figured you'd be still pushing yourself."

"We only have three days to make this operation work after that I can get some rest."

"The only rest you'll be getting is a rest of the permanent type. Have you even eaten lately?"

"Of course I have!"

"When?"

"Recently..." Sarah said as she sat up in her chair.

"Yes dear, and I'm sure Sonluth has smiled recently too."

"He has?" Sarah perked up.

"No, it was sarcasm, and that is exactly why you need some sleep and something to eat."

"But I'm almost done," Sarah said as she rubbed her eyes.

"Well I'll wait here for ten minutes; if you're not done by then I'm picking you up and carrying you to the cafeteria."

"Yes mother," Sarah sighed. Fae walked away from her and leaned on the door to watch Sarah. Her scowl melted to a smile as she watched Sarah's head bob back and forth as it slowly lowered itself onto the desk.

"Silly kids, all the same," Fae laughed to herself as looked at her watch. "Five minutes until time's up, that gives time enough to go secure some foodstuffs for her. Enjoy your nap until I get back," Fae said as she left the room. She came back a few minutes later with some booster rations and a pillow. Sarah was still sleeping when she got back so Fae walked over and nudged her. "Alright, ten minutes is up."

Sarah slowly opened her eyes. "Hmmm?" She then looked over at Fae, and she jolted up. "Oh!" Sarah looked down at her report, "I guess I never did finish it huh?"

"Not at all, but here I brought some food for you since I know you aren't going to listen to reason and put your work down," Fae said as she handed Sarah a packet of rations.

"Thanks, I guess I could use a break," Sarah responded as she took the packet from Fae and opened the packet to eat the contents.

"It's obviously not a proper meal, but it should suffice for a day or so. Just please take care of yourself. No point running yourself ragged and never being able to see the results of what you worked so hard for."

"I will," Sarah said with a nod.

Alex ran in breathing heavily, "Sir, a shuttle just came up from Earth but the passengers are holding each other hostage."

"That makes no type of sense," Sarah responded.

"I suggest we go down and see for ourselves. No one has started shooting, and that is always a good sign when dealing with the UTSF."

Sarah shoved the last bit of the packet into her mouth and grabbed her hat and the trio ran downstairs to the docking bay. Sarah approached the closest officer once they got to the docks, "What is the problem?"

"Sir, the ex-UTSF personnel are refusing to disembark. They claim that we should not have negotiated with the terrorists on Earth as it has compromised the safety of all those living in the colonies."

"Ugh, are they really going to make this argument… again?" Sarah said as she rubbed her temples.

"Hard to teach an old dog new tricks," Fae remarked.

"Well they better used to it," Sarah scowled.

The shuttle door opened and a man came outside. "Is the leader of this farcical group present?"

"Looks like your turn," Jace said as he gave Sarah a soft nudge forward.

"So the rumours were true," the man muttered as Sarah proceeded towards the shuttle. He then spoke up, "Miss Collins while I did hear you were leading a rebel faction within the UTSF, I did not fully believe it until just now. However, I must implore you to reverse this tomfoolery and keep the Earthborns on the planet. We have enough personnel in the colonies and the surviving UTSF to be able to carry on as we did before."

"With all due respect… sir… the UTSF practiced a very divisive regime. No matter how much you hate the Earthborns, with all the discoveries being made in space, chances are we would eventually need them. And even if we didn't need them, we'd need the planet itself as we obviously lack resources on colonies and there are some materials you can only find on planets."

"You can't simply expect a terrorist to forget their ways

and align with civility."

"No more than I expect we've terrorized them. Additionally if we all go back far enough we're all Earthborns. So if we outgrew the habit, I'm sure they'll be just fine."

"So young, so naïve. Not only are you banking on these… terrorists, but you've also working with the Generians *and* the Osmerians, whilst turning your back on our longtime allies the Silicians."

"Oh because you guys have *never* backstabbed anyone before. And let's be real here, as sporadic as the Osmerians are, loyalty is not one of those things they take lightly, it's very much something that's earned, making it highly unlikely that they simply woke up one day and decided, hey guys, let's attack the Terrans. They seem like a dumb bunch."

"You are taking this much too lightly," the man sighed. "Well if you won't change things voluntarily, then we're going to have to do this the hard way. For every minute you don't return things to the way they were, we'll just shoot one of the Earthborn."

"Who's sounding like the terrorist now?" Sarah seethed.

"Just like the Earthborn, it is the only language everyone understands." He walked back into the shuttle and brought out one of the new recruits and shot them in the back of the head then pushed him down the stairs. "There's one," he jeered as he walked back inside.

"Shoot him back! Blow the shuttle up! Don't let him simply shoot the people!" Olaf demanded.

"Because killing them would make such an awesome track record and maybe, you know, kill us in the process,"

Sarah retorted.

"Kids simmer down," Fae said as she stepped between the two.

"No! She's let one person die is she going to let more die? Was this all just a set up to massacre us in space?"

"No, of course not!" Sarah fired back.

"Three more inbound shuttles have also taken up a similar stance," Alex reported.

"Three!" Sarah shrieked.

"I guess they really don't like us huh?" Alex said despondently.

"They'll just have to get used to it! Even if we have to make them get along with you." She then turned to the gathered troops, "We'll follow Olaf's idea and take them by force if need be. If they don't want to play nice, then we shall happily oblige them."

"Sarah wait!" Fae stopped her.

"What?"

"Think about what you're doing. You're not going to make this any easier by crushing them."

"What's wrong with crushing them?" Sarah demanded.

"Isn't that what got us in this mess in the first place?" Sarah looked at Fae for a few moments before she flashed back to her conversation with Curie.

"The UTSF do what they do best... crushing things."

Sarah's eyes dilated and then she collapsed on the ground. "I'm... just like them..." she sobbed. The soldiers had surrounded the shuttle in the docks and were preparing to fire.

"Hijacker of Shuttle one four two six surrender now or face immediate consequences," Olaf ordered.

"Why Fae, why am I still not different from them?" Sarah sobbed.

Fae knelt down to Sarah, "Because you aren't any different from them. You are Terran just like they are. You and them are one in the same."

"Go!" Olaf ordered and the soldiers and they stormed the shuttle in a hail of bullets, grenades and smoke canisters. Sarah collapsed to all fours as she heard the gunshots go off.

"But if we are the same, then why? Why so much hate?"

Fae leaned into Sarah and wiped away her tears, "In Generia, we have a saying that no matter where your body is, your soul belongs to the planet Generia. Terrans have severed that tie. In forging their future they forgot their past. When moving forward, one must never forget their past, or their origins. No matter how painful they may be, let them serve as a lesson, otherwise you just repeat the same mistakes over and over again."

The shooting stopped and Olaf walked back, "We've neutralized the shuttle."

"Why? Why did you act without me?" Sarah demanded.

"You took too long to act, who knows how many others we

may have lost with your hesitation?"

"That is beside the point! You still inflicted losses on both sides that may or may not have happened without your intervention."

"Just because you Spaceborn think highly of your own opinions, I assure you that losses sustained by my course of action were smaller than what you would have incurred via any other." Olaf then walked off and Alex came alongside Sarah.

"The other two shuttles said they'll land without any further trouble," Alex said quietly.

"Thank you," Sarah whispered. Sarah quietly sobbed for a few more minutes before getting up on her feet. "Fae, was my slow reaction really that terrible? Does trying to assess a situation make one weak?"

"Ideally one would want to assess as quick as possible. That being said, the quickest solution isn't always the best solution. Snap decisions are like band-aids, they can hold you over until you get to a medical center, but don't be fooled into believing it's a permanent fix."

"I see…" Sarah said as her posture dropped.

"Sarah, don't be afraid of making mistakes. Be afraid of repeating them. Nothing in life is perfect."

"I guess, but it still hurts, all the same," Sarah sighed. She walked off as the other two shuttles landed.

"Hang in there Sarah, you're almost home now," Fae said as she watched Sarah walk off.

Sarah was still moping as she opened her office door.

She let out a long exhale and as she did she looked to the ground and saw her dad's personal effects.

"Dad, why didn't you ever tell me how hard leadership was? Were you just like everyone else and thought that I could only lead as an experiment?" She poked in the boxes and found postcards from Mars and Pluto. One in particular caught her eye. It was dated from the previous year and was sent from Mars. 'I hear our daughter is doing her maiden voyage on the mechina. She must have really grown since I last saw her. I do sometimes get envious of parents with their children, but I would have been a terrible mother. However, I'm trying to get on the same assignment, but it may conflict with my current assignment with the academy. If I can't get on with you two, I'm sure parent and child will both succeed in completing their mission. Take care, I will write again soon.'

"Why mom? Why wouldn't you join us? We could be a happy family. Why does it seem like everyone is trying to undermine me? Like they don't trust me with the truth." Sarah continued reading the postcards, most of which seemed to be between her parents. She was not aware of how much time had passed when there was a knock on the door.

"Sir, Vice Admiral Gonsalves is arriving at the docks," Alex said as she peered her head into the room.

"Ok, thanks," Sarah replied without taking her eyes off what she was reading. Once Alex closed the door Sarah put down the postcards she had in her hand and stacked them off to the side. Sarah stopped off at the restroom before heading to the docks. "You look like a mess..." She turned on the tap and washed her face. She dried her hands and face, and then fixed her hair before heading to the docks.

"Glad you could make it back," Sarah said as she greeted Gonsalves as he stepped off his mechina.

"Thank you, but I've heard you've had it rough these past few days."

"You could say that," she sulked before quickly adding, "Marina didn't come back with you?"

Gonsalves shook his head, "No. Your order came down to withdraw from Vanius, but we've not heard much from the Osmerians since."

"I hope she's alright," Sarah said with a shiver, "Or maybe her people don't want to ally with us."

Fae laughed, "Marina? In trouble? The only trouble she's in is generally her own doing, be it directly or indirectly. Believe me, she's fine." She then sighed, "As for the ally thing, the Osmerians have been pretty harshly treated. I can't say for sure they'll ally with us, but I'm sure Marina is doing what she can on that front."

"Enemy fleet movements detected! All hands to battle stations! This is not a drill! I repeat, this is not a drill! All hands to battle station!" an alarm sounded and light began flashing red and white.

"That didn't take long," Sarah said. "Guess we'll be fighting them all the way home and back."

"Looks that way," Fae said with a nod. "Are we taking the RAINE out or will you be giving orders from inside?"

"Marina's not here," Sarah said with a frown. "We really should have properly trained a replacement for her."

"It's alright; we'll go up in our mechinas. You watch and

order from HQ." Fae nodded to Gonsalves and the two returned to their mechina and it departed. Sarah tried making her way to the Communications Room, but found herself fighting against the tide of troops going either outside to defend or towards mechina at the docks. The run that should have taken five minutes took almost twenty.

"Commander, are you ready?" Olaf said with a salute as Sarah opened the door.

"What's the battle status?" Sarah demanded as she came along side him.

"We're still waiting for them to reform on this end. The alarm was raised from sensors at the Pluto Base."

"Any visual confirmations?" Sarah asked.

"None that was decipherable. They obviously had knowledge of the sensors around Pluto and passed through when the visual sensors were furthest away."

"Keep on your guard," Sarah ordered as she looked at the holomap of the assembling fleet. If this really is the Silicians, then I want to be ready for them."

"Jump energy building on the third quadrant," one of the detection technicians reported.

"Everyone get ready," Sarah ordered.

"Wait!" there was a yell at the doorway.

"I'm sorry miss but you can't enter, this is restricted access only," the guards said as they held back the person.

"Mandy? What is it?" Sarah said as she took her eyes to

see who was at the door. "Let her through; if she's panicked there is a reason."

"Yes ma'am," the guards said as they released Mandy.

"I analyzed the broadcast signal as they passed Pluto. Although faint, it is neither Silician nor Terran in origin," Mandy said.

"Commander, you can't put the safety of this whole operation because of a suggestion," Olaf spoke up. "The enemy will be here in a few minutes, you should be here observing, not being fed potentially false information from a civilian."

"My computational capacity is far superior to any human's," Mandy rebuffed. "And I most certainly would not use it to mislead a friend."

"Unfortunately he does have a point Mandy," Sarah said with a sigh, "But if you've come this far, get directly to the point, I don't need the calculations, just give me the reason."

"Not Silician, Not Terran, Not Generian, Origin Unknown or Osmerian Origin," Mandy blurted out.

Sarah's eyes and mouth opened as she realized the point Mandy was making. She turned around and yelled at everyone in the room, "Relay everyone to put their shields up, and perform a radio frequency sweep."

"What? Why?" Olaf questioned. "Who else would be flying besides us and the Silicians? A first strike would be optimal against the forces we'd be up against. I know you like to minimize your casualties, but now is not the time for that!"

"No!" Sarah thundered as she narrowed her eyes at Olaf,

"The Osmerians could have possibly had another few mechinas. They had to fly to Generian space somehow, and escape capsules would not have done it in this short of a time. Although Marina was our helmswoman, she'd have no idea what radio frequency we used. Thus she could be trying to communicate on an incorrect frequency. Coupled with the fact of a precision pass at Pluto, it seems like her handy work."

"Energy build up almost complete, expecting mechina within the next minute," the detection officer relayed.

"Those are the orders! Even if I slipped up earlier, I'm in charge here, and if they are wrong they are on my conscience and we can discuss how wrong I was later and how bad of a leader I am, but right now, I'm in charge and that is my call. Issue the order or I will have you relieved and issue it myself."

There was a few seconds of silence before Olaf turned and relayed the order to the outside fleet. The fleet rearranged its formation and formed a phalanx with its shields.

"Emergence in thirty seconds," the detection officer reported.

"You better be right about this," Olaf scowled as he walked back over to Sarah. Sarah did not respond but waited for the next few moments to tick by. As the ships emerged, Sarah saw their black and blue markings and breathed a heavy sigh of relief.

"Everyone stand down, the emerging mechina are friendly," Sarah ordered.

"Message from Vice Admiral Welsch," the

communications officer announced. "She's not using the standard frequency and it may be compromised; do you still want me to patch it through?" Sarah nodded and the communications officer punched in a few keys.

"Lunar HQ do you read?" Marina's voice came through after a few moments.

"Loud and clear, although you might want to check your frequency and wait for a reply before simply flying in like that," Sarah responded.

"Is that why I didn't get any response flying past Pluto," Marina thought aloud before returning to her conversation with Sarah. "In any case, I've convinced my people to aid us in the upcoming battle with the Silicians. Naturally, we're all gung-ho about it, just so long as you guys promise not to turn your weapons on us and give us a planet to inhabit once this is all over."

"That's a lot of mechina," Mandy commented as more mechina emerged from the Chronos Jump, "Perhaps a larger base of operations is needed now."

"Hmmm, Martian Space perhaps?" Sarah thought aloud.

"While that does seem like a good course of action, hasn't it been a long standing dispute that the people of Mars dislike the military almost as much as we did?"

"Well Mandy has a point, this influx of a force is simply too large for the Lunar Base," Sarah said as she rubbed her temples. "Now that I think about it, I should have really thought this through better."

"How about Pluto?" Marina suggested.

"Hmm, that would work too," Sarah replied with a nod.

"We're going to designate Pluto as a rally point for troops coming in from outside Terran Space, since that base is designed to handle the larger influx of troops."

"But is it wise to split the forces so soon?" Olaf questioned Sarah.

Sarah shot him a sharp glance and frowned before replying, "We don't have a choice whether it's good enough. Lunar HQ is an administrative center not a rallying center. Inexperienced I may be, but even you would have to admit that Lunar HQ would never be able to handle such a large scale gathering."

"I suppose you're right," Olaf mumbled and he turned around to face the monitor.

"Vice Admiral Welsch, you have permission to garrison your troops at Pluto. The Generians and Terrans should be prepared to move out sometime within the next forty eight hours. During that time I expect you to have switched over your systems to the UPA Standard."

"Aye sir," Marina replied. "We will station ourselves at Pluto Base and convert over to the UPA Standard."

"Also Marina, be prepared for a pre-mission briefing at twenty hundred hours," Sarah replied. "As much as I hate to admit it, Olaf is right that keeping the forces split would only favour a Silician attack should it come sooner rather than later. Additionally, I'd like to fight them in Silician Space oppose to Terran or Generian space where a planet is easily targetable."

"Aye, sir. Moving fleet out to Pluto, we'll be ready by twenty hundred hours for the briefing. Marina out." The communications channel was cut off and the Osmerian Fleet turned around and Chronos Jumped towards Pluto. Sarah let out a long exhale, "My crew is going to be the death of me yet…" she mumbled before lifting her head and speaking in a louder voice, "Tell the fleet to stand down, we're going back to code yellow." Once the order was relayed, Sarah walked out of the room and headed back to her quarters. Once there she plopped down in her chair and covered her face with her hands letting out a small scream.

"This is *so* stressful!" she thought aloud. "I should probably call up Jace, since he knows more about this Nebula Project than I do." She stood up from her chair and pushed a button for the intercom. "Can Admiral Jace please report to Fleet Commander Collins' office." After making the announcement she rested her head on her desk, "I have time for a quick nap, he'll probably take a while to get here. Yeah, a nap sounds good right now." She closed her eyes, and the next thing she remembered was Jace shaking her.

"Commander Collins wake up," Jace spoke as he shook her.

"Hmmm, oh… OH!" Sarah snapped back in her chair as she realized what was going on.

"If you're tired, you could just get some shut eye," Jace said with a frown as he crossed his arms. "I know the task is daunting, but you shouldn't sacrifice yourself for your organization."

"Yes dad, Fae has already been nice enough to tell me the same thing, but I can sleep afterwards," she said with a yawn. "In any case, the reason I called you is concerning the Nebula Project. I expect it would have to be discussed at the pre-mission debriefing, so would you be able to entertain any questions and possibly talk on the subject?"

"You know you could just, order people to do things," Jace

replied with a slight chuckle. "You are the highest ranking person here; there is no need to ask questions."

"I know, but generally speaking your advice is always more sound than mine," she said as she hung her head down. "You and Sonluth are light years ahead of me, so I feel like I should respect you instead of order you."

Jace grinned a little and spoke, "That maybe true, but as a leader you should never sell yourself short. We couldn't have gotten this far without some of your resolve." He rested a hand on Sarah's shoulder, "Respect has nothing to do with rank. You are the leader that everyone looks up to. Like any other organization, responsibility is filtered down the line, but the ultimate calls lie with the leader. You can respect us by upholding your leadership role and making the right calls. That doesn't mean we *don't* appreciate you engaging us for info and opinions, but the calls are yours to make. No matter how much input we have in your decisions, everyone will remember it as your choice, and you'll be the one blamed or praised."

Sarah looked up at Jace and nodded her head once, "Alright, I'll do that."

"That's the spirit," Jace replied with a smile. He then withdrew his hand and stood back up straight, "I will gladly talk to the group about the Nebula Project during the briefing. Hopefully it will be enough to keep us all alive in the fight that is to come."

"That's the plan," Sarah replied as Jace walked back out the door.

Sarah plopped down in her chair once Jace had left, "So much to do, so little time." She looked over at a nearby clock and sighed. "Well I got a few hours before this briefing starts, might as well look at some Silician Intel before this briefing starts." Sarah pulled out a scratch pad and some files and began writing notes on possible routes and battle plans.

An hour later there was a knock on Sarah's door and it creaked open. Fae peeped her head in and saw Sarah, pencil still in hand with her head down on her desk. She quietly closed the door back shut and spoke to the others who were approaching.

"Shhh, the Commander is taking a nap," Fae said quietly. "We should probably just set up in one of the conference rooms and bring her up to speed when she wakes up."

"But as the commanding officer, she should be present for the meeting," Olaf said with a huff.

"I'd be inclined to agree," Fae said as he turned to face Olaf, "but she probably has not slept since we attacked Mars which was a few days ago. Let her sleep now so that when we do update her and start this operation she'll at least have some form of awareness."

"But this operation involves the whole organization! We can't simply leave her out of it!" Olaf protested.

"With all due respect Vice Admiral, a tired mind will not help with the situation. If you want we can even get a medic up here to confirm that well known fact if you'd like."

He stood there for a few moments looking eye to eye with Fae before moving off towards the conference room. "I still think the leader should be here, especially a shaky one," he mumbled.

About two hours later Sarah woke up and leaned her head over to look at the wall clock. "Oh my God! I'm late for the Officer's Briefing!" she shrieked as she jumped out of her chair. She bolted out of the door and ran to the conference room and threw the door open. The discussion ceased as everyone looked at Sarah who just burst through the door.

"Glad you could make it," Olaf remarked.

"I'm sorry for being late, did I missed a lot," Sarah said with a nervous smile as she looked at the notes on the conference room board.

"Nothing we can't get you caught up on before the actual pre-mission debrief," Jace replied.

"We were just going over strategies to approach Silicia with minimal casualties and the expected military might going in," Golsalves added. "So close the door behind you and get over here so that we can go over this plan with you before you announce it to the troops."

"Sure thing," Sarah said with a nod and she walked over to finalize plans for the Silician Attack.

CHAPTER 12: THE BEGINNING OF THE END

"Welcome all to the pre-mission debriefing for Operation United Front." Sarah spoke a time later to address the officers that had been gathered in the main hall. "This operation will take us into the heart of the Silician System primarily to destroy anything associated with the Nebulizer Project. It has been discussed that destroying the project will greatly hamper the Silician Public from supporting a further war against us. But before we get that far, let's outline what we believe will be the first and main battle of this confrontation. Unlike us, the Silicians have not expanded greatly into their system, mainly all living on the main planet of Silicia. With the senate having approved the nullification of the treaty, we assume that they have begun their war preparation. As per the officer's manual, Silician Rally Points are here over their main HQ, with two smaller points nearer to the poles along the same line of longitude," she indicated with a laser pointer. "Although it may seem foolhardy, the bulk of our forces will warp in with fully charged weapons a little off center from the main rally point near the equator. This is so that while we have the element of surprise we can maximize our damage. Two smaller detachments, one led by Vice Admiral Gonsalves and the other lead by Rear Admiral Olaf will attack the polar rally points to both hamper communications and their ability to send reinforcements from those locations. As the Silicians are preparing for a system invasion, we expect the bulk force in the center to consist of battalions one through fifteen, as well as three support companies. The groups at the poles will probably consist of three fighter battalions, one support, and one artillery contingent. If you should identify these artillery mechinas make it your priority to destroy it as they can use it to pick off the attacking forces near the equator. Admiral Jace will now elaborate more on the Nebulizer Project and what we can expect from it."

Sarah remained standing while Jace came up to the front of the hall to speak. "Project Nebulizer was originally designed by the combined military minds of the Silicians, Terrans, Osmerians, and Generians. The idea was to build an unstoppable weapon that could not be used against them. The result was Project Nebulizer. Four separate mechinas that ran off an energy level similar to that of a star's. Additionally the four when active could channel their energies into a larger mechina, thus activating the mightiest of mechinas ever built. This one would be referred to as the Super Nova. Its long ranged weapons are said to be able to neutralize planets. The black hole at Sector J is a testimony to the scale of energy output from its long range weapons and to this day remains the only active testing it has undergone. To keep an enemy from ever using the weapon against them, originally each race had one pilot attuned to one nebulizer. This spawned a secondary mission known as Operation Free Mind. This operation tracked individuals of mixed heritage and assessed their abilities and phenotypes exhibited in relation to their parental heritage. Upon the conclusion of this Operation, the respective races began seeking out candidates to sync with their nebulizers. Zee Oersted was the Silician Candidate, while Izumi Maehara was the Terran one. Sonluth is the Generian Candidate, while Saku Mystral is the Osmerian one. During this battle we will have all four nebulizers potentially in close proximity of each other. The Silicians would then be able to channel energy from the battle towards the Super Nova. Unlike the Nebulizers, the Super Nova is not synced to a particular pilot, although with the years the Silicians have had to work on it, they may have been able to find a way for only those with Silician abilities and genetics to operate it. This is why we have to make this battle as short as possible, or decrease our reliance on the Fenix and the Kor Hydra."

Jace then pushed a button on the projector and a holomap of the main Silician Planet came up. He clicked a few times to make the map zoom into a location near the equator. "This is where we believe the contents of Project

Nebula are stored; an abandoned laboratory once used to build and house military weapons. We are expecting some resistance, but believe based on preliminary scans that most of the Silician Forces will be preparing to attack our system, and thus leave behind less forces than one would regularly expect. However, one must note that despite its outward appearance it is believed the place is actually an underground fortress. Once we enter, we should disable as much energy conduits as we can to postpone the activation of the Super Nova as long as we possibly can."

One of the officers raised their hands and spoke, "But considering the expected fire power of these mechina, what is to stop the Silicians from engaging them with us in orbit?"

"Because there are limits to how far the channeling can take place, a battle in space would be too far away for the uplink to work, unless they found a way to move the Super Nova up to space. Not saying that it could not be done, but it would effectively be a large sitting duck, that they'd probably spend absurd amount of resources simply defending." The officer lowered his hand with the response and nodded silently.

Olaf then stood up, "How are we going to get to Silician Space without being detected. I'm sure they have early detection systems just like we have ours. Further more due to the former alliance I suspect they even know the route we'd take to get there."

"That would be a concern, one that I admit to not thinking of originally, but the Osmerians who were members of the STARs based in Neptune have devised alternate routes of getting into Silician Space, thus we would not be stopping at any of the expected waypoints. Additionally, Chronos Jumping builds energy at the end of the jump based on the energy build up at the start and the distance jumped, thus we are aiming to use a small jump to initiate our engagement with the Silicians so they have as little time as possible to respond to our attack."

"I see," Olaf said quietly as he sat back down in his chair. Sarah scanned the room for any other hands, but none were raised.

"Well if there are no more questions to be fielded, the mechinas have been divided into four sections; North, Equator, South and Support. The main three will attack at the North, Equatorial and Southern Rally points respectively. Support will be made up of smaller, agile mechina who will be able to swing between the three main attack fleets as well as pick off any stragglers trying to reinforce or escape the rally points. You have all been assigned to your fleets and will report as follows; Vice Admiral Gonsalves shall be in charge of the Northern Fleet, Vice Admiral Olaf will lead the Southern Fleet and I will lead the Equitorial Fleet. Commodore Jenkins will be in charge of coordinating the Support Fleet. Are we all clear?" Sarah spoke as she scanned the audience's facial expressions.

"Aye sir," the gathered officers replied in unison.

"Good," Sarah said with a nod. "Operation United Front will start in three hours at zero four hundred hours. Originally we thought Pluto would be an ideal rally point, but as has been mentioned before, the Silicians are well aware of our usual tactics. Thus we will rally at point zero four seven eight in the sixth quadrant." Everyone in the room saluted and the room reverberated with a cheer as everyone exited.

Sarah afforded herself a smile as she looked at the holomap while everyone filed out of the hall. "Well this is it," she said to herself. "The moment in time we've all waited for; the final battle of this long war." Sarah left the room after a few moments and headed towards the docks and boarded the RAINE. Her crew was already aboard and waiting for her when she arrived.

"Welcome to the bridge Captai... I mean Commander of the Fleet." Kazumi said as she jumped out of her chair and saluted Sarah.

"It's alright," Sarah said with a little laugh. "You don't need to be so formal, or at least not any more formal than you've been so far with me."

"Yes that is true, but alas, our little captain is now all grown up and the Commander of the Fleet. As such we have to show her the respect that everyone expects her to be shown otherwise it reflects bad on crew and commander," Vladmir mused as he finalized a few checks. He then put out a hand to Lucius, "They grow up so fast; do you have a tissue I could use to wipe away the tears?"

"Har, har, very funny," Sarah remarked as she made a face. She then looked over at Marina. "I thought you would have deployed with the Osmerian Fleet."

"And miss all the fun of this mechina?" Marina replied with a grin as she engaged the engines. "I wouldn't miss that for the entire universe," she said with a grin as she turned to face Sarah. "Mind you they are deployed with me, since they are mostly still part of this battalion. That aside, it has been proven that I'm the best at handling the RAINE."

"And that I can't really argue with," Sarah replied. "Alright one final battle and hopefully this will all be over," she said to herself as she sat down in her chair. "Combined Fleet of the United Planetary Alliance, move out! We are following the co-ordinates set out by the STAR unit. Stagger your jumps at five second intervals."

"Aye Admiral came the echoed reply over the radio. The massive force jumped and left the Terran Solar System behind. Sarah closed her eyes and rehearsed the plan they would execute as they came out of the final jump. She ran various scenarios in her mind as the fleet carried out its series of jumps.

Sarah's focus was broken by Marina's announcement, "One minute until we complete final jump."

"Weapons fully charged and loaded?" Sarah said as she opened her eyes and focused her gaze out the front window.

"Yes Ma'am," came the echoed reply of the weapon's crew.

"Alright, in one minute we'll give the Silicians the biggest surprise fire display since the big bang," Sarah said as a small grin spread across her face. She sat up straight as the last few moments ticked by.

There seemed a moment of calm as the RAINE came out of the jump. Everyone's hands hovered over their consoles as they exited.

"Fire *everything!*" Sarah ordered as she jumped out of her chair. The fleet did not need a second invitation as it unleashed everything upon the Silician Fleet that was in front of them.

"Our surprise attack seems to have had the desired effect," Kazumi announced as she performed a sonar sweep. "Silician squads one through eight have suffered severe casualties. The first and second death wings were intercepted by Gonsolves' troops and currently are still engaged. Reports from Gonsolves indicate that his fleet had suffered about thirty percent strength reduction and have gained an upper hand. Olaf's Fleet suffered minimal damage and have forced surrender from Silician squads nine through twelve having obliterated the advance guard with long ranged armaments. There are still no reports of the Nebulizers being deployed."

"They probably wanted to see our numbers before deploying them," Sarah thought aloud. "That or they are keeping them close to the Super Nova to defend it in the event we did break through this upper fleet."

"Jace did mention in the briefing that the closer the nebulizers the faster the energy transfers. It could be that they are being kept close simply to activate the Nebulizer faster," Marina commented.

"Message from Silicia," Kazumi spoke, shattering the relative quiet on the bridge. "Its on a priority channel, do you want me to patch it through?"

"Sure, bring it up," Sarah said as she stood up from her Captain's Chair.

"I must say, I am forever amazed by your ingenuity and resolve. I suppose you get that intelligence from your mother's side of the family," Fen spoke as her expressionless face came up on the hologram.

"I find it somewhat creepy and weird that you can talk so familiarly about my family," Sarah said with a shudder. "But I'm sure you didn't open this channel simply to pat me on the back. And if you did, I'd question what you did with the real Fen."

"Humph, don't get so cocky after winning your first battle," Fen spoke. "That was merely a taste of what is to come. Press forward if you dare, the Silician People will not roll over and accept your invasion. We will fight and we will win.

You may have surprised our space forces, but our ground forces will be more than a match for you until I can fully power up and mobilize the Super Nova."

"Don't you worry Fen, we won't disappoint you," Sarah replied.

"Good, I want to be able to see the expression on your face when your latest endeavour goes down in a hail of fire," Fen said with a smirk. "Until then, I await your arrival." The communication link was then severed and quiet returned to the bridge.

"I've never liked how smug Fen is towards us," Sarah said as she sat back down in her chair. "Its like one of those cheerleaders who no matter how hard you try they always seem to one up you and throw it back in your face."

"Can't say I had that problem with cheerleaders," Marina remarked as she put the RAINE in orbit above the equator.

"Marina, I don't think anyone in their right minds would cause any issues with you," Vladimir said with a slight chuckle. "Remember what happened that time the Silicians had blacked out the upper quadrant and you simply thought a grenade would solve all of life's problems?"

"What is *that* supposed to mean?" Marina said as she crossed her arms and turned towards Vladimir. "You want me to come over there and smack you?"

"I think you just proved his point," Sarah said with a small laugh.

"The remaining Silician Forces that were not destroyed or surrendered are retreating back towards the planet," Kazumi announced. "It would appear they are now trying to converge on the main continent. Other forces not from space are also converging near the capital."

"So all the outlying regions are undefended?" Sarah asked.

"It would certainly appear that way," Kazumi replied as she watched her console.

"They are probably massing on the main continent to protect their capital from falling," Vladmir commented. "It's not the wisest strategy, but it does give them a fighting chance of keeping their vital areas protected."

"Any sign of the Nebulizers?" Sarah asked.

"None," Kazumi replied without taking her eyes off her sensor screens.

"Tell everyone to hold positions until we can determine what their next move is."

"But we should attack now before they regroup!" Olaf interjected. "Once they get organized they will be harder to break down."

"We have space superiority," Sarah responded. "Them regrouping is the least of our worries. I'm more concerned about what hasn't appeared yet. While their ground defenses are pretty good from what I recall at the academy, I'm more concerned that if we pursue they will release the Nebulizers for a strong counter attack."

"Based on observations from when they attacked in Generia, wouldn't their weapons be strong enough to attack from the surface?" Gonsalves asked.

"They would be which would be yet another reason not to

pursue them, since they could simply ambush us with the Nebulizers."

"You're not leaving yourself with many options," Gonsalves responded.

"Kazumi, bring up the known Silician military instillations and laboratories. Distribute their locations to Olaf, Gonsalves and Jenkins."

"Aye Commander."

"Once you guys get the co-ordinates, bombard them as accurately as you can. Do not carpet bomb as not only will you target civilians, but I expect these placed to be heavily fortified and the more damage we do to the fortifications, the less likely they'll retaliate."

"Aye commander," the trio responded.

"Data upload complete," Kazumi said a few minutes later. "Fleets arranging to commence bombardment. No energy gathering from Silicia for a counter attack." Sarah watched as the mechinas spread out around the planet, but kept an especially wary eye on energy levels emanating from Silicia.

"Mechina are all in position and ready to fire," Kazumi announced.

"Fire a single large volley in five…four…three… two… one… fire!" Ballistic and optical weapons rained down on their targets. After they fired their volleys everyone reloaded, but held their fire until the dust settled.

"Barrage damage estimated at eighty percent efficiency," Kazumi announced after a few minutes. "Still no retaliation from Silicia."

"Not even from the senate?"

"Nothing on the radio frequencies other than our own chatter."

"I say we continue the bombardment," Gonsalves suggested.

"No," Sarah said as she leaned forward and rested her head on her fists. "Something is not right here. It is quiet, too quiet. Even if we faced an orbital bombardment, we'd at least deploy shields. It's almost as if they are daring us to destroy the planet. But why would they want us to do that?"

"Destruction of a planet would destroy the abilities of all sensors and automatic lock on weapons," Vladimir said.

"That would make sense, but the numbers still wouldn't add up. A whole planet for fleet?" A flash went off in Sarah's mind causing her to jolt up in her chair. "Kazumi what is the detection behind us?"

"Behind us?" Kazumi echoed.

"Don't question, just do it!"

"Aye commander," Kazumi said as she scrambled on her console. A few moments ticked by before Kazumi responded, "Scanners pick up nothing behind us."

"Nothing?"

"Nothing. Why would you expect something else?"

"That's the trap," she thought aloud as she ignored Kazumi's question. "Well played Silicians, well played." She then added in a more audible tone. "Tell all the fleets to assume defensive formations and fire off a barrage to their rear."

"To the rear? But there is nothing there," Lucius objected.

"That's just it; there is nothing, not even other markers that we use to identify Silician Space. That's the trap. Just like we had the camouflage going into Osmerian Space, they more than likely have the same capabilities. While it works wonders on sensors, it works a bit too well. Close range is fine, but when distant targets are blocked, it's obvious something is there, even if the sensors say otherwise."

"So in other words, we're actually surrounded. But why not just open fire on us now?" Marina asked.

"If they wait for us to descend, we have no chance of evading and our shields would be compromised. It would be shooting fish in a barrel, and an absolute nightmare for us."

"Fleet is in position and ready to fire," Kazumi announced.

"Tell the fleets to spread their fire across a thirty degree arc, sustained for two minutes following our mark."

"Everyone is ready," Kazumi relayed a few minutes later.

"Alright everyone prepare to fire in three… two… one… fire!" As they fired the area around the fleets cracked like glass, and revealed previously hidden mechina of the Silician Fleet. The Silicians returned fire, and the area was soon an expanding debris field as front line mechinas on both sides were destroyed.

"Debris field expanding around the planet and our sensors are being hampered," Kazumi announced.

"Estimated damage to enemy fleet?"

"Judging from our last full reading and inbound counter fire the fleet above us was reduced to around ten percent."

"Vladimir, can we fire the Gravi—"

"Energy release from Silicia!" Kazumi interrupted. Before anything else could be said a large pillar of energy shot up from the planet and went through a large section of the Osmerian Forces as well as the Silician Forces above.

"Hang on!" Marina yelled as she fought to maintain control of the RAINE. The turbulence lessened as the light faded and before them was a giant mechina flanked by the two Nebulizers.

"Talk about an entrance," Lucius whistled.

"The senate has tasked us with defending Silicia, and although your attack came early and your tactics have been commendable, this ends now." Qui Fen's voice started to take on a double tone as she continued, "Now witness the fullest might of the Silician Military." The nebulizers both fired off shots in opposite directions that tore through all four fleet groups.

"Pimea… yo…" Fen spoke slow and methodical as the area went dark.

"Commander, sight nor sensors are working," Kazumi announced.

"So they want to make this a blackout fight," Sarah said as she leaned forward in her chair. "Be ready for anything, this is going to be either a battle of reflexes or a battle of attrition."

CHAPTER 13: FINAL DUEL

The RAINE came out of the darkness in the middle of a debris field. There was no sign of allied or enemy mechina, although below them was what appeared to be a planet.

"Where are we?" Sarah asked as she looked around at their surroundings. "It feels like we've not moved, but I see no sign of any other mechina."

"Welcome to the Remnant," Fen's voice came over the radio. "I applaud your tactics, tenacity and determination to get this far. But like so many other mechina before you, the Remnant will be your final resting place."

"Fen, show yourself!" Sarah yelled.

"Patience young one," Fen replied. "Or are you asking us to reveal ourselves because you can't find us?"

"So you brought allies, but didn't give us the luxury," Sarah responded.

"Not hardly, just merely making this a fair fight, one main mechina with our immediate supports." Her voice then returned to a double toned nature, "Don't worry once the charge is complete, the end will come swiftly. Until then the Gamayun and Kupala should keep you busy. Again, there is no need to worry about time, the more they fight the faster I charge, and once I finish charging I will make you an example to those who would oppose the Silicians." The communication channel was cut out and silence once again returned to the bridge.

"Tell the pilots to form a tight perimeter around the mechina. We will perform sonar sweeps at ten second intervals to prevent the nebulizers from easily zeroing in on us. Other than that, we are going to have to rely heavily on sight," Sarah said as she closed her eyes and folded her arms. "They obviously hold the upper hand with the hiding and we have to seek them. However any rash move on our part would allow them to pick us off and make us less effective."

"Aye Ma'am," the pilots echoed as they prepared to launch.

"Move ahead slowly Marina, I don't want any surprised," Sarah ordered as she stood up from her chair. Her jaw slowly set into a frown and she crossed her arms as she looked out into the debris field. After a few moments Sarah snapped her posture up. "Stop!" she suddenly bursted out as she unfolded her arms.

"Commander?" Marina questioned as she brought the RAINE to a halt.

"Do you not hear that?" Sarah asked as Marina turned around to face Sarah. Marina and the others shook their heads.

"There is nothing on sensors," Kazumi and Lucius both remarked.

"Calm down Commander, if you're paranoid, then you'll only make bad mistakes which we don't have the back up to make," Jace said over the radio. "Take a deep breath, close your eyes, collect your thoughts, then slowly exhale and open your eyes. We don't need rashness right now, we need a calm head."

The bridge crew all watched as she followed Jace's advice. There was a small pause as she held her breath to collect her thoughts. As she opened her eyes she felt her heart rate go down, and the crew returned their attention to their consoles.

"We have some grey noise at four o'clock," Kazumi announced. "Should the pilots investigate?"

"No, we're keeping everyone with us. Marina, bring us around so that we're facing the grey noise. We faced this before in the meteor belt remember? Its more than likely a trap, so I want the Vector Cannon fired at it. That way we aren't only getting rid of a distraction, but we're opening up some of the debris field. Forward Pilots, keep your sights trained on that area incase they reveal themselves."

"Yes ma'am," Jace and Trix echoed. Fae also landed on the top of the RAINE and focused the sniper sites on the blast area. As the dust cleared, the Super Nova revealed itself along with the two Nebulizers. All three were engulfed in an eerie red glow.

"Prepare to fire!" Sarah ordered.

"We can't lock on! Our weapon system is going down! First and secondary weapons have crashed!" Vladimir yelled.

"What!" Sarah spun around to look towards Vladimir.

"Shields are deteriorating, we are facing a cyber attack," Kazumi reported. "Deploying anti-cyber warfare programs; estimated time is five minutes."

"Do what you can," Sarah said as she refocused on the scene in front of her. One of the Nebulizers then began taking shots at the smaller mechina. Jace and the others easily evaded the shots. However after the second rotation of shots the Nebulizer followed up the shots with melee combat. Jace was caught off guard and dodged the initial attack, but was hit by the second attack and then thrown towards Forte before having to evade shots from Fae and Rosita.

"Shoot at the Nebulizer that isn't moving!" Sonluth said as he watched the fight from inside the hanger.

Fae switched her target to the stationary Nebulizer, however the shots had no effect on it, and didn't even so much as dissipate the red hue around it. "Think we're going to need a bigger gun," Fae remarked.

"Hack has been successfully repelled out of weapon systems," Kazumi announced, "we are able to reengage primary and secondary weapons again."

"What about shield power?" Sarah asked.

"Still working on that," Megumi replied. "Shields are at their current maximum, but dividing up resources and combating a cyber attack isn't an easy task."

"Understandable, but do what you must, but prioritize the shields and electronics. We can do without tertiary weapons for a bit longer," Sarah ordered.

"Yes, ma'am!" Kazumi and Megumi echoed.

"Super Nova at twenty five percent charge," a mechanical voice announced over the radio.

"Damn, twenty five already?" Sonluth muttered.

"Is the Vector and Gravity Cannon charged?" Sarah asked looking over at the weapon's consoles.

"Vector, yes. Gravity, no," Vladimir replied. "There is

interference with the Gravity Cannon charging, so estimated charge time is unknown."

"Fine, I've got an idea," Sarah spoke. "If we fire the Vector Cannon at the Super Nova the two nebulizers will break off their attacks and shield it. During that time do you think we can launch a counter offensive on the two Nebulizers?"

"I think we can make that work," Jace replied. "Only thing is if we're all focusing on the Nebulizers there is no one covering you should the Super Nova attack."

"If the Super Nova attacks, I doubt you'd be much help with defending against it. In addition, I doubt Fen would be wanting to sacrifice her battery cells just yet. Besides without Saku and Sonluth being deployed you guys will probably need all the numbers you can get on it."

"Got it," the pilots echoed.

"Vlad fire the Vector Cannon... now!" Sarah ordered. The Vector Cannon fired towards the Super Nova and the Nebulizers fell back to shield it. As they did Jace and Fae moved above while Forte and Rosita moved below and pincered the two Nebulizers. The Super Nova fired off small arms fire, which forced the group to stall its attack long enough for the two Nebulizers to counter attack with their high powered rifles.

"That was close," Jace said as he finally remembered to breath.

"We might be able to try that again if we get some cover for the small arms fire," Forte commented.

"Except we don't know the strength of that firepower, or if our own defenses can stand up to it," Jace responded.

"Good news though guys, that attack seems to have diverted attention from the cyber attack and we are now completely free of it," Kazumi announced and Megumi confirmed a short time later with a nod.

"Graviton Cannon is online and ready to fire,"

"Shields are also coming up to seventy five percent," Kazumi echoed.

"Alright pilots, double up, we're going to try this again with the Graviton Cannon," Sarah ordered.

"Aye," the quartet echoed as they prepared to get into formation.

"Saku, get ready," Sonluth said down in the hanger.

"For what? Our going out would only speed things up."

"Speed up or not, the longer this goes on the further behind they'll be. Soon it won't matter."

"Super Nova forty percent charged, basic weapons online and charging," a mechanical voice relayed over the radio.

"See, basic weapons are already charging. It's only a matter of time before the main weapons charge, and once they charge then we'll be in really deep trouble."

"It would seem so," Saku sighed. "Well let's suit up and let Sarah know we're going out."

"Commander Sarah, Saku and Sonluth leaving to enter the fray," Sonluth said once he had powered up Fennec.

"Confirm that?" Kazumi asked Sarah.

She narrowed her eyes and clenched her fist, "Guess it's our last chance, she looks to be powering up regardless now. It doesn't look like we can manage without them much longer."

"You two are clear to launch," Kazumi relayed to Saku and Sonluth.

Saku and Sonluth both launched and were just in time to see the nebulizers repel another attempted pincer from the quartet already out. As the Nebulizers attempted to counter attack Sonluth and Saku attacked them, but as they drew within melee range, they felt their heads throb.

"What was that?" Sonluth spoke aloud as he fought through the pain.

"Join us," Zee Lynn hissed as a red hue began to form around Saku and Sonluth.

"There are no parameters for this!" Fae yelled as she tried to correct Saku's energy imbalance. Izumi's Nebulizer drew closer to Sonluth and he could feel the pulse in his head getting stronger. His whole body felt as if it were going to be crushed under a tremendous weight. Just as she got within touching distance, she was forced back by Jace and the others.

"You ok in there buddy?" Jace asked.

"Not really," Sonluth said with heavy gasps for air.

"Back off and stay at a distance, we can handle the melee," Jace suggested.

"No, you guys need us up front," Sonluth retorted.

"Sonluth and Saku pull back until we at least know what is

causing your energy fluctuations," Sarah ordered. "Vladmir, take over shielding, I want these two to be able to fully concentrate on any more cyber attacks."

"Aye, sir!" Vladmir responded as he transferred duties from Kazumi's console to his.

"Pilots, your priority target is Izumi. While Zee can put out more damage, these hacks are getting irritatingly effective."

"Understood," the two pilots replied.

"Maiku, use barrage tactics on Zee, to at least keep her off balance. Emphasis on random intervals, I don't want her figuring out a pattern for a counter offensive."

"Super Nova now at fifty percent charge, all weapons online and entering standby mode," the mechanical voice spoke again.

"Dammit, that thing is charging too fast," Sarah muttered as she watched the energy readings flow across the screen.

"Sarah, I have an idea, but I need you guys to trust me," Sonluth came over the radio.

"Speak quickly," Sarah ordered.

"Tell Kazumi to release her security on my electronics," Sonluth said.

"You want her to what!" Sarah exclaimed as she jumped out of her seat. "You can't handle both the hacking and attacking. You were just almost incapacitated from such a tactic!"

"Just trust me on this one, tell her to back off."

"But if you get over run then it'll be three on one," Sarah yelled. "No! I won't give the order."

"Sarah, remember how when this first started and we were in the meteor belt and you gave us the order not to take any sorties in the belt, but we wound up having to anyways? This situation is like that. I know it sounds bad, but trust me, I can do this."

A few moments passed as Sarah went quiet. "Commander?" Kazumi asked, "Your orders?"

"Release the security," she said softly.

"What?" Kazumi asked.

"Release the security!" Sarah yelled as she closed her eyes and they began to water.

"Yes ma'am! Releasing Sonluth's security now!" Kazumi relayed.

"I hope you know what you're doing Sonluth," Sarah whispered. "It's not just the five versus five hundred, this time it's the one for all."

Sonluth felt the invasion almost immediately as Kazumi withdrew. He was a little surprised at the speed at which Izumi seemed to work, but then let out a little grin as he remember how she handled the hack to get into the ship's data and the ATF. "Well Fenix, we have one shot at this, you ready buddy?" The mechina growled its approval. "Then lets not keep them waiting," he said. Sonluth turned on his afterburners and charged directly at Izumi. He could feel the acceleration of her hacking as he closed the gap between them. He raised his sword to strike her but as he brought it down, he stopped short and withdrew the blade and stood next to Izumi.

"Well that didn't last long," Sarah said with a frown. "I guess its up to you now Saku," she added with a sigh.

"No pressure there," Saku replied as he dove in to attack Izumi. However, Izumi did not move as the Fenix moved to intercept Saku.

"Her cyber attacks are accelerating!" Megumi yelled as her console became inundated with warnings. "The defense systems are down again."

"That's just what I want," came Sonluth's reply. Before anyone could respond he turned around to grab Izumi's Nebulizer and brought it around to sever the head with his blade. He felt the release as soon as he cut the head and was quickly able to follow up a downward slice.

"S-S-Sonluth?" Izumi's voice was shaky and staggered. "W-w-what have I done?"

"You have done nothing."

"I-I-I'm so sorry."

"Don't worry, it's all over now." He then thrust his sword around the area he figured the cockpit to be and made an arced cut to slice the top of the Nebulizer away. Izumi's helmet glass was foggy, but Fennec extended its hand.

"Come back to us," Sonluth said. There was a slight hesitation before Izumi reached her hand up and slowly started to move forward.

"Energy building from the Super Nova!" Kazumi warned.

"Jump!" Sonluth yelled as he moved Fennec around to put itself between Izumi and the Super Nova. She pushed off just as the Super Nova's energy attack engulfed them. There were a few moments of quiet tension before the energy passed and Fennec opened up its hand. "We got her, she's safe."

"You're next Fen!" he yelled as he raised his sword and pointed it at the Super Nova.

"Oh my; such illusions of grandeur," Fen replied. "You took out one of the nebulizers. I'm up to sixty percent charge, and you still have one more nebulizer to get through. The odds aren't looking very good for you. Here let me give you a sample of half my power!"

"Energy rapidly rising!" Megumi announced. A split second later a large beam shot out from the Super Nova. Marina rapidly ascended to avoid being caught in the beam, but it grazed past the shields causing a lot of friction onboard the RAINE.

"We lost eighty percent of our lower shields on that one," Vladmir reported once Marina steadied the ship again. "Other than that damage appears nominal and superficial."

"Good to hear, but we need to end this soon, otherwise that thing is going to become too powerful," Sarah remarked. "Everyone transfer consoles back to normal working status, we're going to try attack the Super Nova while Saku and Sonluth try to neutralize Zee."

"Aye ma'am," the crew echoed and for a few moments all that could be heard was furious typing on keyboards and the associated beeps from the consoles. The pilots re-engaged Zee; Sonluth took point with Saku and Jace on his flanks.

"I've got an idea," Fae radioed.

"Let's hear it," Sarah replied.

"Block Zee's line of sight for me while I charge up the sniper rifle. I'll let you know when it's fully charged and when I fire I'll aim for her weapon. Even if she dodges, you guys should be able to follow up quick enough to get in a few good hits."

"Any downside to this plan?" Sarah asked.

"I can't shoot for a few minutes before and after. It'll be an overcharge like Zee done in the meteor belt. Zee might also try to attack if she figures out that the rifle is charging and I will not be able to move during the charge."

"Alright, Trix and Rosita cover and shield Fae, the rest of you keep the Nebulizer busy," Sarah ordered. She then turned to the bridge crew, "Concentrate the forward and top shields. If it looks as if Zee might try to flank, open fire to bring her back around."

"Yes ma'am!" the all echoed. The group furiously typed on their consoles for a few moments before Kazumi updated the bridge status.

"Front shields back up to fifty percent, rear shield's energy have been routed to top and sides," Kazumi announced without taking her eyes off her screen.

"Good," Sarah acknowledged with a nod. "Alright pilots, deploy your side of the plan."

"Aye ma'am," the pilots echoed. Sonluth took point flanked on his right by Saku. Jace provided covering fire from the rear. Fae crouched behind one of the forward turrets on the RAINE and began charging the ATF's sniper rifle. Rosita and Trix took up positions forward of the turret Fae was charging behind and deployed chaff walls. Zee nimbly dodged Sonluth's initial attack and was about to return fire when Jace opened fire on her forcing her to abort her attack.

"Energy levels rising from the Super Nova," Kazumi yelled.

"Forward shields full, prepare for evasive maneuvers," Sarah yelled mere moments before the Super Nova fired another blast. The shot went straight through were the pilots were fighting, Jace, Sonluth and Saku were forced into sharp climbs to disengage from combat and avoid the incoming fire.

"Mission Accomplished," Zee Lynn spoke as the light died down.

"Energy charge complete. Entering standby mode."

"What is *that*?" Sarah said as the Super Nova now began pulsing in red energy.

"Feel the wrath of the firebrand!" Fen exclaimed as the Super Nova morphed the energy into giant red wings. The wings flapped twice before meeting together and formed a giant red energy wave that raced towards the RAINE. Marina fought for control as the energy pulse went past them, forcing them backwards and clearing out all the debris surrounding the immediate battle area.

"Shields down to ten percent. Needless to say we cannot take another hit like that again," Kazumi announced.

"All of them?" Sarah asked

"All of them."

"From one shot?"

"Marina?"

"It's difficult to evade an all encompassing shot like that," Marina groaned. "Even if I had lightning reflexes the sheer area of the attack prevents any type of evasive maneuvering."

"You and your mechina are both too young and naïve to know when you've already lost, and right now, you've lost to a far superior force," Fen's double toned voice spoke.

"Is there really nothing we can do?" Sarah spoke softly to herself. "Is it really going to end like this, after all we've been through, is it still not enough?"

"That's right, feel the despair of knowing you challenged a stronger enemy and have lost. Once I destroy you the rest of the known universe will shortly follow. The Silicians will prove once and for all they always were the superior species. No amount of mixing and cross breeding will ever match the strength and might of the original."

"There is one thing, we can do..." came the strained, weakened voice of Izumi. "Sonluth and Saku will have to remove their limiters and initiate the Essence Program."

"The what?" Sarah demanded.

"The Essence Program is when the energies of the pilots flow through the Nebulizers to launch an extremely strong attack. However, as this most times triggers a sustained PB, the result is fatal to the pilot."

"I'm sorry crew for having us walk into this trap," Sarah said as she drooped her shoulders and hung her head down. "I wasn't able to beat the Silicians after all."

"No, your tactics and leadership have gotten us this far," Vladmir said as he ran a few scans on the ballistic weapons. "Chances are none of the others would have been able to stand up to this assault either. We went in sort of blind, and despite that even though it's a hard choice, we still do have it to pull one for the team."

"We're going to get out of this," Sonluth said with a long exhale. "Izumi's right though, the only way out will be the Essence Program."

"You guys sure?" Sarah asked.

"Do we have a choice?" Saku replied. "It's a pretty dire situation right now. Even if we don't make it, at least you all will make it back and tell everyone what happened and how we won the war."

"Alright, if you two are willing to go through with it, I give the command to initiate the Essence Program," she lowered her head and her voice and spoke to herself quietly, "I guess its pointless to tell you to come back safely, but if there was ever a way to do so, find it, and come back safely." She then clenched her fist and still fighting back the tears gave an order to Vladmir, "Prepare all our remaining ballistics to fire at the Super Nova. All pilots not Sonluth and Saku engage the remaining Nebulizer and keep it at bay as long as you can. We're going to cause as much of a ruckus as we can for the pilots while they charge."

"Alright Saku, you ready for this?" Sonluth radioed.

"Ready as I'll ever be for a one way trip," Saku replied.

"Good," Sonluth replied as he typed in a command.

"Essence Program initiated, two minutes until optimal level is reached," a mechanical voice spoke.

"Ha! Would you really sacrifice your own people for a victory? After you mocked me on Osmeria, you're still going to initiate the same action?"

"Our intentions are not corrupted like yours," Sarah responded. "They are willingly doing this for the betterment of everyone in the universe."

"Emotional, but still futile," Fen spoke with a smirk. "The Super Nova was designed to supersede the nebulizers, without the full power of four you won't be able to break these shields. I've seen the numbers, and for you, it might as well be zero."

"The Super Nova is flying rapidly towards us!" Kazumi yelled.

"Up!" Marina yelled as she maxed out the vertical thrusters to shoot up, causing everyone to fall to the ground.

"A little more warning next time," Sarah said as she staggered back to her feet.

"Be grateful we dodged and didn't need to strain our shields," Marina snapped back.

Zee fired off a hi powered shot just as the RAINE reached its apex and Marina was forced to rapidly descent causing everyone not strapped in to float and then come crashing down to the ground once it finished.

"Marina, can you take it easy on the sudden movements—"

"Vlad, be quiet, a few broken bones are a lot better than a broken life," Marina interrupted Vladimir. "Besides need I remind you of our current shield levels?"

"Saku, Sonluth, how's the charge going?"

"Almost there," Sonluth groaned.

A few moments later, Saku's mechina was now covered in a blue hue while Sonluth's was covered in a black. "Essence Program fully engaged and ready to fire," the console indicated.

"Fire," Saku and Sonluth yelled in unison. Their mechinas became a focal point of energy and it streamed towards the Super Nova. The Super Nova's shields were raised and stopped the attack just short of the mechina proper.

"Your attacks are futile!" Fen laughed even as the shields just barely held the attack in check.

Meanwhile down in the engine room Mandy found Aira looking at the engine.

"You're not thinking of sabotaging the RAINE are you?" Mandy demanded.

"No, not hardly," Aira responded as she looked behind her to see who was addressing her.

"But shouldn't you get Fae or Ned or even me to help you?"

"No," Aira said as she refocused looking at the engine.

"But you're not a mechanic! How can you be alright down here?"

"Mandy, what formula did you program the Vector Cannon on?"

"What does it matter? It has nothing to do with you."

"No, not me." She paused as she looked down at something in her hand. She took in a deep breath and closed her eyes. "It's for… her."

"You're actions are highly irregular," Mandy commented.

"Oh if only you knew the half of it," Aira said as she opened her eyes. "I once promised to do all I could to save my people from annihilation. A promise I thought I could keep. Yet I am so conflicted. Save my people or save the people that have come to stand by and defend me."

"Whatever you're planning, if it's towards the RAINE's detriment I will personally stop you."

"Of course you would," Aira said with a grin. She then took a step forward and Mandy moved to head her off.

"I told you I will not let you sabotage this mechina," Mandy said as she impeded Aira's path forward.

"Mandy, what is the formula?"

"Five A seven A."

"Now put those numbers in old calculator font." Mandy did not answer, and her expression was one of stunned silence as Aira continued past her. "This is my last act, one final act to pay back Sarah for believing in me."

"No, tell me what to do! Organisms are frail, you cannot be rebuilt. If it's dangerous let me go in your stead. You can rebuild me, we can't rebuild you, and I've seen how everyone reacts when someone isn't here. When one goes away… it's like… everyone sinks. When everyone makes it through, everyone is like flying."

Aira paused and held her hands close to her chest, "Not for me Mandy. I'm dead either way. I was dead before I even joined this crew."

"No don't do it!" Mandy yelled as she reached out towards Aira, but narrowly missed as Aira jumped towards the engine.

"Thank you Mandy, Sarah and the whole RAINE crew for believing in me, even when I didn't believe in myself," Aira whispered as she reached out towards the engine. "For all those who believed in the cause, this is my last gift to you. Farewell, and enjoy the future, whatever it may hold."

"Aira! NO!" Mandy yelled one last time as the whole room was engulfed in a pale green light.

"Fire *everything*!" Sarah ordered. "Counter shoot that energy attack with the Vector Cannon."

"Yes ma'am!" the weapon's crew replied without any hesitation. The RAINE fired what remaining armaments it could. As the shots flew out, it felt like time moved in slow motion. She saw the energy lines fade from the Nebulizers and all link back towards the RAINE. She felt the energy of all the pilots and all it seemed all the faces of the pilots and crew of the RAINE flashed through her mind, all seemingly believing in the miracle. Ned and the mechanics working to keep things intact; the bridge working feverishly on their consoles; Marina's unwavering attention on the action in front of her; Izumi crying as Sonluth remained stoic; Saku reaching out to Zee; Jace, Trix and Fae fixed in their defence of the RAINE, and finally she looked over towards Megumi and her mood dissipated as she saw four hundred percent flashing on her console with her head in her hands.

"So that's what this is," Sarah said as she closed her eyes and let the energy flow through her, "To my dear crew of the

RAINE, this is as far as we go. It was an honour to fight by your side." She opened her eyes and smiled as she took one final look at the bridge before it was engulfed in a brilliant flash of light. "Dad, I guess we really are getting out of this one, at what price I don't know, but hopefully, all those gathered here remember what happened."

"They will remember," she heard a response as if whispered on the wind. "Distance and time may move, but memories always stay."

"Good," Sarah whispered. "Then for now, its mission accomplished."

"Shield Failure Imminent. Advise immediate evacuation," droned a mechanical voice from the Super Nova's console and the powered shot broke through the shields and scored a direct hit.

"No, the numbers were perfect!" Fen cried out as the announcement was made. She frantically tried to reroute power, however all she got was a few jolts of electricity. The cockpit began heating up and Fen sat back in her chair and released the controls. Her camera and communicator had stopped working and by the time she attempted to eject the mechanism had seized. She held up her hands and looked at them; a pale green glow began to start fading away from them. "I guess you were right, the daughter is stronger than the parent," Fen said as her eyes watered. "And so I die, by the very same force I scoffed at so many years ago." Fen took out a picture and unfolded it. It showed a much younger Qui Fen holding a child, but the image had cut the child in half. "Sarah, you were created to further our own means, yet it was you who ended up destroying them. In the end, you would have made a fine Silician. I guess this is it John. I'll be at your side once again watching over our daughter," Fen said as she lowered the picture and closed her eyes as she became engulfed in white light as the Super Nova's power source exploded.

EPILOGUE

It's been three months since that final battle. I don't remember much, but Megumi admitted to me afterwards that Aira had asked for a sync program to be installed with the vector Cannon, which explains its wildly fluctuating strength.

Marina returned back to the Osmerians to assume control of the throne. I do say she's a fine Queen and despite her protests, she's curb stomped a few of Saratine's remnant. I don't know why anyone would even bother trying to usurp her, she's the most gung-ho person I've ever met and has the power to back it up.

Gonsalves returned to Generia Space and has begun working on fully re-establishing sovereignty. While the easy way would be to use the Iron Wing hierarchy, he refuses to do so, based on the reasoning that a military should not lead a nation. He also asked Fae, but she refused, instead opting to share her knowledge and skills within the UPA's Mechanical Division. She's remained a true neutral, helping to iron things out diplomatically; always making sure every side gets a fair share of work and reward in the new system.

With provisions and some funds Olaf returned to Earth and has tried to rebuild. He even sent a recent picture of a partially rebuilt steel tower in Paris. He said it was a landmark at one point, Eiffel Tower or some such. I do say it's a rather impressive reuse of the damaged steel, but I was never really good as an art critic. We are still getting Terrans migrating up into space, and some are even having reunions with relatives they never knew they had. Some are also returning to the planet in the hopes of rebuilding what was lost.

On the down side, Saku, Sonluth, Izumi and Zee are all MIA. The only positive we can take from it is that we never found their mechinas or their bodies. Olaf and the others say they swept the entire sector, but were only able to find jump material that led to nowhere. The Silicians have the unusual theory that they ascended, which of course is rather amusing, coming from people who pride themselves on facts and figures. However as I sit here watching the shuttles ferry people in and out of the docks, I can't help but think that wherever they are in this huge universe they're doing what all the rest of us are doing; building that one place that they can finally call... home.

www.ingramcontent.com/pod-product-compliance
Lightning Source LLC
Chambersburg PA
CBHW072205170626
46813CB00003B/803